
★

Something was wrong. The door stood ajar. Did she forget to lock it? No, she was meticulous in that respect.

She listened for sounds from inside. Someone was in there! This was her domain. How dare anyone come in without her permission.

This is ridiculous, she told herself. *Perhpas it's Bruce Hamilton. He has a key and every right to be inside.* With more bravado than she felt, she pushed open the door.

"Who's in here? Mr. Hamilton, is that you?"

A figure clad in black appeared from behind the desk. He ran toward her, growled, "Out o' my way," grabbed her shoulders, shoved her hard and ran out the door. She lost her balance, reached for something, anything, her arms flailing in the air. As she pitched forward, her head hit the side of one of the bookcases and she fell to the floor. The room swirled around in a thick fog, then blackness....

★

Previously published Worldwide Mystery title by
HELEN MACIE OSTERMAN

THE ACCIDENTAL SLEUTH

The

STRANGER
in the

OPERA
HOUSE

Helen Macie Osterman

TORONTO • NEW YORK • LONDON
AMSTERDAM • PARIS • SYDNEY • HAMBURG
STOCKHOLM • ATHENS • TOKYO • MILAN
MADRID • WARSAW • BUDAPEST • AUCKLAND

To my loving family and to opera lovers
all over the world.

Recycling programs
for this product may
not exist in your area.

THE STRANGER IN THE OPERA HOUSE

A Worldwide Mystery/August 2011

First published by Five Star Publishing

ISBN-13: 978-0-373-26764-4

Copyright © 2009 by Helen Macie Osterman

Printed in U.S.A.

Acknowledgments

I would like to thank Five Star for giving me the opportunity
to bring Emma Winberry to the printed page;
the many fans who have enjoyed *The Accidental Sleuth*
and asked for more; and my writer's group, The Southland
Scribes, for their support and valuable critique,
especially Michael Black for his help with police procedure.

I also wish to thank Jack Zimmerman, subscriber relations
manager of Lyric Opera, for answering my endless
questions, and Bill Walters, Super Captain, for supplying me
with information on supernumeraries.

Thanks to Ellen Schuetzler for her expertise in document
analysis, and a special thanks to my supportive editor,
Brittiany Koren.

And, of course, thanks to my family and
loved ones for believing in me.

ONE

EMMA WINBERRY AND Nate Sandler walked toward the Lakeshore Center for the Performing Arts, an opulent building reminiscent of late-eighteenth-century grandeur, located on North Michigan Avenue, alongside the great lake. They had been supernumeraries for the Midwest Opera for a number of years. These were the dedicated people who were willing to stand in crowds onstage, perform simple tasks, and appear at all rehearsals and performances just to be a part of the magic of the opera.

Nate protectively held Emma's hand as he always did as they entered the building.

A high-pitched shriek rent the air.

"What was that?" he exclaimed, searching the lobby area for anything unusual. "It sounded like a scream. Is the soprano having a temper tantrum?"

Emma stopped and listened. "Something's wrong," she said as a chill crawled up her arms. "That's more than a tantrum. Let's find out what's going on."

As cast members and stagehands ran toward the dressing rooms, someone bumped into Emma's slight figure knocking her over. Nate grabbed her.

"What's happening?" she asked.

James Greene, an executive of the Midwest Opera and Emma's son-in-law, appeared pushing his way through the crowd. Emma grabbed his jacket as she and Nate trailed behind him. As they approached the dressing room, they heard a woman's voice moaning.

"Oh, oh—so terrible—so frightening." The svelte soprano, Gina Rienzi, sat on a chair outside her dressing room. The wardrobe mistress handed her a glass of water, steadying it in the woman's trembling hands.

Within minutes, the director and the stage manager arrived and stood next to James. "What happened, Signora?" the director asked.

"A man—a man in my dressing room," she whispered, unaware that she was sloshing water down the front of her costume.

"There's no one in there now," said one of the stagehands. "I checked."

"Are you sure you saw a man?" the director asked her.

"Of course I'm sure. Are you calling me a liar?" Regaining her composure, the irate singer sat up straight and regal.

"No, of course not, *Signora*. Tell me, what did the man look like? Did he say anything? Did he threaten you?" the director continued, a frown on his face.

"Don't you have anything stronger than water?" Signora Rienzi demanded, pushing the glass away. "I have had a terrible shock."

The director raised his eyebrows and whispered something to the stage manager.

"Is she always like this?" Emma asked her son-in-law.

"Worse."

When the soprano had stopped trembling, and eagerly sipped a glass of brandy she had been given, she was ready to tell her story. She assumed a melodramatic pose, turned back to the dressing room, and said in a voice everyone could hear, "He was standing in that corner, over there." Then she pointed to an area near the closet.

"Did he say anything?" the director asked again, clenching his fists.

"Nothing. Just pointed."

"Pointed? At you?"

"No."

"*Signora,* please explain. Security will be here soon and will want to know the details."

"He pointed over there." She shook her head and waved her hand in the air toward the costume closet.

"He didn't speak?"

"No, just pointed."

The director blew out a breath and swore softly. "How was he dressed?"

The singer screwed up her face and thought for a moment. "I couldn't see him very well. He looked dirty and his clothes were torn—like a person from the streets, and he smelled—strange."

"What do you mean by 'strange'?"

"Musty, like something old and rotting." The woman had assumed her stage persona and was obviously relishing the attention.

"All right," the director said. "Our security people will search the entire Center. If they find anything amiss, we will notify the police. Please remain in your dressing room. They will want to question you further."

He turned to a stagehand. "Is there anything in that closet? Another door leading somewhere?"

"No, sir." The man shook his head. "I checked."

"What about the rehearsal?" Emma asked James.

"It's cancelled for today. We'll have to reschedule for tomorrow."

The soprano took the bottle of brandy from the stage manager and sat in a lounge chair with her attendant at her side.

Emma stood still, looked around, and scrunched up her face, thinking.

"Come on, Emma," Nate said. "Let's go where it's quiet."

"Just a minute," she said. "Something isn't right. Do you smell that?"

"Smell what?" He sniffed and shook his head.

"I had a fleeting smell of something stale and musty. I'm not exactly sure." Her mind conjured up a vague image of someone ragged, just as Signora Rienzi had reported. She shook her head to rid it of the image.

"Now what?" Nate shrugged and raised his eyebrows. "Is

that 'sixth sense' of yours telling you something sinister?" he asked in a mocking tone.

Emma gave him one of her looks, eyebrows raised, lips pursed. "Don't make fun of my 'sixth sense,' Nate Sandler. You know all too well what it's done in the past."

"Humph."

They walked down the hall and into the community room to a table filled with bottled water, coffee, and tea. "Shall we have something to drink before we go home?" he asked.

"Yes, please."

Emma sat silently as she sipped a cup of tea and thought about the situation. The Center for the Performing Arts was the home of the Midwest Opera Company. They were rehearsing *Lucia di Lammermoor,* a particularly demanding role for the soprano. Signora Rienzi had agreed to sing three performances for the Midwest. She had just finished singing for the Lyric, Chicago's premier opera company, and was staying on in Chicago for a few weeks. Her voice fit the role to perfection and she was in demand at all the prestigious opera houses of the world. Her performance at the Midwest was a real bonus for the company.

Emma would never have this close contact with such great singers if she hadn't become a supernumerary. She had volunteered to be an extra a number of years ago at the request of her son-in-law and had enjoyed it ever since. Even though she might be relegated to a crowd scene, she was thrilled with the atmosphere onstage—the glorious voices, the music, the dancers. It was like entering a world of enchantment.

She smiled as she remembered her nervousness at her first audition, the enhanced underwear she had purchased to accentuate her nonexistent figure. That was where she had met Nate. It didn't take long for them to fall in love. Now they lived happily together in a condo on Lake Shore Drive.

"You're a million miles away. What thoughts are going through that active brain of yours?" Nate asked.

"I was just thinking, that's all."

"Don't give me that innocent look. You're conjuring up a dramatic scenario. I know you all too well." He added more sugar to his tea and took a sip.

"I think I'll ask James if he puts any credence to this intruder business," Emma said, leaving her tea untouched.

"I'll come with you," Nate said, taking the last swallow.

They made their way to the executive offices where James sat at his desk, rubbing his furrowed brow. He was talking animatedly on the phone. His eyebrows met in a frown and his receding hairline glistened with nervous perspiration.

He looked up when they walked in and waved them to a sofa. As he put the phone back on the charger, he blew out a deep breath. "What a mess," he grumbled.

"This seems like a bad time to bother you," Nate said.

"No, no, it's okay." He sat back in his chair and took a sip of water. "That was head of our security department. His men haven't found anyone, nor is anything missing, so there doesn't seem to be any reason to call in the police. The only explanation they have is that the stage entrance was unmanned for about a half hour. The intruder probably came in that way. We're pretty careful as far as security is concerned." He nervously tapped his fingers on the desk. "Somebody has some explaining to do." He pulled out a handkerchief and wiped his forehead.

"What about the soprano?" Emma asked. "Is she credible?"

James raised his eyebrows and held out his hands as if in supplication. "Are any of them? This one is especially prone to bouts of hysteria, so we can't really be sure of anything."

"Did anyone else see this man?" Emma asked.

"No, only Signora Rienzi," James said. "I have to talk with the director and the stage manager now." He pushed himself up from his chair and preceded them out of the office.

As Emma and Nate left, she thought about the intruder. Something nagged at her. She knew that feeling all too well. She had been plagued by premonitions all her life and they were usually well founded. She had inherited this "gift" from her grandmother Elizabeth. Emma's children had thought she was a witch when her predictions came true. She had a habit of conversing with her Guardian Angel on a regular basis. The celestial guardian had done a good job of protecting her through her six decades of life, but, sometimes, Emma managed to get into trouble anyway.

Guardian Angel, she prayed, *please keep me on the right path this time.*

AS SHE PICKED UP the ringing phone, Emma noted the name on the caller ID as that of her closest friend, Gladys Foster. "Hi, Gladys. How are things on the East Coast?"

"It's not as cold here as it is out your way, but the weather is typical for March. Cornell and I went to see a performance of *Madame Butterfly* at the Met last night. I cried my eyes out at the end."

Emma smiled as she pictured her robust friend dissolving in tears. "I do the same thing. Nate and I saw *Hansel and Gretel* at the Lyric last week. It was delightful."

"So, how do you like living on Chicago's lakeshore now that your first winter is almost over?" Gladys asked.

"It's wonderful. I didn't have to worry about shoveling snow. I've been here less than a year and I don't even think about that old house in Brookfield anymore. It seems like a different lifetime."

She walked into the atrium of the six-room condo, surveyed her many exotic plants and stared out across Michigan Avenue at the waves pounding the shoreline of the mighty lake.

"I'm looking at the water as we speak. It's wild today, white-capped waves rushing in. They're at least three feet high, maybe more." She shivered. "That wind is raw. We were bundled to the hilt when we went to rehearsal." Emma pulled her sweater tighter around her thin body; she felt a sudden chill though the room was warm.

"So what are you rehearsing at the Midwest?" Gladys asked.

"*Lucia di Lammermoor,* and it's not going well."

"How come?"

"Well, yesterday the soprano saw someone in her dressing

room, a man who resembled a street person. She said all he did was point to the closet. The security people searched the entire building, but found nothing."

"That sounds weird. Who is the soprano?" Gladys asked.

"Gina Rienzi."

"Oh, that one. She has a reputation for fits of temper as well as hysteria. It was probably her imagination."

"Perhaps." Emma hesitated for just a moment. "All during the rehearsal today she was visibly nervous. The director stopped her a number of times. Her eyes kept darting from one corner of the stage to another, as though she expected to see someone or something at any minute." Emma sighed. "Finally the conductor and the director called it a day. We're supposed to go back tomorrow."

"She'll probably calm down by then. She's known for that sort of thing. It'll be interesting to see how she handles the mad scene. By the way, shouldn't grandchild number five be here pretty soon?" Gladys asked.

"As a matter of fact, Bertie's due date is just a few weeks from now. I talked with her yesterday. She's a real trouper, taking it all in stride, still working at that clinic dealing with problem teenagers. She was the best thing that ever happened to my son, Martin. She made a man out of an irresponsible boy."

"It'll be interesting to see how he adjusts to fatherhood," Gladys said.

"I'm sure he'll do fine." Emma was pleased with the way her three children had grown through their choices in life.

"Oh," Gladys said, "my loving husband is calling me. I have to go. Talk to you soon. Say hello to Nate."

"I will. Bye, Gladys."

Emma put down the phone but continued to stare at the turbulent lake. To the south she could see the Ferris wheel at Navy Pier. For a long time she stood, mesmerized by the slowly revolving wheel. Finally Emma turned away and tried to concentrate on the coming baby, but she couldn't shake off the feeling that something unpleasant was looming.

TWO

THE FOLLOWING AFTERNOON, Emma and Nate trudged through the slushy snow covering the sidewalks as they headed for the rehearsal. Winter refused to release the Midwest from its grip. The temperature had hovered around the freezing mark for days.

"I hope this goes well," Nate grumbled. "I'm getting tired of this soprano's hysterical outbursts. Last week the staircase was too high, now there's a stranger in her dressing room. What's next?"

"Who knows," Emma said. She looked up at the gray clouds obscuring any hint of blue sky. "Where is spring? There should be some green shoots coming up by now, but the weatherman predicted more of this weather for the rest of the week."

"You know you can't trust March," Nate said with a sigh.

Other supers and chorus members entered at the same time as Emma and Nate. Their moods were no better. They complained of the weather, the soprano, the director, the conductor, anyone who seemed responsible for canceling and rescheduling the recent rehearsals.

At this particular rehearsal, only the principals had to be in costume, so Emma and Nate headed for the community room and a cup of hot tea before the director called them to the stage.

Today the conductor wanted to run through act three where the supers were among the guests at Lammermoor Castle celebrating the marriage of Lucia to Lord Arturo Bucklaw, a man she did not love.

As the act began, Emma and Nate were among the crowd toasting the marriage, each holding a plastic champagne glass filled with ginger ale. Lucia had retired to the bridal chamber.

The scene was one of merriment and festivity, the supers and chorus members conversed in low tones and moved slowly about the stage. Suddenly Lucia's tutor entered and held up his hands to silence the crowd. In an emotional Italian aria, he told the guests that Lucia, in a fit of madness, had stabbed her husband to death.

Signora Rienzi appeared at the top of a winding staircase, her hair, which had been carefully coifed in the previous scene, now hung limply down her shoulders, her white nightgown streaked with theatrical blood. She stared at her hands, as if in confusion. Then she began the familiar strains of the mad scene that had made the woman famous in opera houses around the world.

As she slowly descended the stairs, she presented the picture of a frightened and confused young girl, looking down at her hands, then at her gown, then into space. Her melodious voice mirrored the illusion. Halfway down she stopped. Her hand went to her mouth.

The conductor tapped his baton and the sound of the instruments faded. All eyes were on the soprano.

"There he is," she shouted. "The man from my dressing room."

Everyone turned to the direction she pointed. Emma thought she had the impression of a figure disappearing around the curtain.

"Didn't anyone see him?" the soprano shouted. She brought one hand to her chest and gripped the rail with the other. Her breath came in audible gasps.

Heads shook; people shrugged.

"I think I did," Emma said, hesitating.

The director ran onstage. "Tell me," he said to Emma, "just what did you see?"

"Only a fleeting glimpse." Emma screwed up her face. "But he appeared ragged and dirty, and I think I smelled something."

"See," the soprano said. "It is not my imagination. That woman saw him, too. He was pointing again."

"Where was he pointing?" the director asked, raising his eyes and fisting his hands.

"At the floor," the soprano said. "At the stage floor, then he turned around and disappeared. I don't know if I can sing in this opera house with strange men running about." She fanned herself with one trembling hand still clutching the banister with the other.

By now the director, the stage manager, and the conductor surrounded Signora Rienzi, all trying to placate her.

"We'll take a fifteen-minute break," the director said. "Then we'll resume."

The chorus and the supers retired to the community room where they quizzed Emma.

"Did you really see someone?… What did he look like?… Did he have a weapon?… I didn't see anyone…"

Emma's son-in-law, James, came in and rescued her from the crowd. "Come to my office," he said.

When she and Nate were comfortably seated in the privacy of James's office, he began questioning her. "Emma, it's critical that we verify this woman's story. She's been known for hysterical outbursts in the past, but we have to investigate regardless. Tell me, again, just what you saw."

Emma took a deep breath, sat back, and closed her eyes. She tried to visualize the man. "When the soprano shouted 'there he is,' I looked in the direction she was pointing. I saw the form of a man in ragged clothing turn away and dart behind the curtain and I smelled something, I'm not sure what." She looked from one to the other and shrugged.

"What do you mean by 'the form of a man'?" James asked, a dubious frown on his face.

"It wasn't distinct. Not like a real person," she whispered. Emma felt the familiar goose bumps crawl up her arms at the words she had just spoken. *I could almost see through him,* she thought. *But better not tell James that, or he'll think I'm as mad as Lucia.*

James shook his head. "I don't know what to make of all

this. I just hope Signora Rienzi doesn't try to break her contract thinking she's in some kind of danger. The security guards and the stagehands are searching the building—again."

A half hour later the stage manager called everyone back. The scene progressed with some hesitation on the part of the singers. They all seemed to be expecting something extraordinary to happen.

During the mad scene, Signora Rienzi hesitated at the top of the staircase, her gaze darting from stage left to stage right. Then she took a deep breath and sang her aria to perfection like the seasoned professional she was, even adding a long sustained note at the end.

"All right," the director said. "That was beautiful. The dress rehearsal is Friday afternoon. Everyone on time, please."

As Emma and Nate made their way home through a biting wind that almost knocked her over, he held her as close as possible. The four-block walk seemed more like four miles.

Nate blew out a deep breath as he opened the outer door to the building and the wind literally pushed them inside. "Chicago is aptly named the Windy City," he said, shivering.

Emma also felt a chill, not only from the cold, but from something else. What was it that was bothering her?

When they were settled in the kitchen, each with a cup of hot chocolate, Nate turned to Emma, a concerned expression on his face. He ran his hand through his sparse hair then rubbed the cleft in his chin. "Will you please explain that remark you made to James, about the man you thought you saw?"

Emma pursed her lips and frowned. "I definitely saw someone. It looked like a man, but the form wasn't clear, sort of out of focus." She hesitated for a moment then raised her large gray eyes to Nate's disbelieving face.

"What do you mean by out of focus?"

She thought for a moment. "Kind of like I wasn't sure if he was really there." She scratched her head and pushed her unruly hair behind her ear.

"That doesn't make any sense. He was there or he wasn't

there." He tipped his cup back to get the last drop of chocolate and shook his head. "Didn't you say the other day that your contacts were giving you trouble?"

Emma fiddled with her cup. "They were dirty. After I cleaned them, they seemed to be all right."

"Still, maybe you should see Dr. Fuller and have them checked. You know how bad your eyesight is. Okay?"

"Maybe I will."

"I'm tired of all this foolishness," Nate said, getting up from his chair. He walked out of the room, muttering to himself.

How can I tell him it's not my eyesight? Emma wondered. *How can I say I could almost see through the man? But, I'd better call the doctor for an appointment, just to be sure.*

Oh, Guardian Angel, what does this mean?

Throughout her life Emma had relied on her celestial guardian to help her through trying times. Was this yet another one?

THE DRESS REHEARSAL proceeded with a few minor problems with props, but no more sightings of the mysterious stranger.

On opening night, the late-winter snow had finally blown over, but depressing piles of gray icy mounds still lined the curbs. Emma stepped carefully to avoid slipping on any remaining ice.

Since the supers appeared only in the third act, they had come in later than the singers, and Emma and Nate had time to relax in the community room for a while.

"I hope everything goes well tonight," Nate said, watching some of the other supers standing around. One woman in particular seemed nervous. She walked from one end of the room to the other rubbing her hands together and frowning, then she slowly approached them.

"Can I talk to you?" she asked, addressing Emma.

"Certainly. Sit down here, next to me. Do you want some tea?" Emma noticed the woman's distress and wondered why.

"No, I have water. I need to tell someone, but I don't want to create a fuss," she said.

"Tell someone what?" Nate asked, frowning.

"I think I saw him," she whispered, leaning close.

"Who?" Nate asked, an annoyed tone to his voice now.

"The man, the stranger." She twisted her head from side to side like an animal would watching for a predator.

Emma held her hand up to Nate who was about to say something. "Where did you see him? What did he look like?"

"Well, I was walking down the corridor toward the property room. I lost an earring a few days ago and remembered I had been in that area at the time." She clutched the bottle of water so tightly, her knuckles turned white.

"Go on," Emma urged, ignoring Nate's furrowed brow.

"He was just ahead of me, dressed in ragged clothes, just like you said. He looked like a street person and there was a smell." Her brows knitted together.

"What kind of smell?" Emma asked.

The woman thought for a moment. "Kind of musty, like a damp, old basement. I stopped, and suddenly he wasn't there anymore." The woman began to tremble.

"I squeezed my eyes shut then opened them, but the corridor was empty. I must have imagined him."

"The lighting is poor along that corridor," Nate said, an authoritative tone to his voice.

"Yes, I suppose you're right."

"With all the hysterical outbursts by the soprano this past week, I'm surprised more people haven't reported seeing this elusive stranger," Nate said, shaking his head and waving his hand in the air.

"It is easy to imagine something like that, isn't it?" the woman said. Her hands lost their stranglehold on the bottle and she sat up straighter. "I'd better not tell anyone else."

"That's right. It's better not to get everyone riled up again."

"Thanks." She got up and walked toward the dressing rooms.

"Now, I think we'd better get into our costumes," Nate said. "Emma, is something bothering you? You're making faces."

"No, nothing at all," she said with a slight shake of her head.

He snaked his arm around her and gazed down at her. "Let it go, please."

She nodded and followed him to the dressing room. Her costume had been taken in with large stitches to fit her slim figure. Three petticoats under the skirt filled her out rather well and the tight bodice, with stays, pushed up her small breasts; a white wig covered her unruly hair, and faux jewels completed the illusion. *I'm certainly glad styles have changed through the years,* Emma thought. *I wouldn't want to have to go through this every day.* But when she looked in the mirror she approved of her reflection. Her plain face was almost pretty.

For the rest of the performance, Emma kept searching for the stranger. Now a third person had reported seeing him. It wasn't anyone's imagination, she was sure of that. Someone was roaming about. Was it some street person as James surmised, or was it someone else? And why was he here now? She had a feeling she would be involved whether she liked it or not.

APPRECIATIVE APPLAUSE by the audience and rave reviews by the media concluded the three performances of Lucia. Signora Rienzi bowed to the *bravas* and blew kisses to the patrons.

Though Emma watched closely, she saw no one backstage or in the wings who didn't belong there.

After James said a fond farewell to the soprano, he and his wife, Sylvia, joined Emma and Nate for a late-night snack.

"Who's with the boys tonight?" Emma asked her daughter.

"This wonderful teenager who lives next door. It's great to be free for an evening and not worry about them. They do wear me out."

"Two rambunctious preschoolers are a handful," Emma said. "And James Jr. and Frankie certainly fit the mold." She remembered when her own children were that age, but they grew up so fast. *Those precious years are all too short,* she thought, wallowing in nostalgia.

James gave a deep sigh as he downed his second scotch and water. "You're driving tonight," he said to his wife. "I need to unwind after Signora Rienzi. I've had enough of hysterical singers and sightings of mysterious strangers. I'm sure that's the end of all this nonsense." He and Nate clicked glasses in agreement.

As Emma stared at her chicken salad sandwich, only half eaten, she realized she wasn't hungry anymore. She wasn't sure at all that this episode was over. Something told her they hadn't seen the last of the ragged man. She hoped she was wrong, but experience told her otherwise.

THREE

"So, WHAT DID the eye doctor have to say?" Nate asked as Emma walked in the door.

"He said I needed a minor adjustment to my prescription. It could have caused some blurring of my vision." She knew that was what he wanted to hear, but she wasn't convinced.

"See, I told you. Did you order new ones?"

"Yes, I'm to pick them up next week." She gave him an innocent smile and walked away.

THAT EVENING EMMA SAT in her favorite chair reading a book she had picked up at the Harold Washington Library. It was set in the time of the Civil War, and although it was fiction, the author had thoroughly researched his facts. *Why had she picked this particular book?* She had read three mysteries in a row and was looking for a change. Emma wasn't particularly interested in the Civil War, but something propelled her to the historical fiction section. She smiled as she remembered the almost imperceptible nudge that always came from her Guardian Angel when she was supposed to pay attention to something.

There must be a reason for this book, Emma thought, so she decided to read it and see if she might learn something from it.

"Nate, it says here that the Underground Railroad was active in some areas of Chicago. I didn't know that, did you?"

"Huh?" Nate was engrossed in a particularly challenging crossword puzzle.

"You didn't even hear what I said," Emma chided.

"Sorry, my love, I'm trying to figure out a four-letter word that fits in here starting with the letter 'f' and the answer keeps eluding me. Don't give me that look, it's not the word you're thinking of. Something that means 'brawl.'" He frowned, his bushy eyebrows almost meeting in the middle, his owl-like eyes narrowing in concentration.

Emma got up from her chair and kissed the top of his balding head. "I'm sure it will come to you. It always does. I'll make us a cup of tea." She walked into the kitchen, lit the gas under the teapot, and took two mugs from the cupboard.

"Aha!" Nate shouted.

Emma heard his exclamation and smiled. *What a lucky woman I am. Sometimes I have to pinch myself to make sure I'm not dreaming. Why was I so hesitant to give up that old house in Brookfield with the stairs that got steeper every year? It was time. The only thing I regret is leaving my dear neighbor, Maria, but she's living with her daughter in the city now.*

Everything worked out as it was meant to, her inner voice said.

Yes, it certainly did.

Emma's family approved of her move and were relieved that Nate was there to watch over her. He was there for her last summer when she made some serious blunders that almost cost her life.

The past is gone. Live in the present.

"I got it," Nate said, walking into the kitchen and snaking his arms around her. "Is the tea ready, my little Sparrow?" He planted a kiss on her neck that sent goose bumps down her arms.

"Yes, sit down. And here's a nice slice of apple pie." She had cut a generous wedge and put it in front of him. "What was the word?"

"It was fray—so obvious I didn't see it." He finished the pie in a few bites. "This is great. Are seconds in order?"

Emma gave him a dubious look. "Remember your waistline," she said, cutting another piece. "You promised that you would start working out in the gym, remember?"

"Uh huh, next week." Nate patted his middle with a sigh of

contentment. He had finished the last crumb and loosened his belt a notch.

"That's what you said last week," Emma said, her hands on her hips.

"I promise," he said, raising his hands in submission. "Now, what was it you were asking me earlier about the Underground Railroad?"

"I'm reading this book about the Civil War. The author says there were three authenticated 'stations' as they were called, in Illinois, as well as a number that can't be documented."

"Sure," Nate said. "One is the old Graue Mill near Hinsdale, isn't it?"

"Oh yes," she said warming to the subject. "I had forgotten about that one. Remember when we went there the summer before last to get some freshly ground cornmeal? I seem to recall that it's the only operating waterwheel gristmill in Illinois."

She smiled as she remembered the picturesque stone building dating from the 1850s, the huge grinding stones turning periodically to give visitors a view of early Americana, a woman spinning and weaving wool and flax. What a demanding life that was.

"Let's go there again," she said.

"In the spring," Nate agreed. "I don't believe the wheel is turning in the ice and snow. I think it's closed from November 'til sometime in April."

Emma frowned. "Something else this author said that got me thinking."

"Oh, oh. I can hear the wheels of your brain turning like that old gristmill." Nate tried not to smile, but Emma saw the corners of his lips twitching.

"Are you insinuating I'm old?" she said, sitting up straight in her chair.

"Of course not, my dear, just seasoned, like a fine vintage wine."

"All right. I'll let it slide, this time."

"So, what was it that got you thinking?"

"The author claims there was supposed to be a 'station' some-where near the southern shore of Lake Michigan. The owners of the property dug a tunnel under an old building out to the lake where, under cover of darkness, boats took the escaped slaves across to northern Michigan where some of them went on into Canada. Isn't that exciting? It could have been on this very spot where this building stands."

Nate shook his head. "Sure. It does make for interesting fiction, but it's just that. Now I say we go to bed. I'm tired and full of apple pie."

But it was a long time before Emma could sleep. She felt the terror of desperate people crawling through dank tunnels, then crossing the vast lake in tiny boats. She heard children crying in fear, saw women clutching babies and muttering prayers. How many of them never reached the other shore? She shuddered and vowed to learn more.

FOUR

DRESSED IN BLACK, a figure moved with stealth through the trees and bushes behind the building. Dark clouds obscured the moon, leaving no shadows. He smiled, knowing he wouldn't be detected at this time of night. This was almost too easy.

A large thorn bush obscured the hidden access. As he flattened himself behind it, a branch tore at his face, but the ski mask protected him. He found the large stone that he was looking for, felt the surface for the distinctive marking, a deep depression in the center. Yes, it was the right one. He leaned against it with all his weight and pushed. It moved, but not enough. He planted his feet on the ground and leaned harder into the stone. It finally rolled, just enough to reveal the narrow opening.

He shone his light down into the hole. Satisfied that it was safe, he slid his feet in and squeezed his body through. The small bright disk of the penlight illuminated the way through the narrow space. He wrinkled his nose at the smell of rot and decay. But he would not be long. The light danced along the many recesses in the earthen structure. As he crept along, bits of rotted wood and earth fell onto his head. He noted that it was more pronounced than the last time he was here. This place would not be safe for too much longer.

He looked around, then smiled. There it was, in the hollowed-out space in the wall—a fat envelope. He opened it and quickly counted the money. It was all there, as promised. Then he opened the knapsack he carried, and one by one, took the four packages of high-grade heroin wrapped in brown paper and tied with twine, placed them in plastic bags and tucked them into the recess. He put the envelope in the knapsack, gave it a reassuring pat, then quickly and silently, retraced his steps, pushed the rock back in place, and disappeared into the dark night—unheard and unseen.

FIVE

EMMA LOOKED OUT the atrium window across the roof garden, at the mighty Lake Michigan, its rocky shoreline glistened with an icy sheen. The sunlight danced on the waves belying the chilly temperature that persisted. She was eager to transplant the vegetables and flowers from the starting trays in the atrium to the huge pots that decorated the roof garden. They seemed to be calling for her attention. The tiny plants sat catching the light streaming in from the large windows. Emma lovingly turned the trays daily and made sure the soil didn't dry out.

She heard the phone ring and Nate answer it, his voice slightly raised in an exasperated tone, but she couldn't make out his words. After a few minutes he joined her, plopping down in one of the lounge chairs.

"Who was on the phone? You sounded so annoyed," she said.

"My grandson."

"Which one?"

"Joey. He's writing a paper for school on the Chicago Fire. He got most of his information from the Internet, but he wanted to talk to someone who witnessed it. Can you imagine? He actually thought I was living in 1871, wanted to know what it was like escaping from the flames." Nate frowned and slowly shook his head. "Do I look that old?"

His expression made Emma burst out laughing. "You'll never look old to me," she said, kissing him on the forehead. "What grade is Joey in?"

"Fourth or fifth, I'm not sure."

"Kids that age have no conception of time or when things

actually occurred. I'm sure he didn't mean to insult you. He obviously values your opinion."

"Humph. I wonder what kind of grades he gets in math." Nate got up and went into the living room and retrieved the Sunday paper.

"Emma," he called. "Here's something interesting."

Emma peeked over his shoulder at the article.

"This ties in with what you were reading in that book about the Civil War and the Underground Railroad yesterday," he said. "It seems there was a community in Michigan called Ramptown made up of fugitive slaves. Archaeologists recently discovered artifacts that verify the town's existence. Interesting." He turned to Emma who nodded in agreement.

"So, they might have traveled overland from Illinois to Michigan," she mused, "or they might have crossed the lake under cover of night." Again she thought of the cold waters, small boats bobbing on the waves, women clutching babies and small children. She shivered. How could mankind be so cruel to fellow human beings?

"Take that worried look off your face," he said. "This all happened so long ago. Come on, how about one of those muffins you made this morning? You don't want them to get stale, do you?"

LATER THAT AFTERNOON the phone interrupted Emma's reading and Nate's dozing.

"Hello," she said.

"Hi, Mom, it's Sylvia."

"Yes, dear, how are you and the boys?"

"We're all fine. They're over their sniffles and we're sleeping nights again."

"Good. You sound rested for a change."

"By the way," Sylvia said, "James wants to talk to you and Nate. Here he is."

"Hello, Emma, everything okay over there?" came James's cheery voice.

"We're well." Emma wondered why this concern for their welfare. *He wants a favor, I'll bet.*

"I was wondering if you two would be willing to search through some boxes that are in the basement of the Performing Arts Center. The manager of the building and I were down there with the fire inspectors the other day and they said the place has to be cleared out to meet the new fire codes."

"What's all down there?" Emma asked.

"I don't know. Lots of it is junk that can be trashed. But we found a number of sealed boxes that might hold something of historical significance. Parts of this building are pretty old, you know. The lower area and foundation predate the Chicago Fire."

"Really. I'll talk to Nate. I'm sure he'll be interested." She held up her hand to Nate's inquisitive look.

"I don't trust anyone else," James said. "I know you two will be thorough."

"I'll get back to you later today. Bye now."

"What was that all about?" Nate asked.

"James would like us to look through a few boxes in the basement of the Center that might hold vintage documents or something of interest."

"Sounds like an interesting project. And," Nate continued, "didn't the librarian at the Center retire recently? A stroke or something?"

"I remember that. Volunteers have been pitching in, but it's a hit-and-miss affair. James said they're advertising for someone to take her place. For the time being, maybe we should take over, just temporarily, and get everything categorized properly."

Emma looked at him, a question in her eyes.

Nate shrugged. "We don't have any pressing obligations right now. The next opera isn't until June."

"We might find something interesting," Emma said.

You might find something dangerous, her inner voice said. *Now why would I think that?*

THE FOLLOWING WEEK Emma and Nate ventured into the basement of the Performing Arts Center. James had told Bruce Hamilton, the building manager, to expect them. He gave the project a thumbs-up, delighted to find people willing to spend time amid the dust and spiders, and maybe, an occasional mouse searching for a possible treasure.

Nate carried a backpack loaded with water bottles, flashlights, wipes, and freshly baked muffins, Emma's special recipe. Emma carried a box of plastic sleeves, in case they found any old documents worth investigating.

He flipped a switch on the wall and fluorescent lights lit up the room, the long tubes blinking and buzzing as if resenting being called into service.

"Where do we start?" Emma asked, looking around at the cavernous space housing props, furniture, and old costumes.

"Well, we're not doing anything with this stuff," Nate said. "James told me someone from the props department was going to sort through these. He said there's a storeroom in back filled with boxes. Let's see if we can find it."

He grabbed Emma as she stumbled over a small footstool. "Be careful!"

"Darn," she said, stubbing her toe on something that resembled an anvil.

"There's a door," Nate said, "in the back. See? That's probably it."

She held on to his arm for support and followed through pieces of period furniture, suits of armor, and all the paraphernalia necessary to make a production appear authentic. In the rear of the huge space Emma pulled back.

"What's the matter?" Nate asked.

She hesitated for a moment. "This place has a bad feel to it." She shivered, remembering the case of mistaken identity the previous summer that resulted in her being restrained in an old warehouse. She couldn't erase the memory of that nightmare from her mind. Was this going to be more of the same?

No. This was a new venture and she must view it as such, but she couldn't shake the feeling that something unpleasant loomed.

"I won't let anything happen to you, but if you'd rather not do this, Emma, we can tell James to get someone else." Nate put his arm protectively around her.

"I'm just being foolish. This might be fun, who knows?" She nodded and forced a smile.

"That's my Sparrow." He gave her a hug. "Come on, let's see what's behind that door."

A pile of old costumes and masks barred the way.

"Ugh," Nate said, shoving them aside with his foot. "This stuff is molding down here. They really need a clean-out crew. Okay, let me see if I can get this open." He grabbed the old brass knob and turned it, but nothing happened. Next he heaved his body against the heavy oak. It made a few creaks, but moved barely an inch.

"Is something behind it?" Emma asked.

"I think it's warped. I'll have to try and lift it."

"Don't hurt yourself," she said as Nate grabbed the knob and, straining and groaning, managed to lift the heavy door just a little. He pushed as it scraped along the concrete floor with a rasping sound. Nate blew out a breath and rubbed his hands together. "There, I think I can push it the rest of the way."

"Let me help you." Emma added her meager weight to his, and the door reluctantly opened wide enough for them to get through.

"That was a day's work right there," he said, shining a flash-light into the room.

"Will you look at that," Emma said. Boxes lay piled four deep, almost reaching to the ceiling of the small room. "I thought there were just a few."

"There's a chain hanging from that light bulb," Nate said. He pulled it and was rewarded with a meager glow.

"I can't believe it actually works," Emma said.

"It's probably all of forty watts. Remind me to bring a hundred-watter when we come back tomorrow," he said.

"Where do we start?" Emma felt daunted already. "There's so much here." The smell of must filled the small room. Emma sniffed and scrunched up her nose. Did she smell something else? She looked around at the cobwebs hanging in the corners. She could almost feel them clinging to her face and hair. She wasn't so sure about being down here.

Nate's voice pulled her back to the task at hand. "We have to be methodical about this," he said. "Let's start with the ones closest to the door. Some of them are dated. That might be helpful. I think I saw a couple of old stools among the props. I'll get them so we'll have someplace to sit. Stay put. I'll be right back."

As Emma waited for Nate, she stared, trying to get the feel of the room and its contents. There was something else, all right, but she didn't know what.

Guardian Angel, I feel suffering and pain in here. Is the answer in these boxes? She wasn't sure she wanted to know. Suddenly she had this feeling that she needed to run out, to leave this place and whatever lay hidden here. She clutched her body with her arms to stop the shiver.

"Okay," Nate said, returning with two stools. "Are you all right? You look a little pale."

"I'm fine. It's just all this dust and grime."

"Good. Let's get to work."

AFTER THREE HOURS, they had searched through only a few boxes and found nothing of interest: old bills for costume rentals, receipts dated ten years ago, lists of performers and productions in progress at the time.

Nate stood and stretched. "I've had it for today. How about you?"

"Absolutely. What do we do with these boxes we've examined?"

"I'll push them out of the room and leave them with the props. James said to mark them with an X and they would decide what to do with them." He took out a red marker and put a large X on the boxes. Even without them, they realized they had barely made a dent in the stack.

"This is going to be more work than we bargained for," Nate said, scratching his head. "Maybe we should ask for another volunteer."

"Would there be room in here for three of us?"

"Hmm. We'll clear out a few more boxes first. Right now I need to go home, strip off these clothes, and get in the shower."

"Me, too."

Nate looked at her with a mischievous grin. "Shall we do it together?"

SIX

TRISTANA MORGAN LOOKED out the window of her third-floor studio apartment on Belmont Avenue, in the heart of Chicago's near north side. The gray sky did nothing to dispel her loneliness. A few flakes of snow drifted past the window.

It never snows in southern California, she thought. *Did I make a mistake moving here? There's nothing appealing about this climate. It's cold and damp and I'm chilled to the bone.*

She rubbed her arms as she searched for something heavier to wear. She would have to buy an entirely new wardrobe; she hadn't prepared for the Midwest where weather changes on a whim. Just yesterday it had felt like spring.

Tristana thought she could escape the nightmares if she moved away and started a new life. "Maybe the horrors of what I escaped will be with me until I die," she whispered, sinking into a lumpy chair.

She looked at the empty wine bottles on the table, standing like three sentinels daring her to open another.

"I refuse to go there," she said, picking them up one by one and throwing them in the trash.

The insurance money was almost gone. She would have to get a job soon. She sat on a wobbly wooden chair that was next to a tiny table marred by all the lonely people who had come before. She could feel the loneliness in the aura of this claustrophobic place.

Tristana picked up her pen and examined the list she had started that morning:

1. Get a job.
2. Buy warm clothes.
3. Find an appropriate church.

Then she wrote:

4. Move to a bigger apartment.

That was a start—the beginning of her new life.

What would it be like? Nothing that happened in the past was her fault. Isn't that what the psychologist had told her? If she could only believe it, *really* believe it.

"I must! It's the only way I can survive," she shouted at the walls.

Then with a heavy sigh she looked at the page of newspaper where she had circled an ad that morning:

> *Librarian for Lakeshore Center for the Performing Arts. Call Bruce Hamilton at...*

It probably didn't pay much, but it was a start. She couldn't go back to a big-city library right now anyway, had to get control of her emotions first.

If I start with this job, she reasoned, *maybe I can get my self-confidence back. Then I'll move on. That's it. I'll call tomorrow...*

SEVEN

EMMA WALKED INTO the study and stood for a long time watching Nate. She thought she might break his concentration, but he continued to stare at the computer screen, pressing buttons from time to time. She went to him, leaning over his shoulder. "What has you so mesmerized?"

"I was just looking up some facts about the Chicago Fire and found a good Web site. Here's something Joey may want to add to his paper. The old Water Tower, the only structure in that area that survived the fire, is said to be haunted by the ghost of a man who stayed there and kept pumping water out of it. He waited 'til the last minute, then killed himself by jumping out of the Water Tower rather than burn to death. Some people claim to see his ghost in a window of the tower. I'll call Joey and tell him to access it."

He turned to Emma, made a face, formed his hands into claws and said, "OOO."

"Very funny. Save that for Halloween."

"You have to admit," he said, "it will add a little extra something to a fifth-grade report." Nate reached for his cell phone and called his grandson in Florida.

Emma walked into the atrium thinking of the heroic man who stayed at his post until it was too late to escape. What motives gave people such courage?

Suddenly the picture of the stranger in the opera house came into her mind. When she had seen him onstage, he almost looked like a spirit. *No, it couldn't be. It was my contacts. The prescription needed adjustment. That probably explained it, but still...*

AFTER TWO WEEKS OF dust, dirt, mouse droppings, and spiders darting out of corners, Emma and Nate found nothing of importance in the basement of the Center. Volunteers had carted away boxes they had already searched, so at the very least Emma and Nate weren't tripping over them. After searching through a dozen boxes, they found only a few items of interest from the 1960s that seemed worth saving. Emma slipped them into the plastic sleeves and set them aside.

Nate breathed a sigh of boredom. "Let's take a break from this for a while, okay?"

Emma rubbed the small of her back, stretched and yawned. "That sounds good to me. There are only a few more boxes. We can go through them next week."

"At least the place is less of a fire hazard," Nate said.

Emma frowned as she studied a panel at the back of the room that had been obscured before. "This looks interesting. I wonder what's behind it."

"What are you looking at?" Nate asked, trying to pull her out of the room.

"Just a minute, Nate."

"It's probably more boxes."

"I want to see," she said with the enthusiasm of a child.

"James asked us to look for anything of historic significance, not take the building apart. It was probably put there to reinforce crumbling concrete. Come on, let's go."

Reluctantly she followed him, but the panel intrigued her. She had felt something behind it, perhaps something important. She'd make sure to check it out later.

They found James on the phone, as usual, an exasperated frown on his face. "I'll have to get back to you on that later." He gripped the instrument and looked as if he intended to throw it across the room. Then he took a deep breath, blew it out slowly, placed the phone back on the charger, and gave them a smile.

"Nate, do you want my job?" he asked, rubbing his hand over his eyes.

"No, thank you. I'm retired and don't intend going back to the corporate world."

"Smart man. How about some coffee?"

"Now that sounds more like it." Nate chuckled.

As James set two cups of steaming coffee in front of them, he scanned the material they had placed on his desk. "Nothing exciting, is it?"

"Not really," Nate said. "There are only another six or seven boxes left. We decided to take the rest of the week off."

"Of course. Maybe they're not even worth bothering with," James said.

"No, no," Emma said. "We may find a treasure yet."

"By the way," James said, "we have a new librarian. Bruce interviewed her yesterday. She just moved here from California, was working at a school library out there. She seems well qualified. Her name is, ah…" He picked up a note on his desk. "Tristana Morgan. How's that for an operatic moniker? With a name like that she belongs in this place. She starts next week. I'll introduce you to her then."

"WHAT ARE YOUR PLANS for today?" Emma asked Nate as she cleared the breakfast dishes.

"I had better finish that article I'm writing for the investment newsletter. It's due next week."

She nodded, knew that Nate needed to keep involved in the world of stocks and bonds in which he had invested so wisely in the past, the reason they were living in this beautiful condo. This was an area as foreign to her as the theory of relativity.

"I think I'll go to the Performing Arts Center and meet the new librarian. Perhaps I can give her a hand," Emma said.

"Good idea."

Emma knew he'd be in his own world for a number of hours in the study. She put on her coat, pulled a denim cap over her unruly hair, and slipped out the door. As she left the building, Emma took a deep breath of the brisk air that heralded spring.

It seemed to hover over the Midwest, but Mother Nature refused to let it loose.

The four-block walk invigorated Emma. She felt younger than her sixty-plus years. Yes, it was good to be alive, to be loved, and to be living in this vibrant city.

She found herself humming as she went into the stage entrance of the Performing Arts Center. She climbed the stairs to James's office, but found the door locked.

Going back down the flight of stairs, she heard raised voices coming from the office marked Bruce Hamilton, General Manager.

"Because I authorized it!" Bruce's angry voice shouted.

This is none of my business, Emma thought, tempted to tiptoe closer.

"But why didn't someone tell me?" a whiny voice asked.

"Because I make the decisions around here on these matters. There was no reason for you to be involved. When you're the manager, you can call the shots. Until then, I do."

"Yes, sir, but…"

"No buts. If you don't have enough work to do, Mr. Quiller, I can always assign you other duties."

With that, Emma decided she had heard enough. She had no idea what was going on and really shouldn't care, but her innate curiosity did cause her to wonder.

She headed for the library where she found James talking to an attractive middle-aged brunette. Her shoulder-length brown hair was peppered with just enough gray to give it a sheen. Her tall, well-built frame looked professional in the pinstriped, tailored suit, though it did sag, just a little, as if she had recently lost weight.

James turned to see Emma and smiled his usual warm greeting. "Emma, just the person I need right now." He walked over and gave her a warm hug.

"Mrs. Morgan, this is Emma Winberry, my mother-in-law,

one of our supernumeraries, and one of our gracious volunteers. Emma, meet our new librarian, Tristana Morgan."

"How do you do," the woman said hesitantly, extending her hand.

Emma shook it but noticed how cold the woman's hand felt. Emma smiled and gazed into brown eyes that reflected pain and sadness. Makeup didn't quite cover the dark circles around them.

"Bruce asked me to show Mrs. Morgan around," James said, "but I have a meeting in a few minutes." He said, turning to Emma, "I wonder if you could take over here for me. I think I've overloaded Mrs. Morgan." He gave Emma a pleading look.

"Of course, I came to help."

"Bless you, and thanks." With a wave, he was out the door.

"Why don't we get acquainted?" Emma said. "I think a cup of coffee is in order."

"All right," the woman said. "Where do we go?"

"There's a coffee machine down the hall, but the stuff is vile. Let's slip out to the café on the corner. They have lovely scones there."

"Can we do that?"

"My dear, the nice part about being a volunteer is that they can't fire me, and I consider this part of your orientation." Emma gave her a wink. "Besides, after a while, your mind stops absorbing information. Your batteries need recharging."

Tristana gave her a weak smile as she grabbed her coat.

The women walked outside to be hit by a cold wind from off the lake. "That coat isn't warm enough for Chicago weather," Emma said, looking over at her companion.

"I found that out." Tristana Morgan pulled the thin fabric around herself and shivered. "I have to do some serious shopping. Perhaps you can tell me where I can find the best priced stores."

"Well, right now you can get some good buys on winter clothes. Go to any store on State Street. You should find what you need there." She smiled, hoping she had sounded encouraging, but the woman simply nodded and sighed.

The mid-morning lull in the café gave them their choice of seats. The breakfast crowd had left and the staff was preparing for the lunch rush. The homey décor was welcoming; vintage pictures of fruits and vegetables lining the walls. The booths upholstered in a plum-colored vinyl left enough leg room for comfort. Emma slid into one.

"This is the best time to come here," she said, "no rushing."

Tristana sat opposite her. She only wanted coffee, but Emma talked her into trying the scones. With the first bite she agreed that they were delicious.

"So, tell me about yourself," Emma said as she poured cream into her coffee.

The woman looked past Emma, out the window at the barren trees and sighed again. "I recently moved here from California. That's why I don't have proper clothes. I have a furnished apartment on Belmont Avenue that's too small. It's such a congested area, and I don't know anyone in the Chicago area. I feel lost."

"Well, now you know me," Emma said.

Tristana stared at her half-eaten scone, pushed it around the plate, and let out a grief-filled groan. "I'm sorry," she said, pulling a tissue out of her purse. "My husband died six months ago."

Emma waited while the woman regained her composure, then reached out her hand. "I know your pain. I'm a widow, too."

"How long ago?"

"About twelve years," Emma answered. "You don't get over it, but you do get used to it." She leaned forward. "Believe me, after a while the pain does ease up. And, one day, you're surprised to find that it's gone, you can take a deep breath again, remember your husband with love, and you can go on with your life."

The woman nodded and looked away. "I've been to counseling, but it hasn't helped."

"You need more time," Emma said. She felt there was a lot left unsaid, but she didn't prod.

"Do you have children?" Emma couldn't help asking.

"No," Tristana answered, a little too quickly. "It never happened."

She seems so alone, Emma thought. *I wonder if she has family? I'd better not intimidate her by asking too many questions, at least not until I know her a little better.*

"Well," Emma said, "there's plenty going on at the Performing Arts Center. I think it's time for us to go back now. I'll give you a tour of the building, and then we'll go to the library and start working."

"Yes," Tristana said, "I'm eager to get to work."

"DID YOU FINISH your article?" Emma asked, handing Nate a cup of tea.

"Just about. It needs a little polishing, that's all. And did you meet the new librarian, Tristana somebody?"

"Yes. She's such a sad soul. Her husband died six months ago and she moved here from California for a change of pace. But she's lost, and seems so lonely."

"Hmm." Nate looked at Emma, his brows furrowed, his mouth turned down. "I have a feeling that means you plan to take her under your maternal wing."

"I just want to give the woman a little support. When Frank died, I had lots of loving folks around me. This woman doesn't."

"Hmm," was all he said in reply.

Emma wanted to tell Nate about the argument she overheard outside Bruce Hamilton's office, but thought better of it. *He'll only tell me to mind my own business, as usual.*

EIGHT

A SLIGHT FIGURE dressed in a dark tracksuit followed the same route taken by the hooded figure in black earlier. He looked up and cursed the moon intermittently sneaking out from behind a mass of moving clouds. He needed the merchandise, badly. His contacts were threatening. But he dared not take the chance of coming out on a clear night. It was too dangerous. He could not risk being caught. It would be the end of everything.

Why did I get myself involved in this tangled mess? He berated himself often, but it did little good. He couldn't seem to break the pattern.

As he lowered himself into the narrow space, he looked around in disgust. The scurrying rats made his skin crawl. A spider's web plastered his face with its sticky silk, the irate creature scurrying away.

Quickly he shone the penlight around and noticed with some alarm that the roof had loosed more mud and rotted wood. A shudder shook his body as he went straight for the niche. Yes, there they were—four thick packets in plastic bags—and the rats hadn't gotten to them. Then he laughed. Rodents were too smart for that. They would find the scent repulsive. Only man was foolish enough to pad his pockets with this contraband. He grabbed the packets and stowed them in the canvas bag he carried. Then, as fast as he could, he left the cursed place.

NINE

EMMA AND NATE procrastinated over examining the remaining boxes in the storeroom. They had made the commitment, but found the task ponderous and unrewarding. Now they would both prefer to forget the entire venture. Nate kept revising his article and Emma spent more time with Tristana in the library.

"We're making headway," Emma said, arranging books on a shelf.

"Hmm," Tristana said and nodded to Emma. "I would like to computerize this entire library. That way everyone can easily find what they're looking for."

She sat at the desk, glasses perched on the tip of her nose, a few strands of dark hair coming loose from behind her ears.

Emma smiled. In the past two weeks the woman's color had improved, and she even smiled occasionally. She had found a challenge. Emma knew how therapeutic that could be.

They both looked up as a tall, graceful figure almost danced into the room, a long scarf trailing around his thin neck.

"Emma," he said, his scowl turning into a smile. "There's no one I'd rather see right now than you." He sank into a chair waving his arms gracefully to the sides, and heaving a deep sigh.

Emma chuckled. "Claude, let me introduce you to the new librarian, Tristana Morgan." She turned to the startled woman. "This is Claude Doran, choreographer for the ballet that's presently rehearsing, and my next-door neighbor."

Tristana stood and extended her hand in welcome.

Claude bounded from the chair and bent low, his lips brushing Tristana's hand. "My pleasure," he said.

Tristana blushed, then smiled and let him hold her hand for just a moment.

"What's the problem?" Emma asked.

Claude's face took on a pained expression. "These dancers move like a troop of cattle. When I think of my days as a dancer..." He rolled his eyes and shook his head from side to side. A receding hairline and a little puffiness beneath the eyes belied his youthful appearance.

As the women waited for the histrionics to subside, Emma winked at Tristana.

"Where are the tomes on ballet techniques?" he asked, pressing the back of his hand to his forehead.

"I believe they're on the top shelf," Tristana said, pointing towards the ballet volumes.

"Merci." He pranced to the area and mumbled to himself as he searched through the collection. "May I take these out? Perhaps I can get through to these dunderheads with pictures of the great ones."

Tristana turned to Emma. "This is a reference library and the books don't usually leave the room."

"I think we can break the rules occasionally, don't you?" She winked at Tristana. "How soon can you have them back, Claude?"

"In two hours. You have my word."

"I suppose it's all right," Tristana agreed.

With his arm upraised in a graceful motion, he danced out of the room.

"Well," Tristana said, "he certainly is a colorful character."

Emma sat down, laughing. "He's somewhat affected, but he's really very sweet. I remember when he and his partner, Thomas, an interior designer, bought the condo next door to ours just last year. I was taken aback at first, but quickly got used to the idea. They're lovely neighbors, quiet and considerate, nothing like the previous ones." Emma remembered the terrible experiences with the Evans couple and their niece. She shivered.

Tristana looked at her, a question on her face.

"Someday I'll tell you the whole unpleasant adventure about how I accidentally became a sleuth," Emma said. "But now, let's get back to work."

"ALL RIGHT," NATE SAID, a determined expression on his face, "today we finish the boxes, okay?"

Emma stretched, already feeling the ache in her lower back that inevitably followed such activity. "I guess so. Let's get it over with."

"What started as an interesting challenge has turned out to be a dull chore," he said, pulling an old sweatshirt over his head.

"That's because we expected to find something of historical value," Emma muttered, searching her dresser drawers for something appropriate. She finally drew out an old shirt with a faded Lyric Opera logo on the front. "Do I dare wear this? A logo of a competing opera company?"

"The Midwest is not competing with the Lyric, my dear. That will never happen." Nate looked out the window at the balmy spring day. "I'd rather be walking along the lakeshore."

"If we finish early enough, we may still be able to do it. A walk will get the kinks out after all that bending." Emma slipped on a light jacket and followed Nate out the door.

It took most of the morning to search the remaining boxes. They both had to admit they weren't as thorough as they had been at the beginning.

"That's the last one," Nate said, blowing out a deep breath and stretching his back. "I think we deserve an afternoon in the Jacuzzi." He gave Emma a mischievous grin.

"I would still like to know what's behind this panel," she said, looking closely at the piece of plywood. "Look, it's loose on the bottom." She slipped her fingers underneath and gave a gentle pull. She hesitated a moment fearing they might be met by spiderwebs, or worse, rats.

"Emma, stop that. We're not supposed to take the building apart," Nate said, shining the flashlight behind the panel. "Wait, I think there is something back there."

"Rats?" Emma asked.

"I don't see any, but there appears to be another room."

"I knew it! I could feel it." Emma peeked through the small space. "Come on, let's get this thing off." She began pulling as hard as she could.

Nate grabbed the edge and gave it a yank. The plywood reluctantly came away amid a shower of concrete dust and cobwebs. They drew back—coughing and rubbing their eyes. The flashlight illuminated a tiny room constructed of stone and crumbling cement. Old rotting boards made up the floor. Cobwebs hung from the low ceiling. As Nate swept the light across the area, Emma felt an overwhelming sadness here. Why? She couldn't understand the reason.

She looked around the small area. In a corner sat a shredded spider's web, long ago deserted by its occupant. Parts of desiccated insects were still wrapped in their silken shrouds.

"This looks dangerous," Nate said. "That's probably why it was boarded up."

"I'll bet this was a root cellar," Emma said. "See how it slopes downward? Almost as if it was built underground."

"It probably is," Nate said, again shining the flashlight around the room. "What's that back there in the corner?" He bent his head and cautiously crept into the area avoiding the webs.

"Be careful," Emma said, following close behind.

"Emma, stay out. This place might collapse."

"If it does, I want to be with you."

"That's a cheery thought, buried alive, just like Aida and Rhadames." He bent over and shone the flashlight on something. "I do believe this is an old steamer trunk." He grabbed the handle and pulled. "Watch out. It's heavy."

Emma grabbed the other side, and amid grunts and groans, they managed to pull it out into the storeroom.

"Whew!" Nate sat back on one of the stools and slugged down more water. Emma did the same.

"You've got cobwebs in your hair," he said, brushing them off, making her hair more disheveled than usual.

"Never mind that. I want to see what's in this trunk." Eagerly she fiddled with the rusted lock that literally fell apart in her hands.

Nate pulled on the lid, and, with a few creaks, it opened. On top lay an old quilt sewn by hand from scraps of fabric of varying designs and colors.

"Wow," Emma said. "Look at this." She carefully lifted it from the trunk, and placed it on one of the stools. As she held it, she felt vibrations coming from the material, as if it were trying to tell her something. It smelled old and moldy.

She hurried back to the trunk to find Nate staring at articles of clothing: a child's dress, a poke bonnet, an old flannel shirt.

"Be careful," Emma said. "These are really old. Where are those large plastic bags we brought?"

Gingerly they removed the clothing and transferred it to the plastic bags. Underneath lay yellowed papers.

"I think we hit pay dirt!" Nate said. "Be very careful with these documents. They might fall apart. Hand me a few of those plastic sleeves."

Cautiously he picked up a yellowed, folded parchment from the trunk. He unfolded it and stared, squinting. "Look, this is actually the architectural plan for the original house on this site!"

Emma felt a thrill of excitement. "Let me see it." She got off her stool and leaned over his shoulder.

"Careful. It appears this was originally a three-story house. These are the original dimensions. There's even the plan for an outhouse. Apparently plumbing was not available then. See, the well went there." He pointed to a round area away from the house.

"They even show a root cellar off the basement. That must be where we are. See? According to this plan it went deep into the ground, but was much more extensive than that room. The rest must have collapsed or probably filled in when they built the present structure."

Emma had a strange feeling, as if she were going back in time. In her mind she saw figures huddled together, hiding, crying, afraid.

No, there's more to it than a root cellar, her inner voice said, but she didn't tell Nate about her feelings.

He smiled triumphantly as he methodically folded the document and slipped it into the plastic sleeve.

"What else is in here?" Emma asked, picking up another piece of yellowed paper. "Nate, this seems to be the legal description of the property. I can barely read it. It looks like the property originally consisted of five acres from the lake to the west. I don't think they farmed this land. It had to be pretty rocky and sandy so close to the water. There's a plan for trees off to the west, maybe a small orchard."

"Hmmm." He studied the blueprint while Emma thought of what life must have been like back then.

"Is there a date anywhere?" she asked.

"I'm looking. Here's a date, but it's smudged. It looks like 1840 something, either a seven or a one. When James said the foundation predated the Chicago Fire, he wasn't kidding."

"What else does it show?" Emma could hardly contain her excitement at the significance of their find.

"There's a barn and a few other structures. They probably raised chickens, maybe cows and some pigs. They had to have a horse and wagon for transportation."

Nate carefully folded the document and slipped it into another plastic sleeve.

"What else is in here?" He took out another paper and tried to read it. Emma leaned over his shoulder shining the flashlight on the print. A list of supplies written in a spidery hand filled the page. So many bales of hay and straw, oats, flour, sugar, cornmeal, coffee, and bolts of cloth.

"That certainly looks nothing like my shopping list," she mused.

"Be grateful for that," he said. "I can't visualize either of us slopping the hogs." He slipped the paper into another sleeve.

"Here's a ledger." He opened the cover, the binding loose and crumbling. He squinted at the tiny scrawl. "It appears they took in lodgers, people traveling through the area. Here are names and dates and length of stay. That's probably how they supplemented their income."

The box produced numerous documents chronicling a meager existence: letters of condolence from friends and relatives at the death of two children from cholera, a letter from an uncle promising to send money, and a child's crude drawing.

Emma felt drawn into this life. She saw herself in a gingham dress sitting at the bedside of a dying child. As she read the letter from the uncle, she imagined why the family needed the money. Perhaps for burial expenses? She shook her head and came back to the present.

"Are you all right?" Nate asked.

"Yes, I just got lost in the past for a minute."

At the bottom of the trunk, they found the real treasure, the family bible. Emma's hands shook as she carefully removed the old bible from the trunk. The leather cover was cracked and worn, the binding barely holding the pages together. She placed it on her lap with the reverence of a holy relic. "These old tomes usually chronicled the life and death of an entire family," she whispered.

On the first page they found the births and deaths of the family.

Charles Perkins Born—1832, Lay'd to rest—1872
Sarah Perkins Born—1833, Lay'd to rest—1874
Mary Perkins Born—1852, Lay'd to rest—1852
(Cholera)
William Perkins Born—1852, Lay'd to rest—1897
Alice Perkins Born—1853, Lay'd to rest—1855
(Smallpox)
David Perkins Born—1854, Lay'd to rest—1855
(Smallpox)
Francis Perkins Born—1856, Lay'd to rest—
Levi Perkins Born—1858, Lay'd to rest—1898

"Oh, Nate, how sad. Half of their children died—cholera, smallpox. How awful." Emma felt the mother's pain. To stand helpless and watch her babies die such horrible deaths. It was too much to bear.

"Life was hard in those days," he said. "They had to have a lot of children because, statistically, half of them died. Not to mention the number of women who died in childbirth." He shook his head. "It was a time of survival of the fittest."

"These pages are so fragile," Emma said, turning a few. "We'd better not disturb them." She slid the volume into a large plastic sleeve, looked at Nate and smiled. "This must be the way archaeologists feel when they unearth a new tomb. We really accomplished something here."

"We certainly did. Now it's time to take our find up to the library and tell James."

THEY DECIDED TO go to James's office first. As usual, he was on the phone, his voice mirroring his frustration.

"Singers," he muttered, hanging up a little too forcefully. "Canceling at the last minute. Where have you two been?" He smiled, looking up at the disheveled pair. "You're a welcome break."

"Wait 'til you see what we found," Emma said, unable to keep the excitement out of her voice. She carried the quilt in her arms as if it were a newborn babe.

Carefully Nate lay all the plastic sleeves on the desk.

James was speechless as he examined one after another. "I had no idea there was anything this old in those boxes."

"They weren't in the boxes," Nate said, looking at Emma. "Mrs. Sleuth, here, insisted on peeking behind a plywood panel at the back of the room. There's another room back there. That's where we found an old trunk with all these things inside."

"Wait until Bruce hears about this. He'll be delighted. He's a real history buff. This confirms the fact that the original foundation predates the Chicago Fire. I wonder if the house was destroyed then?"

Nate shook his head. "I don't think so. The fire was supposed to have burned itself out at Lincoln Park. Everything north of there, including this property, was prairie. Of course, flying embers could have ignited a wooden structure that far away, depending on which way the wind was blowing."

"Bruce will know," James said. "He'll research the area and get as many details as he can. He isn't here this afternoon or I'd call him right now. Let's take these things to the library for safekeeping. Tristana Morgan is proving to be an absolute jewel. She's done wonders already. She'll be ecstatic over this."

TEN

THE FOLLOWING DAY, loaded down with groceries, Emma walked into the condo just as a petite blond woman with a young boy in tow, was being buzzed in. They exchanged smiles and walked to the elevator.

Something about the woman looked familiar, as if she had seen her before. From the corner of her eye Emma watched the boy. He appeared to be about nine or ten, but something about his facial expression told her he wasn't quite normal. His eyes were too close together and his mouth remained slightly open, the tip of his tongue protruding. His sandy-colored hair sported a crew cut and he kept rubbing his left hand over it. His right hand clutched the woman's so tightly that his knuckles were turning white.

When the elevator door opened, he hesitated and looked up at the woman.

"Come on, Oliver, remember what I told you. The elevator is going to take us up all the way to the top." She smiled patiently. Hesitantly he followed her into the elevator with Emma close behind.

"Now you can press the button," the woman continued. "Do you remember which one?"

He looked at her, a deep furrow forming between his eyes. Slowly he shook his head.

"Number six. Can you find it?"

His eyes lit up as he stared at the number panel and pressed the right one. Then he looked back at the woman, a triumphant expression on his face.

"Very good." She turned to Emma. "Thank you for being so patient. Which floor did you want?"

"I'm also going to six," she said, as the elevator commenced its upward journey.

The boy looked questioningly at Emma. "Are you going to see Daddy, too?"

Emma's eyes widened in surprise. Did she hear correctly? There were only two units on the sixth floor and her neighbors were two gay men. Did he mean one of them?

She smiled at the boy. "There are two houses on the sixth floor and I live in one of them."

That seemed to satisfy him. He turned his attention to the front as the movement stopped and the door began to open.

Thomas stood in his front doorway, a huge smile on his face. He nodded to Emma, hugged the boy, and ushered him and the woman inside.

Emma stood for a moment, dumbfounded. She quickly unlocked her door and hurried inside. "Nate, Nate," she called.

"What's going on?" He walked in from the kitchen holding a screwdriver.

"You'll never believe what just happened."

"Try me," he said with a shake of his head.

She told him about the woman and the boy referring to Daddy. "There was something familiar about that woman. When Thomas opened the door, I realized they resembled one another. What do you make of that?"

"It does sound odd, but, as I have told you a hundred times, it's none of our business."

"I suppose," she agreed, taking her parcels into the kitchen, "but it does make me wonder. And, by the way, what were you doing with that screwdriver?"

"Nothing major. I was just tightening that cover plate on the outlet beside the sink."

"You mean the one I asked you to fix a month ago?" she said, suppressing a grin.

"Don't goad me, woman. We haven't exactly been sitting around twiddling our thumbs lately."

"You're right." She gave him a resounding kiss and busied herself putting the groceries away.

THAT EVENING AFTER DINNER, Emma and Nate relaxed, satisfied with the result of their efforts. Emma read another book about the Underground Railroad. She was becoming fascinated with the subject: visualized slaves crowded into musty basements, transported in wagons hidden underneath bales of cotton and sacks of grain, lying on the bottom of boats soaked with water, crossing rivers and lakes—going North—always North—to freedom.

All right, Guardian Angel, this isn't anything but normal curiosity about the past, is it?

A voice in her head seemed to say, *keep an open mind about everything around you.*

I don't know what that's supposed to mean, because I never close my mind to anything.

Nate put the newspaper down and went to answer a knock at the door.

"Hello, Claude, please come in."

"I hope I'm not disturbing you," he said, waltzing into the room. He stopped and examined a pencil drawing on the wall.

"What a lovely piece of work," he exclaimed, taking a closer look. "Where did you get this?" A single, delicate line executed a kitten at play. The simplicity of the work portrayed the sensitivity of the artist.

"It is lovely, isn't it?" Emma said, walking up to the drawing. "Tracie Adams, a very talented young lady, gave it to us for Christmas. In fact, she lived in your condo for a while with her aunt and uncle." Emma didn't feel the need to tell the neighbors of Tracie's psychological problems.

"I hope she's pursuing her artistic talent," Claude said.

"Oh, yes, she's studying Art Therapy and plans to work with troubled teenagers."

"Hmm." Claude seemed preoccupied for a moment, then turned to them, smiling. His long blond hair, pulled back in a ponytail, accentuated the fine bone structure of his thin face. His eyes glowed a luminous blue, his mouth an almost perfect bow. "I came to give you tickets to the opening performance of the ballet."

"How kind," Emma said, then suddenly remembered her manners. "Would you like a cup of tea? I made cookies this afternoon."

"That sounds divine. Thomas is visiting his mother this evening and I do hate being alone."

"Oh?" This was the first Emma had heard of a mother. Emma wanted to ask about the woman she had seen that afternoon, but she bit her tongue. Both men were extremely private about their personal lives and she had no right to pry, but she supposed they would find out eventually. "Does she live nearby?"

Claude sighed. "She's ninety-five and in a nursing home in Des Plaines. He tries to go as often as he can." He looked as if he wanted to say more, hesitated, furrowed his brow, and bit down on his lip. Then he turned to Nate and began chatting about the ballet as Emma went into the kitchen and prepared a pot of tea.

"So how are the rehearsals going?" Nate asked.

"Much better. The dancers are actually behaving like true ballet performers." He sat back, quite pleased with himself.

"What ballet are you rehearsing?"

Claude hesitated, then replied, "Oh, something new. I think you'll be pleased." He offered no further explanation and Nate, unlike Emma, didn't pursue the issue.

As Emma arranged oatmeal cookies on a gold-rimmed plate, her mind kept conjuring up various scenarios. *I wonder if Claude was about to tell us who that boy is? Could he possibly be related to Thomas?* Her innate curiosity wouldn't let it go.

When she carried the tray into the living room she found the two men standing at the piano, Claude testing the tone.

"This is a fine instrument. Who plays?"

"I play with it," Nate admitted. "Nothing like the sounds that come from your condo."

"Oh, I hope I don't disturb you," Claude said, placing a hand to his chest.

"On the contrary," Nate said. "You play extremely well. Are some of those your own compositions?"

He lowered his eyes to the keys and fingered them lovingly. "Yes. I'm working on a new ballet. I've tried writing a few in the past, but nothing that's been performed as yet." He looked up at the two of them. "Music and dance are my life. Now that my performing days as a dancer are over, I choreograph and compose. It's as close as I can get to the stage." He looked across the room, a wistful expression on his face.

"Come and have some tea," Emma said.

"You didn't have to go through so much trouble. Are those oatmeal? I do love oatmeal," he said with the enthusiasm of a child. His long, graceful fingers almost caressed a cookie as he took it off the plate. "Umm, delicious," he said savoring the confection.

They shared a pleasant half hour talking about the ballet, the Performing Arts Center, and Emma and Nate's experiences as supernumeraries.

During a lull in the conversation, Emma noticed a frown on Claude's face. "Is something bothering you?"

He glanced at her, his hand stroking his chin. "Who is that man roaming around the Center?"

"What man?" Nate asked, leaning forward.

"I've seen him a few times. He never says anything, just looks at me. In fact, yesterday he motioned, as if he wanted me to fol-low him."

"What does he look like?" Emma asked, holding her breath, even though she already knew.

"He looks dirty and grubby and there seems to be a sadness about him. He resembles a person of the streets, and I think I noted an odor of mustiness. Have you seen him?"

"I have," Emma said.

For a moment she and Claude communicated with their eyes. Then Emma gave an almost imperceptible shake of her head. Claude nodded.

Nate looked at the two of them and grimaced. "People keep seeing this person, but he never says a word. He's probably a vagrant who's found a spot in the building where he's hiding out for the winter."

"Perhaps," Claude said. "But if I see him again, I'm going to try and speak to him, perhaps even follow him." He stared at Emma, but neither said anything.

"Now I had better get home. Thomas should be back soon."

"Take him some cookies," Emma said.

"Oh, he will love that."

She went into the kitchen and returned with a plastic bag filled with cookies.

"Too generous," Claude said, brushing his lips across her hand.

As THEY PREPARED for bed, Nate stared at Emma, a deep furrow between his eyes. "I saw the look that passed between you and Claude. That 'stranger' is a street person, a vagrant, nothing more. If I catch him, I'll set him straight, mighty quick."

"I'm sure you will, dear," Emma said. *But you'll never catch him.*

ELEVEN

ON THE OPENING NIGHT of the ballet, the Performing Arts Center buzzed with excitement. Nate wore his dark gray Italian silk suit, the cuffs peeking out from the sleeves of the jacket at precisely the right length. A black tie with diagonal red and silver threads added the finishing touch. There wasn't much he could do about his features, his owlish eyes, his thinning hair, but, if the old adage that clothes made the man was true, he looked satisfied.

Emma had examined her figure in the bedroom's full-length mirror, turning from side to side. She had nodded with approval. Her ten pound weight gain since meeting Nate had served her well. She was no longer shaped like a stick. Now she had curves, albeit, small ones, but nevertheless, curves.

Her midnight blue velvet dress was designed with an empire waist to downplay her slim hips. She wore a single strand of pearls just above her breasts. Pearl earrings adorned her ears. She had gone to the beauty salon to get her unruly locks tamed. They lay in a perfect cut capping her head, curling toward her thin face in a saucy wave.

As Nate and Emma entered the building, they chatted with a few patrons they had come to know through the years. The seats Claude had given them were in the fifth row, center, on the main floor.

Emma smiled in genuine surprise when she saw Thomas in a seat next to them. His round, homely face always reflected a bit of sadness; his eyes drooped like those of a hound dog. His short, graying hair lay trim and neat as always. A warm smile lit up his face as he greeted Emma and Nate. They exchanged pleasantries for a few moments.

"This is great," Emma said, settling back in her seat. "We'll be able to see every expression and subtle move."

Emma opened the program and exclaimed in astonishment. "Look, the first ballet is *Le Sylphide* followed by a new ballet, *The Huntsman,* music and choreography by Claude Doran."

"That's why he was evasive when I asked him about the ballet," Nate said.

"He wanted to surprise you. He's been working so hard on this," Thomas said.

"Now I am excited." Emma clasped her hands.

At that moment the conductor walked onto the podium to a generous sound of applause. The first number was familiar to the audience, comprised of music by Frederick Chopin. The dancers—in tutus and tights—waltzed with grace and charm, captivating the audience.

At intermission Emma and Nate walked out into the foyer. Thomas went backstage to check on Claude.

"Wow, Claude really whipped them into shape," Emma commented, remembering his frustration when he had come into the library complaining to her and Tristana.

"Don't you think he was overreacting just a little when he criticized them?" Nate asked, heading for a corner to escape the milling crowd. "We've seen them before and they performed all right as far as I could see."

"He's a perfectionist," Emma said, "and in the artistic world, that's not a bad thing."

"How about a glass of champagne?" Nate asked. "I think tonight warrants a toast."

"Agreed."

Nate disappeared into the crowd and came back a few minutes later carefully carrying two flutes of bubbly. He handed one to Emma and raised the other in his hand. "To Claude."

"To Claude," she answered, "and to a successful performance."

A short time later, the bells rang heralding the second act. As they made their way back to their seats, Emma caught a glimpse of a figure ducking behind the curtain. She frowned.

Was it the mysterious stranger? Did anyone else see him? Did he intend to disrupt the performance?

She fidgeted after she sat down, her eyes darting back and forth, searching.

"What's wrong with you?" Nate asked.

"I'm nervous, that's all. I want Claude's ballet to be a success." *I can't tell him what I saw. He'll say it's all in my imagination and I know it's not. There's meaning to these sightings, if I can only figure it out.*

Thomas joined them just as Claude mounted the podium and turned to the audience, graciously accepting their applause.

The curtain parted to reveal a lone figure onstage in a costume representing a deer. The forest background was dark and foreboding. A single spot bathed the dancer with light. He darted gracefully from one end of the stage to the other. The music reflected an air of mystery and fear.

Suddenly Emma noticed a shadowy figure among the trees. *Was he supposed to be there? Was it part of the performance?*

The ballet continued with the hunter soon coming onstage chasing the deer. The dancers expertly executed difficult leaps almost suspended in the air, contouring their bodies into positions that appeared impossible. Still the figure lurked in the background, barely perceptible.

But Emma *saw* him. Goose bumps climbed up her bare arms. The dancers continued their leaps and pirouettes as the music reached a crescendo. The huntsman raised his bow and shot an arrow through the heart of the deer. The dancer crumpled gracefully to the stage.

When the curtain descended, the Center erupted in applause. The dancers took their bows. And Claude climbed onto the stage and bowed low.

Thomas jumped up, clapping and shouting "Bravo." Others joined him, until the entire audience was on its feet.

Emma saw tears streaming down Thomas's face. She, too, had a lump in her throat.

They went backstage to congratulate an exuberant, but exhausted, Claude.

"Magnificent, Claude. It was breathtaking," Emma said.

"I need to make a change in a few bars," he said, jotting a note.

"Not tonight," Thomas said. "We're going out to celebrate." He turned to Emma and Nate. "Will you join us?"

"No, thank you," Emma said, knowing the night belonged to the two of them.

But as they were leaving, Claude pulled Emma aside. "Did you see him? The man?"

"Yes, but I don't think anyone else did."

"Who is he? What does he want?"

"I don't know, but I have a feeling we'll soon find out."

TWELVE

Tristana opened one desk drawer after another—clutter—nothing but clutter. She decided to take one drawer at a time. After an hour she had a wastebasket full of useless papers. The former librarian must have saved everything.

She stopped for a break and made a list of the things she needed to order: hanging files, legal pads, a box of pencils... then went back to the drawers. At the bottom of another one she found a box of crayons and a manila envelope filled with a child's drawings. She looked at them one by one—charming. One was an obvious attempt to duplicate the library. The child hadn't used a ruler so the shelves slanted at an angle. But books in bright colors stood side by side. She wondered who the child was and spent a moment in regret.

"Mrs. Morgan." James knocked, then entered the room. "How are you doing? Do you need anything?"

"Mr. Greene, I made a list of supplies and I found this envelope of drawings. Do you know who did them?"

James smiled as he looked at the pictures. "The former librarian's daughter and grandson came to visit her occasionally. He was a budding artist."

"I can see that. What shall I do with them?"

"I'm sure she'd like to have them. I'll have the secretary look up her address and send them to her."

"Thanks."

After James had gone, Tristana looked at the box of crayons, some broken, others intact. She thought for a moment, then tucked them in the corner of the drawer.

LATER AN EXCITED EMMA burst into the library to see Tristana. The auditions for supernumerary roles for the next opera, *The Ghosts of Versailles,* were scheduled for the following week. Emma thought she might encourage the woman to try out.

"Tristana, where are you?" Emma called, looking about the room. Books, magazines, and librettos lay in piles on the floor and on the desk.

"I'm down here," a voice said.

"Where?"

A disheveled head popped out from behind the desk. The usually neat, organized woman appeared as though she had been in the basement going through boxes. She pushed her brown hair back behind her ears and rubbed a smudge from her nose.

"What in the world are you doing?" Emma asked, leaning over the desk.

Tristana stood up, placed her hands on her lower back and stretched. "I was in that position too long." She looked at Emma and laughed. "I was organizing the bottom shelves. While I was at it, I decided to clean out all the desk drawers. They were crammed with papers. So I'm cleaning everything out. I want to put the documents you found in this bottom drawer, the one with the lock."

"I'll help you," Emma said, taking off her coat and pushing up the sleeves of her sweater.

"Let's get some coffee first," the other woman said. "I need a caffeine boost."

"Good idea. You sit here and relax and I'll go to the machine and get some. It will have to do."

Emma passed Bruce Hamilton's office on the way to the small kitchenette. Again she heard raised voices outside his door. *It's none of my business,* she thought, flattening herself against the wall.

"Listen, Quiller, I don't know what your problem is, but these items give this building historical value," a booming voice shouted.

"But...but...this center is dedicated to the arts, not history."

These words from the same whiny voice she had heard the last time.

"We may decide to donate the items to the Chicago History Museum. That's up to the board, not me, and certainly not you."

"Well, I don't think anyone should be poking around that storeroom. It isn't safe."

Emma heard an exasperated sound. "In case you haven't noticed, steel support beams were added to that entire basement when this building was built. Otherwise the whole thing would have collapsed long ago. The storeroom and the things that were found there have nothing to do with you, or your duties. Is that clear, Mr. Quiller?"

Emma had heard enough. This was the second argument she had heard between those two. Who is this Quiller? She would have to ask James.

When she returned to the library with the coffee, she found Tristana sitting in a chair staring out the window. Her face wore a pensive expression.

"Spring is finally here," Emma said, following her gaze to the trees, their buds swelling, their branches waving like awakening arms in the breeze.

"Oh, yes it is."

"Here's what passes for coffee from that machine." She handed the cup to Tristana. "You were a million miles away, weren't you?" Emma asked. She was rewarded with a smile, but nothing more.

"I wish you had seen the ballet last night," Emma said. "It was fabulous." She went on to describe Claude's music and the amazing choreography.

"It sounds like an unforgettable evening," Tristana said, a regretful look on her face.

A wave of guilt flooded through Emma. *I should have taken her along, but I couldn't have asked Claude for another ticket. The house was sold out and he pulled strings to get the two he gave us.*

"By the way, the audition for supernumeraries for *The Ghosts of Versailles* is scheduled for next Wednesday. Why don't you come?"

Tristana cowered. "I couldn't possibly do that, be on the stage in front of all those people." She twisted her hands, frowned, and squirmed in her chair.

"That's the way I felt the first time, too, dear, but you get over it quickly. It's fun. Please, won't you say you'll come?" Emma gave the woman her most appealing look.

Tristana laughed. "You do have a way about you, Emma."

Emma felt a flush rise up her long neck. "Thank you. Does that mean yes?"

"It means maybe. Let me think about it."

"I'll take that," Emma said. "Now let's finish this job."

EMMA SAID NOTHING to Nate about the argument she had overheard.

"You're unusually quiet," he said, watching her repot a large bromeliad.

"I'm trying to be careful and not spill soil all over the atrium tile. Oh, damn!"

"Here, let me help you," he said, kneeling on the floor and scooping up a mound of soil with his hands. He put it in the pot around the roots and tapped it down. "There, do I pass for a gardener?" He gave her a grin.

"Absolutely."

She picked up a broom and dustpan and swept the floor.

"Does this need water now?" he asked.

"Yes, please."

The chore finished, Nate took both Emma's hands in his and led her to a couch. "Now, what's on your mind?"

"You know me too well, Nate Sandler." She sighed, thought for a moment, then decided to tell him. "Twice now I've overheard an argument between Bruce Hamilton and someone named Quiller. It seemed to revolve around the storeroom in the basement."

"And how did you manage to overhear these discussions?" He pursed his lips and raised his eyebrows.

"Well…I was just passing the office and I heard raised voices."

"And, instead of walking by, as any normal person would, you stopped to listen, am I right?"

She shrugged. "Well, sort of."

She ignored the scowl she got in return. "I'm going to ask James who this man is. I don't like him," she said with a shake of her head. "It seems as though he knows something about the storeroom and doesn't want anyone to find out about it. Could we have missed something?"

"Nonsense," Nate said, "it's only an empty room now that all the boxes are gone. Stop imagining things."

There's something else, I feel it, Emma thought. *Guardian Angel, please keep me out of there. I got into so much trouble last year that I don't want a repeat.*

"We're going to James and Sylvia's new house on Sunday, aren't we? You can ask him then if it's so important to you."

Emma nodded, pulling her thoughts back to the present. "We have to decide on a housewarming gift. Shall we go shopping?" She batted her eyelashes at him.

"Come on." He pulled himself off the couch and headed for the coat closet.

"Oh, and I think Tristana is going to audition next Wednesday," Emma said. "It will be good for her to get involved in something besides the library. She's alone too much." She slipped on a jacket and her navy blue denim hat.

Nate looked at her and grinned.

The hat had a special meaning for them both. She had bought it after her harrowing experience the previous summer.

"I heard a lot of new people are expected to audition," Nate said as they walked out the door. "They need quite a few for the crowd scene in the second act."

"I'm not familiar with that opera," Emma said as they waited for the elevator.

"Nor am I. I'll bet there's a copy of the libretto in the library. Next time you go, check it out."

"I will do that."

THEY WERE SOON walking down Michigan Avenue inhaling the fresh spring air, heading toward Water Tower Place. It was a good hike, but they needed the exercise.

Spring invigorated Emma. She thought about planting her roof garden pots, about visiting with her family on Sunday, and how her life had changed in the past year. She was content. The question in her mind about the arguments she overheard, her feelings that they weren't finished with the storeroom yet, and the mysterious stranger, all retreated into the recesses of her mind. Today she was with the man she loved, on a beautiful spring day in a vibrant city. She would simply enjoy the here and now.

THIRTEEN

SUNDAY MORNING DAWNED clear and sunny. Emma spent her half hour practicing yoga. It had become almost a religious experience. She hadn't missed a day in the past six months. Now she was limber and fit and pleased with herself. Nate, true to his word, had spent some time in the exercise room on the first floor.

"Are you ready for coffee?" he asked, standing in the doorway, two cups in hand.

"Yes, sir." She took one, plopped in a chair and inhaled the aroma of the Colombian roast. "How did people live before coffee?"

"I believe they drank ale. The water was contaminated with all kinds of nasty stuff."

Emma shivered at the thought. "I think my stomach would revolt at a glass of ale first thing in the morning."

She gazed out the huge glass window at the blue waters of Lake Michigan. A few waves marred the surface as shorebirds circled, looking for a meal. "I pinch myself every morning to make sure I'm not dreaming."

Nate put his coffee cup down on a small table. He took Emma's out of her hand and set it beside his. He snaked his arms around her, nuzzling her neck and flicking his tongue at her earlobe. "I want to spend the rest of my life making you happy, Sparrow. I do believe that was what I was put on this earth for."

"Why, Nate." She turned and buried her face in his chest to hide the tears that welled up. "That's so romantic."

"I don't know. Let's not try to explain life. Let's just enjoy it. Now I'm becoming maudlin. How about a walk along the lake before we go to James and Sylvia's this afternoon?"

"Good idea. A walk, then breakfast at that new pancake house. Okay?"

"You're on."

THAT AFTERNOON Nate drove up to the two-story Victorian-style brick house in Wicker Park. Large trees lined the street, their leaves beginning to bud, their curving branches almost meeting in the center. Arcs cut in the sidewalks accommodated the massive trunks.

"This is impressive," Emma said, walking up the inlaid brick walk.

"This door is really old," Nate said, examining the heavy carved oak and the leaded glass insert at the top. "No one could kick this door in. They'd break a foot trying." When he depressed the doorbell, they heard melodic chimes from inside.

Sylvia opened the door and hugged and kissed them both. James came up from behind her and shook hands, then proudly gave them a tour of the large rooms, the high ceilings, the long windows. Crown moldings, chair railings, and baseboards of solid oak decorated every room. The kitchen had been updated and sported all the modern conveniences.

"We were lucky," James said. "The previous owners were in the middle of a bitter divorce and needed a quick sale. They accepted our offer, even though I thought it was ridiculously low. We sold our town house in two days, and here we are." He extended his arms, a satisfied look on his face.

"Wonderful," Emma said. "Where are the boys?"

"In the backyard with Stephen and Pat and their two," Sylvia answered.

"Here, a little housewarming gift," Nate said as he picked up a package he had left in the foyer.

James unwrapped a watercolor painting of children playing at the seashore.

"Oh, it's beautiful," Sylvia said. "Mom, Nate, thank you so much. Look, James, won't it be perfect right there on that wall?"

She pointed to a spot directly above a lounge chair. "The muted tones really complement the colors of the room."

James agreed and, within minutes, hung the picture to everyone's satisfaction.

"Now I want to see my grandchildren," Emma said.

They walked out into a fenced yard sporting a swing set, slide and sandbox in one corner.

"Did this all come with the house?" Emma asked, a surprised look on her face.

"Yes, they left a lot of things," Sylvia said. "Amazing what people will do when they're under stress."

"Grandma, come and see me," a little voice shouted from the play area.

"My public is calling," Emma said as she walked over holding out her arms. The impact of small bodies loaded with energy almost knocked her down.

Nate stood back with James and watched her sit on a swing with young Frankie on her lap. "Right now she's as much of a child as they are," Nate said, a grin on his face.

"How about a drink?" James asked.

"Sounds good to me."

"Stephen," James called to Emma's older son. "We're headed for the liquor cabinet. Care to join us?"

"You're on."

The men disappeared into the house leaving the women to supervise the children.

Four-year-old Susan ran up to Emma and whispered, "Grandma, are there really angels?"

Emma stooped down to the level of the child. "Why are you asking me, honey?"

"My Sunday school teacher said I have a guarding angel watching over me." The innocent eyes gazed at Emma for confirmation.

"Of course we have Guardian Angels. I talk to mine all the time."

"Really?" The eyes grew wider. "Can you see her?"

"No," Emma said, "we can't see angels because they don't have any bodies. They're spirits."

"But they have wings," the child persisted.

"People draw pictures of angels with wings, dear, but no one knows for sure."

Susan pursed her lips and frowned. "I think I'll talk to my guarding angel, too. Come on, Angel, let's go for a ride on the swing."

Emma smiled as she watched the child skipping along and murmuring.

At that moment Sylvia called everyone in for lunch.

Emma's younger son, Martin, and his very pregnant wife, Bertie, had just arrived.

"How soon?" Sylvia asked her sister-in-law.

"Three more weeks," Bertie said, slowly lowering her cumbersome body into a chair.

"Are you still working?"

"Oh yes. I'd go crazy at home arranging and rearranging baby things all day. How many times can you change the layout of a room?"

"I refuse to move that crib one more time," Martin said.

"See what I mean? I'll stay on at the clinic as long as I can. After all, counseling and social work are not physically taxing jobs," Bertie said.

They enjoyed a lunch of sandwiches, salads, and finger foods for the children. Emma produced three different kinds of cookies for dessert with ice cream.

Stephen and Pat left early because of another commitment. Frankie fell asleep and James Jr. busied himself with a train set.

"James," Emma asked, "who is that man named Quiller?" She ignored Nate's frown and pursed lips.

"Why do you ask?"

"Well, I accidentally overheard an argument between him and Bruce Hamilton the other day as I was walking by the office on my way to the kitchen."

"Accidentally," Nate muttered.

Emma waved her hand at him.

James thought for a moment. "There's something strange about that guy. I'm not sure what it is. He's Bruce's assistant, only been in the position for a few months. He's really antsy and short-tempered. Personally, I think he may have a drinking problem. Bruce thinks he might be a gambler. He's already asked for a raise but hasn't done anything to warrant one." He shook his head and reached for another beer.

"Well, he seemed upset that we were cleaning out the storeroom in the basement. Can you think of any reason for that?" Emma persisted despite Nate's expressions of annoyance.

"I think the guy's got issues. He disagrees with every decision of the Board of Directors. I don't think he'll last long. Bruce has about had it with him."

They soon took their leave with hugs and kisses and wishes of good luck to James and Sylvia in the new house.

"You had to let James know you were eavesdropping, didn't you?" Nate said as they drove toward home.

"I had to learn more about this man. Something is nagging at me and I can't let it go."

Nate gave a sigh that came out as a grunt but said no more about it.

Emma's mind kept turning over the thought of the storeroom. *There had to be a reason he didn't want anyone in there. What* could *it be?*

FOURTEEN

As EMMA WALKED into the library, she saw Tristana bent over the desk, deeply engrossed in something. Her usually neat brown hair hung down over her face.

"Hello, Tristana. What's got you so interested?"

"Oh." The woman looked up, her eyes wide with excitement. "I didn't hear you come in. Look what I found in this old bible from the storeroom. These pages were sewn into the back cover. A corner was unglued, and when I tried to repair it the cover came right off revealing these." She held out her hand in a theatrical gesture.

Without taking off her jacket, Emma hurried behind the desk and stared at the pieces of thin, yellowed paper carefully laid out before her.

"What are they?" she asked.

"Documents," Tristana said mysteriously. "Names and dates. By the sound of these names, I think they may have been slaves."

"Slaves?" At first, Emma had difficulty grasping the concept.

Tristana's voice climbed an octave as the words tumbled out. "I've been comparing the dates here with the ones we found for the family members in the front of the bible. I think the original farm was used as a 'safe house' for runaway slaves." She whispered the last sentence, then sat back, pushed the hair out of her eyes and grinned at Emma.

"Oh my!" Emma scanned the names and dates on one page:

Zechial and Mandy—March, 1850
Big Jim, Little Jim, Liza—April, 1850
Mose, Zenobia, Eulaly—June, 1850

"These could have been families or groups that escaped together. But why here?" Emma asked.

"Look at this," Tristana said, a triumphant note in her voice. "A diagram showing the root cellar and what looks like a tunnel deep underground."

Emma's eyes widened as she peered at the crude drawing. "It could be just that, a drawing, or..."

"This is so exciting," Tristana said.

"That quilt we found in the trunk," Emma whispered. "I read that the slaves who were seamstresses made quilts with designs that were an actual means of communication." She remembered the vibrations she had felt from the fabric. "They hung them on clotheslines and the slaves used the designs as a kind of road map. Pretty ingenious, don't you think?"

Tristana shook her head. "Yes, most people would do anything to be free."

Something in her tone told Emma that there might be a personal meaning to her words. She put that thought away and again scanned the names and dates on the yellowed paper. "But how can we authenticate these documents?"

Tristana blew out a breath and sat back. "I've never had to deal with anything this old. I'll have to do some investigating."

Emma looked more closely. "This wavy line here could indicate a body of water. It could be Lake Michigan, or just a line."

She screwed up her face and thought a moment. "You know, I've been reading a book about the Underground Railroad. It said that in 1850, the Fugitive Slave Act was passed. Before then, if slaves reached the Northern States, they were considered free. But after the act was passed, they could be caught and returned to their owners. Anyone found harboring slaves was fined, or sometimes imprisoned."

"I'm impressed," Tristana said, her eyebrows arching.

Emma preened. "These dates are all 1850 and later." More names and dates appeared on three other pages, then abruptly stopped after 1855. Emma turned back to the first page of the bible. "Two children died of smallpox in 1855. It must have been after that they stopped harboring slaves. Was there an epidemic? Were they afraid of the authorities? Divine retribution?" She shrugged her shoulders and held out her hands.

"The family could have hidden the slaves in the root cellar and led them out through the tunnel where someone else took them across the lake by boat and into Michigan and on to Canada." Emma took a deep breath and blew it out. She felt the fear and panic of the poor souls literally running for their lives. If they were caught, the punishment was terrible: neck chains with spikes, leg irons, beatings, and even toes cut off. She shivered.

Tristana's voice brought her back to the present. "Let's put all of this into protective sleeves. Then we can take our find to Bruce Hamilton."

"Yes, yes," Emma said, still unable to get the terrifying pictures out of her mind.

Tristana put the sleeves in a large manila envelope; Emma carried the bible, and together they walked quickly down the hall to the director's office.

Through the open door the women saw Bruce Hamilton sitting behind his large oak desk making notations on a small stack of papers. His glasses had trailed down his long nose until they perched on the very tip. He pushed them back and reached for a nonexistent cup. Puzzled that it wasn't there, he looked up. A surprised smile crossed his face when he saw Emma and Tristana.

"Come in, ladies. Whatever you have clutched in your hands is a welcome break from this endless paperwork."

He rose from his chair and walked toward them. He had a slight limp that Emma hadn't noticed before. His shoulders hunched forward a little, a common stance for exceptionally tall men. The thick glasses made his deep-set eyes look abnormally large.

"Sit down, please. I was just going for coffee, would you like some?" he asked.

"Not right now," Emma said. "We're eager to show you our find."

They sat in the proffered chairs and Tristana carefully removed the plastic sleeves from the envelope. Hamilton sat back in his chair and reached for them, one at a time. He thoroughly examined the diagram, then the spidery hand that had documented the names and dates so many years ago. He handled them as if they were holy relics, then leaned back in his chair and closed his eyes.

Emma and Tristana looked at each other. Emma shrugged, wondering if the man had fallen asleep.

After a moment he opened his eyes and stared at them. "Does this mean what I think it does? Could these be the names of runaway slaves?"

"That's exactly what we thought," Tristana said, jumping up from her chair. She pointed to the crude drawing. "This could indicate a tunnel under the root cellar that could possibly have led to the lake." She indicated the wavy line. "Emma and I think the original farmhouse may have been a 'station' in the Underground Railroad." She took a deep breath and pushed back a lock of hair that had fallen over her face.

He slowly shook his head. "If these can be authenticated, it will be quite an historical find." He looked at the women and grinned, the smile lighting up an otherwise plain face.

Emma noticed a maintenance man repairing an electric outlet in a corner of the room. Did Bruce know he was there? He appeared interested in what they were saying. But after a moment he turned back to his task.

Just then a thin, wiry man came sidling into the office. "Mr. Hamilton, can I talk… Oh, I didn't know you were busy." His eyes darted around suspiciously. His nose twitched, the edges of his mouth turned down and kept moving with some kind of tic.

"Come in, Quiller, come in. Let me introduce you to our librarian, Tristana Morgan, and Emma Winberry, James Greene's mother-in-law. Ladies, this is Norman Quiller, my assistant."

The man frowned, then bobbed his head at the women, moving in jerking motions toward the desk. He reeked of a particular scent of aftershave that Emma disliked. She wrinkled her nose.

"Look at these, Norman. You didn't think anything of value could be found in that old storeroom in the basement, but these ladies have brought me what may be a very important historical find."

Quiller almost jumped when the director mentioned the storeroom. Emma took an immediate dislike to the man; something about him didn't ring true.

As Bruce Hamilton explained the possible significance of the documents to Quiller, Emma never took her eyes off the man, watching his jerky movements and expressions, running the gamut from surprise to suspicion, or was it fear?

"These don't prove anything," the assistant said. "They could have been planted there by anybody. I say leave the storeroom alone and forget about tunnels that don't exist. It's all fictitious nonsense."

Tunnels? We never mentioned that, Emma thought. *Why did he allude to the tunnel?* Emma wondered. *He's hiding something. Why do these thoughts come into my mind?*

Don't trust him, her inner voice said. *Watch out!*

Bruce frowned at his assistant. "What was it you wanted to see me about?" he asked, putting the documents back in the manila envelope.

"It can wait 'til later. I have to check on something now," he said, turning and almost running out the door.

Tristana glanced at Emma. "What a strange man," she whispered.

Emma nodded.

"Mrs. Morgan, lock these in your desk, along with the bible, until we decide what to do with them. Good work, ladies." He smiled as he handed Tristana the envelope, and Emma the bible.

As they walked out the door, the maintenance man packed up his tools and left the room. They saw Mr. Quiller turning the corner. Had he been listening?

Yes, Guardian Angel, I will watch him closely, Emma mused as they walked back to the library.

"NATE, WHERE ARE YOU?" Emma burst into the condo, her excitement mirrored in her voice.

"I'm right here," he said, walking out of the study. "What happened, did you win the lottery?" He grinned and planted a kiss on the tip of her nose.

She threw her arms around him and hugged him tight. Then she pulled back, opened her eyes wide, and clasped her hands. "Oh, Nate, you'll never guess what Tristana found in that old bible from the storeroom."

"Old currency hidden in the pages?"

"No." She bit down on her lower lip.

He screwed up his face. "Ah…pressed flowers?"

"No." She began to giggle.

"We're not playing Twenty Questions, are we?" he asked.

"We found names and dates that could be a list of runaway slaves, and a diagram of a tunnel leading from the root cellar to the lake." She dug into her purse and pulled out copies they had made of the documents before locking the originals in Tristana's desk.

Nate examined the papers then let out a low whistle. "If these can be authenticated, it would mean the original house was …"

Before he could finish, she whispered, "A 'station' on the Underground Railroad."

"I see why you're so worked up," he said. "Where are the originals?"

"Under lock and key in the library. Bruce Hamilton was as thrilled as we were with the find." She frowned. "His assistant came in as we were examining the papers, and when Bruce explained the possible significance of the documents, his assistant became very upset."

"He's an oddball," Nate said. "I met him only once and thought there was something strange about him."

"Exactly," Emma agreed. "He seemed fixated on the tunnel, sent out bad vibes. He reminds me of a weasel."

Nate laughed. "All right, Sparrow, so he's a little peculiar. Don't read any more into it than that. Say, why don't we go out for a celebratory dinner? Call Tristana and see if she wants to come along."

With no need for further discussion, Emma checked the number in her book, reached for the phone, and punched it in. She waited through five rings and was just about to hang up when a soft voice answered.

"Hello."

"Tristana? It's Emma."

"Oh, hi."

"Are you all right? You sound kind of—weak," Emma said, concern in her voice.

"I'm okay, I guess. I was unpacking a box and came across some old photos of Jim and me. I started remembering too much of the past. I must stop doing that."

Emma heard a sniff and realized the woman was crying. "Well, I have the antidote for that. I told Nate about the find and he suggested we go out to dinner, the three of us."

Tristana hesitated for a moment. "I don't think I'm up to socializing tonight."

Emma remembered how she had felt after Frank died and couples had invited her out. She always felt like the third wheel on a two-wheel bicycle.

"This is not just socializing. We can consider it a working dinner. We have to come up with a plan to authenticate those documents and we need your expertise." Was she pushing a little too hard? *Guardian Angel, give her a nudge*.

"You are persistent," the woman said. After a pause, she agreed. "All right, I'll come."

"Good. Give me your address and we'll pick you up in an hour."

As Emma put the phone down, she turned to see Nate smiling but shaking his head. "You had to do some persuading there, my dear, and you did a damn good job, too."

"I could tell by her voice she had been crying, looking at old photographs she said. That could have gone on all night. I remember all too well."

He put his arms around her, kissed her hard and held her tight. "You're a good woman, Sparrow, and I'm a lucky man."

She looked up at him and grinned. "And don't you forget it."

LATER THE THREE OF THEM sat in a quiet restaurant close to Tristana's apartment. Even though she had on a colorful outfit and was wearing quite a bit of makeup, she still appeared to be fighting for self-control. Her designer glasses did nothing to mask her red, puffy eyes.

"I wonder if they serve wine here," Nate said. "I don't see a wine list."

Tristana shrugged. "I've never been here before."

At that moment the waiter greeted them and passed out menus. "Would you like something to drink before your meal?" he asked.

"Do you have wine by the bottle?" Nate asked.

"Yes, sir." He handed Nate a wine list. "I'm sorry, sir, one should have been on your table. Any of the wines listed by the glass can be ordered by the bottle."

Nate nodded. "Any preferences, ladies?"

"Anything is all right with me," Tristana said, her eyes looking down, her hands clutching the napkin.

He reviewed the list and ordered a bottle of dry red wine. The waiter left and they studied the menu.

"I'm not very hungry," Tristana said, putting her menu aside.

"They have these lovely wraps," Emma said. "They're light and you can always take half home with you." She looked at the other woman, feeling her pain, or was it something else? Emma wasn't sure. "I'll have the chicken and veggie wrap." With that decision made, Emma closed the menu.

"I guess I'll have the same," Tristana said without enthusiasm.

"All right," Nate agreed. "We'll make it three, keep it simple." He raised his eyebrows and pointed his chin.

After they gave their order to the waiter, and each had a glass of wine in hand, Nate raised his in a toast. "To the historical 'find' and the lovely ladies who uncovered it."

Tristana blushed as she raised her glass in the toast. She sipped the wine, then took a rather large gulp. "It's good. Just what the doctor ordered." She finished the wine and Nate poured her another.

"Since you are the experienced librarian, how do we authenticate these documents?" he asked.

"That's a good question. We need someone who can date the paper and the ink," she answered. "I remember once in California we needed to authenticate a signature on a letter. We used a forensic lab that specialized in that sort of thing."

"There should be someplace like that in the area," Emma said.

"I don't think it was anywhere in California," Tristana said. "It was a long time ago and I can't remember." She took another swallow of wine.

Emma hoped their order would arrive soon, before the woman became inebriated. She was already finishing her second glass.

"We can always use the Internet," Nate said. "You can find anything there."

When their meal arrived, Nate called the waiter and asked for another bottle of wine.

Emma tried to signal him with her eyes, but he didn't seem to notice. When the bottle arrived, he refilled all the glasses.

Tristana smiled as she reached for hers. "Thank you both for including me. I do get lonely in the evenings." She took another gulp. "I'm afraid I've been drinking a little too much of this lately, too."

Emma reached for her hand. "Any time you feel the need for a night out, just call. We're usually available, aren't we, Nate?" She raised her eyes to him.

"You bet," he agreed. "And, if you don't mind children, you're welcome to come along when Emma's family converges. It's noisy, but fun."

"Thank you. I may take you up on that."

FIFTEEN

"I'LL BE SPENDING most of the morning working on this article for the investment journal," Nate said after they finished breakfast.

"Okay. I have some errands to run," Emma said. She kissed him on the top of his head, put on a jacket and hat and left the condo.

The brisk March air put a spring in her step. Soon she would be able to put her plants out on the roof garden. She couldn't wait. But, she must control herself. Putting them out too early could end their young, tender lives. They were doing fine in the atrium, but Emma was eager to taste the sweet, juicy tomatoes. The thought made her mouth water.

She walked to Water Tower Place and browsed through a few stores. She wasn't looking for anything in particular although a new store selling children's clothes caught her eye. The tiny mannequins in the window wore white shirts and khaki trouser outfits. Emma smiled as she pictured her rambunctious grandsons in those clothes. The pants would be muddy in a few minutes and the white shirts covered with handprints.

Bertie's baby was due soon, she mused. *Maybe I'll pick up a few things. Pat and Sylvia will have plenty of clothes to give her from their children, but it's always nice to have something new.*

Emma went in and looked around. A woman piled an entire layette on the counter. The salesperson eagerly helped her choose too many tiny outfits. *That baby will outgrow them before it can wear half of that stuff,* Emma thought.

She picked up a couple of all-in-one sets of underwear and a cute bib with a teddy bear print. *That's enough,* her inner voice said. *A nice check will be appreciated much more.*

"I hear you," Emma muttered. She paid for her purchases and left the store carrying the bag over her arm. Another customer was still piling items on the counter.

I think I'll browse the bookstore, Emma thought. She left Water Tower Place and walked down Michigan Avenue glancing into store windows at summer wear. Nothing like being ahead of the game.

As she walked into her favorite bookstore, she felt like she was visiting an old friend. She couldn't wait to get into one of those comfy chairs in the corner with a book in her hand.

Let me see now, what's new? She looked at the new arrivals in hardcover and in paperback, but nothing in particular shouted out, *buy me!*

She heaved a sigh and walked up to the information desk. She'd been procrastinating, but now it was time to do some research. What she had in mind was not the history of Chicago, but an entirely different field. A young man stood punching something into a computer; a frown creased his forehead. Something resembling a hatpin protruded from his eyebrow. Emma grimaced and decided not to break his concentration. She was in no hurry.

"I'm sorry," he said, looking up. "These things don't always work the way you want them to. How can I help you?"

Such nice manners, Emma thought. "Uh, where can I find books on the—occult?" she whispered.

"I'll show you." He walked out from behind the desk and led her to an area marked *Paranormal.* "Are you looking for anything in particular?" he asked.

"No, I'll just browse. Thank you."

He must think I'm one of those crazy old ladies trying to contact the spirits. What am I looking for?

She looked through the titles lining the shelves; so many books on a topic totally foreign to her. She picked up one titled, *The Encyclopedia of Ghosts and Spirits,* and opened it. The text started with A and went all the way to Z, just like a dictionary. She was about to settle herself into a chair when she sensed someone behind her.

"Hello, Emma."

She jumped, almost dropping the book, turning to see who it was.

"Claude."

"I didn't mean to startle you," he said. "I'm so sorry." He stepped back raising his slender hands dramatically.

"No, no," Emma stammered. "I wasn't expecting to see anyone I knew."

He looked down at the book she held, then up into her eyes. Was that fear she saw?

"Do you believe it?" he whispered.

"Believe what?"

"The stranger. I saw him again," Claude said, moving his head slowly from side to side.

"When? Where?" she asked. A chill ran down her spine.

Claude turned around again as if expecting to see someone or something standing next to him. "I was in the wardrobe room the other day checking on costumes for the ballet. Suddenly there he was! I almost wet myself." He blushed at his own words.

"Did he say anything to you?" Emma asked, clutching the book to her chest.

Claude shook his head. "Nothing. But I got a good look at him. He was a black man with close-cropped gray hair. His clothes were dirty, appeared to be covered with mud, but none of it fell off onto the floor. And there was a strange smell about him, like decay."

Emma saw a shiver shake the dancer.

"He wasn't frightening. He seemed kind of—sad. He beckoned me to follow him, but I shook my head and backed away. I bumped into one of the racks of costumes and almost fell. When I looked up again, he was gone."

"He's trying to tell us something," Emma said. *Now what*

made me say that? But as the words came out of her mouth, she believed them.

"Do you think the answer lies in that book?" Claude asked, pointing to the volume in Emma's hands.

"I don't know, but I intend to find out." She thought for a moment, then added, "For the time being, we'd better not discuss this with too many people."

He nodded, put his finger to his lips, and moved gracefully down the aisle.

WHEN EMMA GOT HOME her mind was still whirling with thoughts of the stranger and who, or exactly what, he might be. Did the odor of decay mean something? More important was why was he roaming about and what did he want?

Nate walked out of the kitchen carrying a cup of coffee. He put it down on an end table, gave her a kiss, heaved a sigh, and plopped into an armchair.

"I'm drained," he said, "but I finished the article and sent it off to the publisher. I hope he doesn't want another one for a while."

"He will," Emma said. "You write well and you know all the answers when it comes to investing." She looked around the spacious condo, a testimonial to his skill.

"Well," he said. "You're right. I guess I am considered an authority." He sat up a little straighter. "Now, what did you buy?"

"Just a couple of things for the baby."

"I see the logo from the bookstore, another mystery?"

"Uh-huh," she mumbled. It could be considered a mystery. She walked into the bedroom and slid the volume beneath her underwear in the dresser drawer.

"Want some coffee?" Nate called to her.

"Sure do. I'll be right out." She closely examined her reflection in the mirror. Nate is going to know as soon as he looks at my face that something isn't quite right. Shall I tell him?

Tell him the truth, her inner voice said. *He is your life partner, isn't he?*

"You're right, but he isn't going to understand," she said aloud.

"Who isn't going to understand what?" Emma turned to see Nate standing in the doorway, his arms crossed over his chest.

"Oh, you startled me. I thought you were in the living room."

"I knew as soon as you walked in that door that something was disturbing you. Do you want to tell me about it?"

He walked up to her and wrapped his arms around her trim body. "Are you trembling, Sparrow?"

"Let's go in the living room." She walked to the couch, took a swallow of the coffee Nate had set on the table for her, and closed her eyes for a moment.

"I met Claude in the bookstore," she began.

He raised his eyebrows. "Is anything wrong next door?"

"No, no, nothing like that." She looked into Nate's eyes, bit down on her lip, and, even though she had cautioned Claude not to say anything, blurted out, "He saw the stranger again. He was in the wardrobe room."

Nate let out a deep breath. "This has got to stop! Why can't someone catch this guy? He can't be allowed to roam around the building like that. Who knows what he might steal." He frowned and shook his head. "Did Claude ask him what the hell he wants?"

"He didn't speak," Emma said. *How can I phrase this so he believes me? Guardian Angel, help me.* "He wanted Claude to follow him."

"Follow him? Where?"

"I don't know. When Claude refused, he just—disappeared." She whispered the last word.

"What do you mean *disappeared?*"

"Just what I said. He has never spoken to anyone. He appears out of nowhere and disappears just as quickly. Not everyone sees him." She felt that was all the explanation she could give him.

"Are you suggesting what I think you are?"

"I don't know, Nate. I just don't know."

SIXTEEN

"THIS IS A REAL CHALLENGE," James said as he handed the libretto across his desk to Emma.

She had come to talk to him about the stranger, but found him engrossed in the planning of the next opera, *The Ghosts of Versailles.*

"It actually takes place on three different planes: the ghost plane, the theatrical plane, and the world of history." He frowned and rubbed his chin. "The stage director is doing a first-rate job with this. The ghost world has to look mysterious while the other worlds need to appear realistic."

"How is he going to do that?" she asked, disturbed by the reference to a ghost world.

James shrugged and held up his hands. "That's his field of expertise. I think he plans to use a theatrical mist as well as a skrim surrounding the unearthly realm." He opened his eyes wide and formed his mouth in an O.

"This talk of ghosts gives me the willies. Why would anyone want to incorporate such a premise into an opera?" Emma asked, rubbing her arms.

"Modern," he answered. "It's really supposed to be very clever if it's done well."

"Have you seen it performed?" she asked.

"No, but it got good reviews when the Lyric did it a few years ago." He looked up at Emma, a question in his eyes. "What did you want to talk to me about?"

"Oh, nothing important." She decided this was not the time to mention strangers and ghosts. "When are the auditions for the supers scheduled?"

"Very soon. Didn't you get a notice from the super captain? We need a lot of folks for some of those mob scenes."

"Of course, how foolish of me. I have it right on the refrigerator. I have to be going now. Love to Sylvia and the boys."

She hurried out of the office and down the stairs. *Now my son-in-law probably thinks I'm losing it. Why couldn't I bring up the topic of the stranger to him? Oh, why does my life always seem to be so complicated?*

Because you put yourself in these situations, her inner voice said.

Emma heaved a deep sigh as she made her way out of the building. *If I would learn to mind my own business, life would be much simpler.* But she knew she couldn't. It wasn't her nature.

"Hɪ, Gʟᴀᴅʏs," Emma said, picking up the phone on the second ring and looking at the caller ID. "How are things on the East Coast?"

"All is well. You'll be proud of me," Gladys said with a lilt to her voice.

"How so?"

"Cornell and I have been diligently exercising and eating a sensible diet. We've each lost between fifteen and twenty pounds."

"Fantastic," Emma said. "Soon you'll have to buy a new wardrobe."

"Not yet," her friend said. "I want to make sure I keep it off before I go on a spending spree."

"That sounds like a wise decision."

"Say, has your daughter-in-law had her baby yet?" Gladys asked.

"No, and she's overdue. Poor thing is so uncomfortable. The doctor is giving her until Monday. If she doesn't go into labor by then, he'll induce her." Emma felt edgy. Something didn't feel right. She walked into the atrium and examined her plants. They always had a calming effect.

Emma hesitated for a moment, then made a decision. "I want to ask you something."

"My, your tone sounds serious. Go ahead. I'm all ears."

"Have you ever seen *The Ghosts of Versailles?*" Emma thought this was safe ground before she introduced the topic of the stranger.

"I saw it last year. Why do you ask?"

"The Midwest is putting it on this season and Nate and I are going to audition for supernumerary roles. I'm trying to encourage the new librarian to join us. What did you think of the opera?"

"It's a challenge," Gladys said. "I'm not much for modern opera, but I must say, it was interesting, especially the way they portrayed the ghost world."

Emma felt a chill at the last words. "Gladys—there's something I have to talk to you about."

"I figured. I can always tell when you're leading up to something. What, pray tell, is on your imaginative mind?"

Emma walked back out into the living room, pacing the floor. She was glad Nate had gone out so he wouldn't hear her end of the conversation.

"Remember when I told you the soprano, Gina Rienzi, saw a man in her dressing room?"

"Yeah, I remember that. Did they ever catch him?"

"No, but others have seen him, too. They describe him as a ragged-looking man in muddy clothes. Some claim to smell a kind of musty, decaying odor about him." *I've gone this far,* Emma thought, *might as well go all the way.* "Not everyone can see him and he never says anything, just appears and disappears." She let out a deep sigh.

"Wait a minute," Gladys said. "Are you telling me this guy's a—spirit?"

"I don't know. He seems to want someone to follow him. If he is a spirit, he's trying to tell us something." Walking into the atrium again, she looked out over the lake as if expecting to see the stranger there.

"Have *you* seen him?" Gladys asked, her usually booming voice toned down to almost a whisper.

"Twice, the first time he just ducked behind the curtain during rehearsal. I wasn't really sure that time. But the second time I saw him onstage during the ballet. I saw him lurking in the artificial forest." She felt the chill again as she remembered the dim figure. He appeared to be there and not be there, all at the same time.

"Okay, let's get this straight. You're saying there's a ghost wandering around the opera house and some people see him and others don't. If I didn't know you better, I'd say you're getting soft in the head." Gladys hesitated a moment. "But, you seem to know things that other people don't. Listen, my friend, be careful. Remember what happened last summer. Stay out of trouble!"

"I will," Emma said with more assurance than she felt. "I promised myself to mind my own business."

"Ha! I want to see that. Keep me informed, and if you ever decide to write a book about your escapades, Cornell will publish it in a heartbeat. I'm certain it would be a bestseller."

"I'll keep that in mind. Bye now."

As Emma disconnected the line, the phone rang again.

"Hello."

"Ma, I'm at the hospital. Bertie started bleeding!" Emma's son, Martin, almost shouted the words.

"Oh, my God! I'll be there as soon as I can."

EMMA SCRIBBLED A NOTE and left it on the table for Nate, grabbed a jacket and her purse, and ran out the door. She punched the DOWN button on the elevator three times bouncing from one foot to the other. When the door finally opened, there stood Nate.

"What in the world?" he asked.

"Oh, I'm so glad you're here," she said as she pushed him back into the elevator, got in, and punched the button to the garage. "Bertie started bleeding. We have to get to the hospital right away."

He nodded and put his arm around her. Neither one said a word on the way down. When they reached the garage, they rushed to the car and Nate careened out of the garage. He tried to be supportive on the ride to the hospital, but Emma didn't hear a word he said. He drove as fast as traffic would allow, but it was the beginning of the afternoon rush hour and the streets were jammed.

From time to time Emma let out a frustrated sigh, wished she had a police escort, but there was nothing either of them could do.

When Nate pulled into the parking lot of the visitors' section, Emma jumped out of the car.

"Wait a minute," he said, following and grabbing her arm. "There's no need for you to get flattened by an SUV. That won't help anyone."

"You're right. I'm just so worried. Bertie's such a petite little thing and the doctor said she'll have a big baby, and besides that, she's late." Her voice raised in tone with each word.

"But she's tough," Nate said. "And we don't know anything yet, so stop imagining the worst."

They walked through the continually revolving doors of the new hospital wing which looked more like a four star hotel than an institution of healing.

"Where can we find Bertie Winberry?" Emma asked the woman behind the information counter.

"How do you spell that, please?" the woman asked, peering at Emma over half-glasses.

"W-i-n-b-e-r-r-y."

Nate held her hand tightly. She was glad for his strong presence beside her. *Oh, Guardian Angel,* she prayed, *please watch over mother and child.* Was her Guardian Angel able to watch over someone else? Emma wasn't sure, but angels could certainly communicate with one another.

"Labor and delivery," the woman said. "Take the elevators on the left to the third floor."

"Thank you."

Emma and Nate hurried to the bank of elevators and squeezed into one that was just about to close.

When they got off on the third floor, Emma spotted Martin waiting at the nurse's station. "Martin," she called.

"Oh, Ma." He turned to her as she clasped him in her arms. "They're taking her to surgery—have to do a C-Section. The placenta started to come loose the doctor said, causing the bleeding."

"The baby?" Emma asked.

"So far, it seems okay, but they have to deliver the baby right away. I'm so glad you two are here." He grabbed Nate's hand.

"Did you call Bertie's parents?" Emma asked.

"Yeah, they're on their way, but it'll take them quite a while to get here from Naperville."

Nate walked over to a coffeepot sitting on a counter and poured three cups. He handed one to Martin and one to Emma. "None of us needs more stimulation at this time," he said, opening three packets of sugar into his. "But coffee seems to be the only hot beverage readily available in hospitals."

"Thanks," Martin said, settling back in a chair. "I'm wiped out. We were up all last night. She was having contractions on and off." He took a swallow of coffee and let out a breath.

"The doctor asked me if I wanted to watch, but I almost passed out just thinking about it."

"I know," Emma said, squeezing her son's hand. "You were always squeamish when anyone was bleeding." She remembered his screams with every little scrape and scratch.

Martin visibly shivered and took another swallow of coffee. "Bertie knows I can't stand the sight of blood. She said she didn't want the staff to have to revive me in the middle of the delivery."

The trio alternately sat sipping coffee, pacing from one window to another, and sitting down again. Nate tried to engage Martin in conversation, but the younger man couldn't concentrate.

After what seemed like hours but was only forty-five minutes, a door opened and a woman wearing surgical scrubs walked out.

"Mr. Winberry," she said, smiling at Martin. "You have a beautiful, healthy eight-pound daughter, and your wife is fine."

Nate grabbed Martin's arm as he bounded out of the chair.

"Oh, thank you, Doctor." Tears pooled in his eyes. "When can I see them?"

"In a few minutes. Relax. The nurse will call you." She nodded, then turned, and walked back through the doors that said AUTHORIZED PERSONNEL ONLY.

"That's a big baby for a tiny girl like Bertie," Nate said, shaking his head.

"Bertie said she was a big baby, too. What about me, Ma?" He turned to Emma.

"You were a pip-squeak, not even seven pounds. And look at you now, shoulders like a football player. You're built like your father."

Emma turned away feeling her eyes stinging. She walked to the window and stared out at the pink-streaked western sky. "Happy birthday, baby," she whispered.

LATER EMMA LOOKED DOWN at the sleeping infant lying in Bertie's arms, so perfect, so innocent, untouched by the world.

"Take her, Emma," Bertie said, smiling.

The new grandmother gently took the newborn from her mother's arms. "She's beautiful, looks just like you."

"She has a little birthmark," Bertie said, "shaped like a fish. It's so cute."

Emma's eyes widened. "A fish? Where is the birthmark?"

"On the inside of her right thigh. Look at it."

Emma sat down, carefully unwrapped the blanket and stared at the tiny red fish-shaped mark. She tried to smile but felt a chill as the baby opened her eyes and seemed to look directly at Emma. Then the infant yawned and went back to sleep.

Oh, little one, Emma thought, *have you, too, inherited this* gift? *I have the same birthmark and so did my grandmother Lizzie. She passed the sixth sense on to me, and I fear I may have passed it to you.* Emma wrapped the blanket around the baby and held her close willing her not to have this *sixth sense*.

"I almost forgot to ask, what name did you chose? You hadn't decided the last time we spoke about it," Emma asked, trying to concentrate on something else.

"We're going to call her Robin."

"What a lovely name." Emma sighed and looked at Martin strutting proudly around the room.

"Robin Elizabeth," Bertie continued, "after my mother."

Elizabeth—Grandma Lizzie—that's also my middle name, Emma thought. *And today is Friday the thirteenth. Grandma and I were also born on that day of the month. Oh, little Robin, may your Guardian Angel watch over you, always.*

SEVENTEEN

TRISTANA STOOD IN FRONT of the tall bronze doors of Holy Name Cathedral. She thought that the Gothic-style church with its spire soaring into the sky would give her a feeling of solace, but instead it seemed impersonal and foreboding. She felt that if she entered those enormous doors, she might be entombed inside forever.

Hesitantly, she climbed the stairs. She had always found comfort in a church, any church, regardless of denomination.

She touched the metal bar on the side and, controlled by some inner mechanism, the doors slowly opened. It gave Tristana an eerie feeling, as if unseen hands beckoned her inside.

She walked slowly into the vestibule and then into the nave of the massive cathedral. She caught her breath as she gazed at the light streaming through the stained-glass windows. Dark blues and reds on one side progressed to lighter colors until they culminated in whites and golds behind the altar and crucifix.

Slowly she made her way toward the altar, slid into the second pew and sat back expecting to feel *something* in this holy place. She closed her eyes and tried to pray, but no words came. *How do I go about this? I must let go of the past.*

She looked at the bronze bas-relief circling the pedestal of the altar—scenes from the Old Testament depicting sacrifice and atonement.

How much had she sacrificed in her life? *Hadn't she atoned for her sins?*

EIGHTEEN

"COME ON, Tristana," Emma said, bursting into the library. "It's time for the auditions." She stood in the center of the room, hands on hips, a determined expression on her face.

"Oh, I don't know," Tristana said. "I've never been on a stage before. I really think I'll pass on this."

"Absolutely not," Emma said. "We talked about this and you said you'd consider it." Emma felt she had to do something to get help this woman to reconnect to life. "Please, will you try it, just once?"

"You'd better go along with her," Nate said, coming into the room, "or she'll niggle you to death."

Tristana shrugged and held out her hands in a gesture of submission. A smile sneaked across her face. "All right, I guess I'll give it a try."

"Good," Emma said.

"Let me run a comb through my hair and put on a little makeup. I won't be a minute." Tristana hurried down the hall to the ladies' room.

"I'll lock up," Emma called after her.

FIFTEEN MINUTES LATER the trio walked into a room crowded with people. It was familiar to Emma and Nate. They had gone through this routine many times. Emma looked around at the newcomers. She recognized the nervous movements of hands and legs, the glances at one another. She took Tristana's cold hand and led her to a chair.

"All these people," the woman whispered.

"Don't worry, most of them are as nervous as you are. See

those two over there?" Emma indicated a man and woman chatting in a relaxed manner. "They've been here before. I recognize them, but don't remember their names." Emma screwed up her face trying to recall a name. *I hate this,* she thought. *I used to be so good at names. Now I'm lucky if I remember my own.*

The years are passing, her inner voice said.

"Don't remind me."

"Don't remind you of what?" Nate asked.

"I'm talking to myself."

"As usual," Nate said.

A short, burly man wearing an expensive-looking suit swaggered into the room. His eyes scanned the area as if he were looking for someone. He gave a slight shrug and walked up to Nate extending his hand.

"Dominic Orso."

Nate shook the man's hand. "Nate Sandler."

"You done this before?" the man asked.

"Many times," Nate answered, pulling his hand away.

"I'll give it a try." With that he walked off and took a seat.

"He's aptly named," Emma whispered. "Looks like a bear." She wrinkled her nose at the aroma of his aftershave. Like Norman Quiller who was prone to overdo the stuff.

"His hand was sweaty," Nate said, taking out his handkerchief and wiping his hand. "I hate shaking a sweaty palm."

At that moment a tall, attractive brunette glided into the room, as graceful as a dancer. Her movements reminded Emma of Claude's. *I'll bet she danced when she was younger,* Emma thought. The woman smiled as she recognized the regulars and nodded to Emma and Nate.

"Good morning, everyone. I'm delighted to see such a big turnout. We do need quite a few supers for this production. My name is Cecily Cunningham, and I'm the super captain. I'm responsible for notifying you of when rehearsals are scheduled or cancelled. If you have any questions at any time, please direct them to me. I'll pass out cards with my phone number and E-mail address. Here comes George Ross, the stage manager."

A portly man wearing a sport shirt, a loose-fitting jacket and baggy pants came into the room.

"Boy, is he putting on weight," Emma whispered to Nate.

He nodded and held his finger up to his mouth.

George Ross went into the talk he had given many times before. It sounded memorized. In a monotone he told the assembled would-be supernumeraries what their responsibilities were: the rehearsals they must attend, the costumes they would wear, and their expected deportment onstage. "We request that you do not speak to the singers unless they speak to you first." He looked around the room making eye contact with each person.

"We realize that this is a big commitment of your time, so, if anyone wishes to bow out, now is the time to do it."

"Are rehearsals held during working hours?" one man asked.

"Some of them are. We try to schedule them in the afternoon on weekdays and on weekends, but some will be required during normal working hours. You see, there is nothing 'normal'—" he mimed quotation marks with his fingers "—about opera."

Most of the group smiled, but others let out frustrated sighs.

"I don't think I can put in that much time," the man said. "I will have to excuse myself."

George Ross nodded then asked, "Anyone else?"

An older couple stood, smiled, and walked out the door.

"All right, then, let's take you on the stage and show you what it feels like to be behind the footlights."

Tristana let out a little gasp and grabbed Emma's hand.

Emma smiled. "There's nothing to be afraid of. Come on."

The group followed George Ross and Cecily Cunningham through long hallways and toward the stage.

"Is all this necessary?" Dominic Orso asked, letting out a frustrated breath. "I thought we were just supposed to stand around in a crowd."

Emma frowned, shaking her head. *What bad manners.* There was something about the man that bothered her, but she couldn't identify what it was. It would come to her—eventually.

When they reached the stage, Tristana pulled back as she looked out over the auditorium.

"I can't do this," she whispered.

"Yes, you can," Emma said with authority. "I felt the same way the first time. Just try to relax. Take some deep breaths." She heard the woman's almost labored breathing.

"Slowly," Emma said. "That's it. Just let the tension go."

"It's not as intimidating as it looks," a tall, soft-spoken man said, looking down at the two women. He smiled at Tristana.

Emma recognized him as someone she had seen before. *Yes, I think he was a super last year,* she thought. *At least I remembered that, though I don't recall his name.*

They turned their attention back to George Ross who was directing each of them to perform a small task, place a bowl of artificial flowers on a table then walk over to a mark on the floor.

Nate went first, as he was a veteran and had been doing this for ten years. Emma followed, remembering how she had knocked over a jug the first time.

"Go on," the kind man said to Tristana, "I'll be right behind you."

Emma watched her walk across the stage with natural grace. *Nothing like my clumsiness,* she thought. She felt the woman's trembling body as she took her place and heard her let out a deep breath. "I did it," she whispered, a note of pride in her voice.

The man with the nice smile stepped next to them and nodded to Tristana.

I do believe he's attracted to her, Emma thought. She felt vibes coming from him, but they were mixed. She let it go as she relived her first meeting with Nate in this very situation three years earlier. Was it only three years? It seemed as though they had been together for a lifetime. She could barely remember being without him. She wished the same for Tristana. Perhaps this man will be good for her.

And perhaps he won't, her inner voice said.

Emma frowned, and for once, disregarded her inner voice.

"In this opera the supers are usually men," the voice of the stage manager broke her reverie, "but the director has decided he will use women, too, for this production."

George Ross again gave them general instructions, then passed out cards with his phone number and E-mail address. "Be sure we have all your information with the correct spelling of your name, phone number and E-mail address. If there are no more questions, that's all for today.

"Cecily will notify you when the first rehearsal is scheduled. We'll fit you for costumes at that time. Those of you who haven't been here before are welcome to continue with a tour of the back-stage area including costumes, props, and the makeup and wig room. It is helpful to familiarize yourself with the facility."

Emma watched as Dominic Orso, the loudmouth, came up to Tristana. "Hi, cookie," he said, winking. "You want to go on the tour?"

Tristana drew back as the man came a little too close to her and reached out his hand.

Nate appeared about to intervene when the kind man stepped between the two.

"The lady is going with me," he said, smiling at Tristana.

"Sorry," Orso said, shrugging. "Didn't know she was with you." He looked closely at the tall man as if he were studying him, then he turned, uttered a few words under his breath, and stalked out of the room.

"I'm sorry," the man said, looking at Tristana, then at Emma and Nate. "I didn't mean to be forward, but you appeared un-comfortable."

"Thank you," Tristana said.

"Are you going on the tour?" he asked.

"No, I've seen the facility. You go ahead."

"I've been here before," he said, "but it doesn't hurt to refresh the memory." He smiled, nodded and followed the group.

"He's nice," Emma whispered to Tristana.

"Yes, he is." She turned away but not quickly enough. Emma noticed the blush in her cheeks.

NINETEEN

W<small>HEN</small> E<small>MMA</small> <small>WALKED</small> into the library the following day, Tristana was glued to the computer monitor. A few wisps of her shiny hair had escaped from behind her ears and tickled her face. From time to time she blew it away out of the corner of her mouth.

Emma smiled as she stood there, just inside the door, watching and wondering how long it would take the woman to become aware of her presence.

Finally Tristana said, "There, that's it," jabbed a key, and the printer came alive, spitting out pages. She sat back and smiled, obviously pleased with herself. Only then did she raise her eyes.

"Emma, how long have you been standing there?"

"Only a few minutes," Emma said, walking toward the desk. "I didn't want to break your concentration."

Tristana pushed the errant locks behind her ear. "I found a list of people qualified to authenticate the documents we found. Mr. Hamilton asked me to do the research." She reached out and retrieved the pages from the printer.

"That's exciting," Emma said, walking around the desk and reading over the other woman's shoulder. The page listed experts in ink analysis, comparison of papers, and handwriting.

"Here's one who's a Board Certified Forensic Document Examiner. Unfortunately she's located in Texas. Here's another one in California. There are quite a few. Oh, here's one in Ohio, another in Missouri, New York, Georgia, everywhere but Illinois."

"I wonder why there aren't any in Chicago," Emma said. "It's a big enough city and there's plenty of crime that would warrant such services."

"Here's another site with more information on document

analysis," Tristana said, reading from the screen. "'Paper and ink must be compared to that used at the time period, but antique paper and ink can be purchased.' Hmm," she said, sitting back. "I really don't think these are forgeries. What would anyone stand to gain? They're only valuable from an historical perspective."

Emma stood behind Tristana, her eyes scanning the words on the monitor. "Look, it says the examiners need to be proficient in microscopy, photography, chromatography, and methods of document alteration. What's chromatography anyway?" She straightened up and rubbed a sudden ache in her back.

"I know it has something to do with color," Tristana said, reaching for the dictionary.

Emma shook her head. "That's a little too technical for my brain," she said, stretching out the kinks in her back.

Tristana put the dictionary aside and turned back to the list. "Most of these experts deal in forged documents. I'll give the pages to Mr. Hamilton and let him decide what to do."

THE WOMEN KNOCKED ON Bruce Hamilton's door, Tristana clutching the computer printouts. They heard two voices inside, one whining, the other slightly raised in volume.

"Maybe this isn't a good time," Tristana said, turning to Emma.

"Come in," they heard Bruce Hamilton say, his tone less than inviting.

Emma turned the knob and pushed the door partway open.

The director greeted them with a smile as he rose from his chair and walked toward the women. His limp seemed more pronounced today.

"Ladies, what a pleasant break." He turned to his assistant and frowned. "Mr. Quiller—" he emphasized the *Mr.* "—you know these ladies, I believe."

The man jerked his head, rising from his chair with obvious reluctance. "Yes," he muttered, his displeasure reflected in his beady eyes.

"Ladies, please sit down and tell me what's on your minds."
He indicated the two chairs in front of his desk.

"Sorry to interrupt," Tristana began, "I just wanted to bring
you this information on forensic labs available for authenticating the documents. I couldn't find any in Illinois." She handed
the printouts to Bruce who scanned them eagerly, pulling on his
lower lip.

"The State Police Crime Lab," he said excitedly. "I'll give
them a call. Bet they have a source.

"This is exciting, isn't it?" He turned to Quiller who was still
standing, squirming, and trying to inch his way toward the door.

Emma watched him closely, feeling the negativity emanat-
ing from him.

"You know," Bruce continued, oblivious to the attitude of his
assistant, "if these documents are authentic, and I believe they
are, we can convert that old storeroom into a sort of museum,
displaying the documents and artifacts from the original farmhouse." He seemed pleased with the idea.

But Emma's eyes never left Norman Quiller. He clenched his
fists and leaned forward. She saw his expression change from
one of surprise to shock, or was it fear?

Watch him, her inner voice said.

"This is a Center for the Performing Arts," he blurted out.
"I...I thought you were going to donate everything to the Chicago History Museum." His face reddened as he bounced from
one foot to the other.

"Calm down, Norman. Of course we focus on the performing arts, but a bit of the history of the original site would be a
nice addition to our routine tours of the building."

"That's a great idea," Tristana said, looking at Emma. "In
the meantime I'll be sure to keep them locked in my desk."

Emma's eyes remained on Norman Quiller. He didn't agree
with his boss, but there was more to it than that. There was
something secretive about the man, something unpleasant.

As if hearing her thoughts, Quiller looked at Emma. His eyes
met hers for only a moment, then he looked away.

But that was enough to give Emma the familiar chill that always warned her of trouble. Yes, she would heed her Guardian Angel and steer clear of Norman Quiller.

TWENTY

Now that the responsibility for authenticating the documents was in Bruce Hamilton's hands, Tristana felt the adrenaline rush ebbing. The search had perked up her spirits, made her feel more alive. And the prospect of being a supernumerary was exciting, although it was also frightening.

She walked around the tiny apartment and looked out the window facing Belmont Avenue. No rush-hour traffic filled the Sunday morning street.

She picked up the newspaper, checked the movie section, but found nothing that intrigued her.

She had been going to church for the past few weeks and still found no comfort there.

She looked around the small room then remembered, "Damn, I left the book I was reading at the library yesterday." Should she make the trip and retrieve the book, or just start another? She peered outside at the sunny day. A walk would do her good. She'd go to the Center, get the book, then maybe stop at the café for a cup of coffee and a scone.

She put on a jacket, picked up her purse, made sure she had the keys to the Performing Arts Center, and slowly walked out the door.

The crisp spring air did little to lift her mood. She hardly noticed the daffodils poking out of the ground, tiny buds just visible among the leaves and a swatch of crocuses filling one area with a spiral design of purple and white.

As she walked on, she felt tired, for no reason other than she was depressed and uncertain where life was leading her. She was tempted to turn around, go back and crawl into bed. *No!* she scolded herself, *I need to keep going.*

She passed a building she had seen every day since she came to Chicago. The sign in the window said *Psychic Readings by appointment,* and underneath, the phone number.

Tristana stopped, took out a pad and pen and jotted down the number. She had consulted a psychic in California, but the woman was no help. *Most of them are charlatans,* she thought, *but maybe I'll call.*

She looked up at the building and saw a curtain move on an upper floor. Was someone watching her? Now she was being paranoid. She shook her head and moved on.

WHEN SHE ARRIVED AT the Center, she unlocked the side door that led to the offices and the library. The building appeared to be deserted. She knew there would be a lot of activity later on, a theater group had been performing a new play the past few weeks. The papers gave it good reviews. She would like to see the play but she didn't like going alone.

She hesitated a few moments. It was so quiet. All Tristana heard were her own footsteps echoing through the deserted corridors. Did she hear a sound from somewhere? No, just her imagination. *It's a little spooky,* she thought. For a moment she was tempted to turn around and run out. *Fool, you're not a child, just go to the library, get the book, and leave. It should take all of ten minutes.*

As she climbed the stairs to the second floor she noticed the lights were out in the corridor. That didn't seem right. She looked around, but the area was deserted. *I'll have to report it to maintenance tomorrow.*

Again she was tempted to turn around and leave, but at the library door, she stopped. Something was wrong. The door stood ajar. Did she forget to lock it? No, she was meticulous in that respect.

She listened for sounds from inside. Someone was in there! This was her domain. How dare anyone come in without her permission.

This is ridiculous, she told herself. *Perhaps it's Bruce Hamilton. He has a key and every right to be inside.* With more bravado than she felt, she pushed open the door.

"Who's in here? Mr. Hamilton, is that you?"

A figure clad in black appeared from behind the desk. He ran toward her, growled, "Out o' my way," grabbed her shoulders, shoved her hard, and ran out the door. She lost her balance, reached for something, anything, her arms flailing in the air. As she pitched forward, her head hit the side of one of the bookcases and she fell to the floor. The room swirled around in a thick fog, then blackness...

TWENTY-ONE

WHEN TRISTANA CAME TO, she was momentarily confused. A dull throb at the side of her head reminded her of the fall; then she remembered the figure in black. A little light shone through the closed venetian blinds on the windows. She slowly sat up, trying to shake away the feeling of light-headedness, and struggled to her feet, wavered for a moment, then holding on to the furniture, made her way to the desk. With a groan she gingerly sat in the chair. For a long time she sat there, elbows resting on the desk, her hands supporting her aching head.

I must call someone, Bruce Hamilton, the police? Something might be missing. She reached for the desk lamp, switched it on, and winced as the sudden light stabbed at her eyes. She rested her head on the desk until her eyes adjusted to the light.

I have to get a hold of myself. She grabbed the phone and punched in 9-1-1. She heard her voice tell the dispatcher what happened, but the words sounded distant and disconnected as if someone else were talking.

Have to call Mr. Hamilton, but her thoughts were all in a jumble. *Have to find the Rolodex...everything out of focus.*

Emma, I'll call Emma. She'll know what to do. That number she remembered. She punched it into the phone and prayed they were home.

"Hello," Emma's friendly voice answered.

"It's Tristana. I'm at the library. Someone broke in—pushed me—I hit my head—called police..."

"Tristana, are you all right?"

"I don't know."

"Hang on. Nate and I will be right over."

WHEN EMMA AND NATE ran into the entrance of the Center, they saw James talking to a policeman. Emma had called him on her cell phone as they ran out of the condo.

"James, is Tristana all right?" she asked, grabbing his arm.

"The paramedics are with her now. It seems to be just a bad bump on the head, but they want to take her to the hospital for a thorough checkup." He looked worried, rubbed his hand over his face and blew out a deep breath.

"Do you think it might have been that stranger who's been lurking around the Center?" Nate asked.

"Who knows?" James shrugged.

"No," Emma said. "It was definitely not the stranger."

"How can you be so sure?" James asked.

"I just know. You'll have to trust me on that one." She ignored the nudge from Nate and the deep frown on his face.

"Can we go up? I must see her," Emma asked, fidgeting with her purse.

"Go ahead. I'll be up as soon as I finish here," James said, turning back to the officer.

When Emma and Nate entered the library, they saw a policeman dusting the desk for fingerprints and Tristana lying on a gurney, the paramedics starting an intravenous drip. Wires snaked from under her blouse hooked to an EKG machine. The paramedic was transferring the data to the hospital through his cell phone.

"Tristana," Emma said, rushing in. "Are you badly hurt?"

"I think I'm all right, but I'm a little disoriented and my head aches." She pressed an ice pack to the side of her head.

When the paramedic was finished, he told the Emergency Room they were on their way.

"Is this necessary?" Tristana asked, her voice weak.

"Yes," Emma said emphatically.

"What hospital are you taking her to?" Nate asked the paramedic.

"Northwestern."

Nate nodded. "We'll be there as soon as we can."

NATE TURNED TO JAMES who was scanning the bookshelves. "What are you looking for?"

"I don't know." James shrugged. "Anything that's missing or out of place. What a time for Bruce to be out of town." He blew out a breath and sat heavily in a chair.

Emma sat in a chair biting her lip and trying to think, but nothing came to her.

At that moment the policeman who had been examining the desk looked up. "This locked drawer has been tampered with. It appears someone was trying to open it."

"The locked drawer?" James asked.

"Was there something significant in there?" Nate asked.

"The historic document that we found," Emma said, getting out of her chair. "That's where Tristana put them."

"Who has the key?" the officer asked.

"The librarian does," James answered. "Here's her key ring that I found on the floor when I came in. She must have dropped it. It may be one of these." He handed the keys to the officer.

"This one fits," the man said, opening the drawer and extracting a large manila envelope.

James took it, and with trembling fingers, extracted the plastic sleeves. He examined them carefully then breathed a sigh of relief. "Everything seems to be here. There may be some significance to these that we're not aware of," he said. "They're not secure here, that's for sure. I'll put them in the safe in Bruce's office. Only he and I have the combination."

James turned to Nate and Emma. "I'm sure the police will question Tristana at the hospital when she's stabilized. Now I better try and contact Bruce." He shook his head, suddenly overcome with weariness. "When is this all going to end?"

"When we find that stranger," Nate said. "I'm sure he has something to do with this."

WHEN EMMA AND NATE walked into the hospital they asked for Tristana Morgan.

"She's having an MRI at the moment," a nurse told them.

"I think I'll have some of that coffee while we wait," Nate said. "Do you want some?" Emma shook her head. He walked over to the machine, put change into the slot, and retrieved a cup of dark brew. He poured in three sugars and walked back to Emma. "What are you thinking about? Your face is all scrunched up."

She sighed. "I was trying to make some sense of this whole thing, but no answers are coming to me."

"I still think that once we find the stranger everything will straighten itself out," Nate said with conviction.

Emma shook her head and turned to him. "Nate, if the stranger is a homeless person as you seem to believe, what would he possibly want with some old documents? It doesn't make sense."

"There doesn't seem to be any other explanation," Nate said.

"Oh, there is," Emma said with conviction. "We just haven't found it yet."

At that moment Tristana returned from the MRI. She sat in a wheelchair and appeared a little better than she had at the Center.

An officer came into the room and asked if Tristana could answer some questions.

She gave him a blank look. "I'm not sure what I can tell you. Can't seem to remember much."

"Did you see the man's face?" the officer asked.

She thought for a moment. "Not really. He had something covering it. I don't know what it was."

"How about his voice. Did he say anything?"

"No," she hesitated. "Just mumbled something. I'm not being much help, am I?"

"You're doing fine," the officer said. "Just relax. How about his height, was he a big man?"

"No, just average." She gave him an apologetic look.

"All right," he said. "Here's my card. If you remember anything, no matter how insignificant, please call."

Tristana nodded, then turned to Emma and Nate. "This is so perplexing. What could he be after?"

"The documents," Nate said. "The locked drawer had been tampered with. James found your keys on the floor. When the officer opened the drawer, the envelope was intact so James locked the documents in the safe."

They sat in silence unable to come up with an answer when a doctor came into the room and examined Tristana's pupils. He shone a flashlight in her eyes then had her stand up and walk a straight line.

"The MRI was negative," he said. "It's a mild concussion. You can go home, but I suggest you not be left alone for the next twenty-four hours."

Emma and Nate looked at each other. "How about staying with us?" Emma suggested.

The doctor agreed it would be a good idea; otherwise she would need to stay in the hospital overnight.

"I don't want to be any bother," Tristana answered.

"Nonsense. We can stop by your apartment and get anything you might need," Nate said.

Tristana nodded and murmured her thanks.

EMMA TUCKED TRISTANA in bed in the spare room. "You'll feel better after a nap. But I'm supposed to check on you every half hour. That's what the doctor said."

Tristana smiled and grabbed Emma's hand. A frightened look crossed her face. "Do you think this could possibly be connected to the stranger?"

"No," Emma said emphatically. "This is something entirely unrelated."

AFTER A NAP, Tristana felt renewed. She even helped Emma prepare a dinner of linguine with clam sauce and crusty bread dipped in olive oil. Afterwards the trio sat quietly in the living room, each with their own thoughts.

A knock at the door broke the silence. Nate opened it to see Claude holding a covered plate in his hands.

"Am I intruding?" he asked with some drama.

"Not at all, Claude, come in."

He placed the plate on the coffee table and raised his eyebrows in surprise. "Tristana, how pleasant." He bent over and kissed her hand, then Emma's.

"And what have you brought on that plate?" Emma asked.

He gave a wry smile. "Since you are always so graciously baking cookies and those glorious muffins, I tried my hand at a bundt cake." With a flourish, he removed the plastic cover to reveal a slightly lop-sided cake with white icing dribbled down the sides.

"It looks wonderful," Emma said. "Let me put on a pot of coffee and we'll sample your culinary skills, kind sir."

Claude pressed his hand to his chest and bowed as Emma disappeared into the kitchen, still within earshot of the conversation.

"Dear lady, are you ill? You look quite pale," he said to Tristana.

"There's been an incident at the Performing Arts Center," Nate said.

"What happened? Was it…the stranger?" His voice dropped to a whisper.

"No," Tristana said. "It was someone else."

Nate began the story and by the time Emma returned with a tray of coffee and plates for the cake, he was just finishing the explanation.

"So," Claude said, "whoever it was seemed to be after the historical documents."

"So it seems," Emma said, slicing into the moist cake. "This looks delicious."

"Hope so. Was the lock to the library door tampered with?" Claude asked.

Tristana shook her head. "Not a mark. Whoever it was had a key."

"Or a good lock pick," Nate said.

"What about the window?" Claude asked.

Emma shook her head. "It was locked, and that's a two-story drop to the sidewalk. No way anyone could get in there without a ladder."

"Why would anyone want those documents?" Tristana asked, gently touching the side of her head. "I've been asking myself that question over and over."

"Perhaps to sell them?" Claude suggested.

"Who'd want to buy them?" Emma asked.

He shrugged. "Maybe a collector."

"That's not too likely," Nate said. "The more important questions are: who knew about the documents and who has keys to the library?"

Emma opened a drawer to an end table and took out a pen and pad of paper. "We'll make a list. I'll label it: Those who had knowledge of the documents. We must be thorough." She began to write, and when she had finished, she had six names on the list.

1. Bruce Hamilton
2. Norman Quiller
3. James Greene
4. Tristana Morgan
5. Emma Winberry
6. Nate Sandler

She read them off one by one.

"Thomas and I knew about them. Add our names," Claude said. "As you said, we must be thorough."

Emma nodded and added their names.

7. Claude Doran
8. Thomas Aherne

"That makes eight people," she said.

"I think one of the maintenance men may have overheard

us talking to Mr. Hamilton," Tristana said. "He was fixing the electric outlet in the office when we brought the documents to the director. Remember, Emma?"

Emma bit the side of her cheek. "Vaguely—a tall, thin fellow. I'll add him to the list. And he would have keys to all the offices, right?" She was warming to the task, scribbling furiously on her pad of paper. "I'll ask James about him. Now that you mention it, he did seem interested in what we were saying."

"Of course, it could be just that, interest," Nate said.

"Perhaps, but then again…" Emma didn't finish the sentence.

"I've had enough for one night," Claude said. "This intrigue is too much for my artistic brain. I must say good night."

With a dramatic wave of his hand, he waltzed out the door.

After Emma settled Tristana in the spare room, Nate yawned and stretched. "I think I'll turn in, too," he said. "Are you coming?"

She frowned. "I'll be in shortly. My mind isn't ready to settle down yet. You go along."

He kissed her, yawned again, and headed for the bedroom.

Emma knew she wouldn't be able to sleep—too many thoughts mixing around in her brain. She warmed a cup of milk, sat in her favorite chair in the atrium, and looked out over the placid lake. A full moon reflected off the water filling the room with a mysterious glow.

Emma twisted in the chair until she was in just the right position. Then, she began to rethink the names on the list and mentally cross off any who couldn't be the intruder.

She could discount her own, Nate and James, of course. But Claude and Thomas. What about those two? They seemed like a nice couple, but what did she really know about them? And who was that woman and child she had encountered in the elevator? The boy who referred to one of them as Daddy? *No, they may have secrets, but they're not involved in this. I won't cross them off just yet.*

Bruce Hamilton was out of town, so it couldn't be him. But was he really out of town? Could he have come back and entered the library unseen? He would have no reason to steal the documents. He was the one most interested in verifying them. But Tristana said the intruder was average height and Bruce was extremely tall. She would have noticed that. No, it wasn't him.

Norman Quiller is a shifty weasel, but he doesn't have the gumption to pull off something like this. Mentally she struck a line through his name.

The maintenance man seems the most likely suspect. James and Bruce will have to question him. Perhaps he thinks he can make a few extra dollars by selling the documents. That's the simplest explanation.

But the simplest explanation is not necessarily the correct one, her inner voice said.

All right, Guardian Angel, if it quacks like a duck, it's a duck. Don't be too sure.

Emma frowned, then went back to her ruminating. She thought hard as she tried to remember what the maintenance man looked like. He was fairly tall. But Tristana said the intruder was average height. She could have been mistaken. After that nasty bump on her head she might not have remembered too much.

The last name on the list was Tristana. Emma had been avoiding considering her. She certainly didn't knock herself out. She's a widow, never talks about her husband. Does she have any family, siblings? Would she hit herself on the head just to fake an attempted robbery? Of course not. *My intuition tells me there's something secretive about that woman, but it doesn't have anything to do with the documents.*

There was always the stranger, lurking in the background. *Could this be his way of attracting our attention? I wish I knew who he was and what he wants.*

Put it away for now, her inner voice said. *The answers will come.*

"You're right. They always do—eventually."

Emma heaved a deep sigh. *This* sixth sense *is such a burden sometimes.*

TWENTY-TWO

The following morning Emma decided to go with Tristana to the library. Although she still had a slight bump on her head, she was feeling much better. Nate stayed behind to work on the finances and another article.

When they walked into the library, they encountered a livid Bruce Hamilton examining the tampered desk lock and swearing. Norman Quiller stood behind him, twitching and shifting from one foot to the other. Emma studied him closely.

For a moment their eyes met, then he quickly looked away. She gritted her teeth and pursed her lips, barely able to contain her dislike for the man.

"Mrs. Morgan," the director said, looking up. "How are you?" He hurried over and took Tristana's hand, examining her face for some signs of injury. "That's a nasty bruise on the side of your head."

"I'm quite all right, Mr. Hamilton. Don't worry about me," Tristana said with a slight tremor in her voice.

"Rest assured that our insurance will cover all of your medical bills." He sighed. "This has to be the work of that strange man roaming about the center. We must find him and have him arrested." Bruce paced the floor, his limp becoming more pronounced with each step.

Emma and Tristana exchanged knowing glances, but said nothing.

"What about the maintenance man who was in your office the day we brought in the documents?" Emma asked.

"Oh, yes, James mentioned him to me. Quiller, go out and

find that man, whoever he is, and bring him to my office. I want to speak to him—now!"

Quiller sidled out of the room, nodding in nervous jerks. Emma noticed that he avoided eye contact. *Obnoxious little man,* she thought; her body inadvertently shivered.

"Ladies, please sit down. Let me get you some coffee," Bruce Hamilton said. "Of all the times I had to be gone…" He retreated from the room toward the coffee machine.

"I'm not used to all this fuss," Tristana said. "Do you think we'll ever find out who's responsible?" She turned to Emma as if to find the answer.

"I'm sure we will, eventually. If we knew the reason why, the who might present itself."

"Yes, but for the life of me, I can't come up with any logical answer."

"It might be something entirely unconnected with the intrinsic value of the documents themselves, something we know nothing about."

Now what made me say that? Guardian Angel, are you trying to tell me something?

Just observe, her inner voice said, *and keep an open mind.*

BRUCE HAMILTON RETURNED with the coffee, his brow furrowed, his face set in a frown. "I am going to take these documents myself to someone for verification. Where is that list you printed off the Internet?" he asked, looking at Tristana.

"I left a copy on your desk, but I have another, in case you misplaced it." She found the list on her desk and handed it to him, then sat down again.

"Thanks," he said, scanning the list. "Oh, yes, the Crime Lab. I did decide to start there. I'll call right now and see what I can find out, and Mrs. Morgan, please be careful." He limped out of the room and down the hall.

EMMA STAYED WITH TRISTANA until noon when they both decided to lock up and go home. Tristana said she still felt a little shaky.

"You look pale. Do you want to come back to my place?" Emma asked.

"No thanks, I'll be fine. I just need rest."

The two women said good-bye, and Emma thought for a moment as she watched Tristana walk away. *She needs more than rest. Something is bothering that woman, something other than the trouble at the Center. I wonder what it could be?*

TWENTY-THREE

As TRISTANA WENT from the bus stop toward her apartment, she stopped again in front of the building with the sign advertising psychic readings. *If I don't go now, I may lose my nerve. Why not?* she thought.

She gripped the cold iron railing and began climbing the stone steps. There were only seven, but with each one, her feet seemed to grow heavier and the stairs steeper. By the time she reached the ornate oak door, she was trembling. Maybe she should just turn around and go home.

At that moment the door opened. A short rotund woman greeted her with a smile. Her hair was stark white, not the graying of age, but completely devoid of color. As she squinted slightly, Tristana noticed the pink of the irises. *She's an albino,* Tristana thought.

A dark blue caftan flowed around her body in soft folds. "Won't you come in?" the woman said in a soft, velvety voice. "I've been expecting you." Her tone was inviting.

"You must have me mistaken for someone else," Tristana stammered. "I didn't have an appointment."

"I know, but I've been watching you, the way you hesitate as you walk by, look at the sign then up at the window. I knew it was only a matter of time. Do come in. I just made a pot of herbal tea."

Hesitantly, Tristana followed the woman. The room she entered looked like an ordinary living room, no crystal ball sat on the coffee table, no candles burned anywhere. A brown couch, two matching armchairs adorned with old-fashioned antimacassars and a table were the only pieces of furniture. Plain beige drapes hung on the windows. A few brightly colored pillows broke up the austere atmosphere of the room. A black-and-white picture in a plain frame hung on a wall—the circular pattern of the yin and yang.

"Make yourself comfortable while I get the tea," the woman said.

Tristana sank into one of the chairs, suddenly realizing how weary she felt. She leaned back and closed her eyes. Only then did she become aware of a soft chanting sound, some type of oriental music accented by tinkling bells. It's soothing melody soon put her at ease. She breathed in deeply as the woman returned carrying a tray with two steaming cups of a fragrant brew.

"That's a lovely sound," Tristana said.

"Yes, it helps to dispel nervousness and fear. Just relax, my dear, and let the tension leave your body. When you're ready, you can tell me what's troubling you and how I can help." As she smiled, tiny wrinkles creased the corners of her eyes. She reminded Tristana of the fairy godmother she had read about in children's books.

Tristana took a cup of tea and sipped. She didn't recognize the taste, but it was pleasant, slightly sweet, and floral.

For a while neither of them spoke. Tristana felt the despair and loneliness slowly begin to leave her body. The tea seemed to have a revitalizing effect.

"There," the woman said, "your color is better already. Now, give me your right hand, please."

Tristana put down the tea cup and hesitated for a moment before she held out her hand.

The woman stared at the palm, stroked it, and closed her eyes. When she opened them, she looked directly at Tristana. "You are harboring a great deal of pain and resentment about your past."

Tristana stiffened and tried to pull her hand away.

"Please," the woman said, "let me finish." She stroked the palm until Tristana again relaxed.

"Unless you are able to release the past, you will be forever bound to it. It's time to forgive, and let go."

Tristana pulled her hand away. "I can't. There's too much hurt and sadness." Tears streaked from her eyes and down her face. She quickly brushed them away.

"You will heal only with release," the woman said, leaning closer. Then she sat back. "You can't change the past, only the present. Learn from your mistakes. That is their purpose. There is a new life awaiting you, but you must let go of the old one first."

Tristana leaned her head on the back of the chair and wept openly, tears of sorrow, pain, and regret.

"That's right," the woman said, "let it go." She stood up and walked behind Tristana. "Close your eyes and relax. I'm going to transmit my energy to you, using my hand as a ball around your head. I won't touch you, but you may feel a slight tingling sensation. Relax…relax."

Tristana inhaled deeply and slowly let out the breath. After a few moments she felt a sensation of warmth around her head. She sighed, and without realizing it, drifted off into a semi-sleep. She didn't know how much time passed, but when she opened her eyes the woman was again sitting across from her, smiling.

"That's all for today, my dear." She hesitated, then a frown crossed her face. "Let me warn you that I sense danger around you, but until we get past this impediment, I can't go any further."

Tristana nodded. Already she felt a lightening of the burden she had carried for so long. "How much do I owe you?" she asked.

"There's no charge for today, *if,* when you return, you feel that I have helped you, then you can pay me."

"I don't even know your name."

"Just call me Rose." She gave her a card with only the name *ROSE* and the phone number printed on it. "Call me anytime you need me."

Tristana walked back down the seven stairs with a spring

in her step. She held her head higher and felt energized. It was only then that she realized the woman had never asked her for her name.

TWENTY-FOUR

"Nate," Emma said as they finished a breakfast of muffins and fruit, "I would like to spend some time at the library with Tristana. You don't mind, do you?" She looked at him with her large gray eyes, widening them just a little.

"No need to give me that disarming look, Sparrow. I know you're up to something. What is it?"

Emma shook her head. "I'm not up to anything other than concern. I just want to keep an eye on her, to make sure she's all right. Something's troubling that woman."

"You just can't let people sort out their own problems, can you?" He gave her a stern look, then softened it into a smile. "I know—you can't. Go ahead. I'll keep myself occupied. I want to look at that kitchen sink. I think the drain is clogged; it's been running kind of slow lately."

"You're a dear." She kissed him on the forehead and caressed his cheek with her hand.

"Go on. I'll clean up," he said, returning the kiss.

She needed no further urging. Grabbing a jacket and her purse, she was out the door.

"You look better today. Did you get a good night's sleep?" Emma asked as she entered the library and scrutinized the woman's face.

"As a matter of fact, I did. And what brings you here this morning?" Her smile was genuine and welcoming.

"Oh, I had some time on my hands and thought you might need some help."

"I certainly do."

Emma hung up her jacket and busied herself to help categorize books and check in new arrivals.

A little later Bruce Hamilton came in. "Ladies, I have some encouraging news." A smile lit up his craggy face. "I called the Crime Lab and they gave me the name of a woman here in the Chicago area who does this sort of thing. When I called her, she seemed eager to look at the papers, made it a point to tell me that she's certified by the American Board of Forensic Examiners. I have an appointment with her this afternoon." He sat his long frame into a chair as he exhaled a deep breath.

"That's wonderful," Emma said. "At least you'll have some idea of their worth, in case that was what the thief had in mind." Somehow, she didn't think that was the reason, but she kept those thoughts to herself.

"I've been thinking," he said, rubbing his large hand over his prominent forehead. "Wouldn't it be interesting if we could locate the descendents of this family?" He turned his head, looking from one woman to the other.

"Why would you want to do that?" Emma asked. It seemed like a daunting task.

He shrugged. "I don't know. I just thought it might be interesting."

Tristana frowned. "If you actually found someone, they might want the family bible with all the documents, as well as all the other artifacts. That would be the end of your display."

"You have a point, Mrs. Morgan. I'd better give that some thought. On the other hand, if there are descendents, we might need their permission to display the items."

Emma frowned. Another challenge, she thought. "How would you go about searching for them?"

"I have no idea," he said, unfolding his long frame from the chair. "Now I have work to do. I'll let you know what the document expert has to say." He turned, and with his characteristic limp, walked out the door.

"I wonder why he limps?" Tristana wondered aloud.

"I asked James about that. He said Bruce mentioned an accident when he was a boy but nothing more." Emma noted a wince of pain cross Tristana's face, but she quickly composed herself and Emma didn't ask about it. In silence, the women went back to work.

"I'M ABOUT READY for lunch, how about you?" Emma asked, looking at the clock.

"Yes, I think so," Tristana said with a deep sigh.

"Is something bothering you?"

She hesitated for a moment. "Can I talk to you—about a personal matter?" The woman wrung her hands and began to pace.

"Certainly. We can discuss it over lunch, away from here." Emma looked around, almost expecting to see someone eavesdropping.

Tristana nodded. She took her jacket out of the closet and carefully locked the door as they left and headed toward the small café a short distance away.

As they walked in, Emma scanned the room just beginning to fill up with the lunch crowd, a noisy group at one table filling the area with raucous laughter.

"We won't be able to talk in here," she said. "Say, why don't we get a couple of sandwiches and coffee and sit on one of the benches along the lakeshore. It's a lovely day and only a two-block walk. The exercise will do us good."

"All right."

They ordered two ham on ryes with a large dill pickle on the side, two coffees to go, and extra napkins; then they headed toward the lakeshore.

Gulls screeched as they swooped down seeking possible food. The spring breeze brought the scents of damp earth and new growth. Emma found it invigorating and wondered if Tristana did, too. They found a bench, and after Emma wiped off the remaining dew with a few napkins, they sat down.

Tristana made no attempt to unwrap her sandwich. She sipped the hot coffee and stared into the distance.

Emma waited, took a bite of her sandwich along with the pickle and washed it down with coffee. It was a bit dry.

"I went to see a psychic," Tristana said, still staring at the water.

"Oh?"

"She told me she felt an aura of danger around me." Tristana turned to Emma, a frightened look in her eyes.

"What sort of danger?"

"She couldn't tell. It seems my psyche is filled with pain and resentment over something that happened long ago. She said she couldn't get past it."

I knew it, Emma thought. "Do you want to talk about it?"

Tristana shook her head. "I can't," she whispered.

Emma sat back and ruminated. She brought up memories she had put away years ago, but if she could help this woman, she might want to bring them back. They weren't painful anymore; in fact, they seemed to have happened to someone else a long time ago.

"I'm going to tell you an experience of mine that you might find helpful," Emma said, looking at the waves lapping the shoreline. "Many years ago I was filled with resentment over the cruel turn my life had taken." Emma hesitated for a moment, then continued, "When my last child was just a year old, my mother-in-law had a stroke. She was a good woman, claimed I was like the daughter she never had. She had been a great help to me through the years, but now, she needed care." Emma took another swallow of coffee. She put the sandwich aside, not feeling hungry anymore, turned to Tristana, and looked into her eyes.

"My husband didn't want to put her in a home and neither did I. His brother was unable to care for Grandma, so we took her in. We did hire a woman to clean and help out, but Grandma was my responsibility. She and my baby were both in diapers. Nothing was disposable at that time, and we couldn't afford diaper service. So I ended up changing and washing diapers for Grandma and my son every day." Emma stopped for a moment and gazed at the blue sky. Puffs of clouds drifted by as if the memory of that time was carried along with them.

"I grew so resentful of my life, that I didn't think I could go on. My daughter helped as much as she could, but she was only a child. I was riddled with guilt. Here was a woman who had been so good to me, and all I wanted was to be rid of her."

Emma shook her head and waited a few moments. Tristana said nothing.

"One day I went to church, a nondenominational church in the neighborhood. The minister gave a sermon that seemed to be directed specifically at me. He talked about resentment, said any situation that we resent, we hold to us. We must learn to release it to be truly free."

Tristana looked at her now with rapt attention, taking in every word. "How did you do it? How did you let go?"

"Well, it took me a few days of talking to my Guardian Angel before I came up with a plan." Emma noticed the skeptical look on Tristana's face. "I know it sounds silly but I've been doing it all my life. My angel usually tells me what to do. Every time I went to minister to Grandma, I put my arms around her and told her I loved her."

"That's all?"

Emma nodded. "Within two weeks I no longer minded the distasteful tasks. The burden was somehow lifted from my shoulders. And, six weeks later Grandma died quietly in her sleep."

Tristana said nothing, simply continued to stare at the lake. "I don't know if that'll work for me."

"Give it a try," Emma said, swallowing the lump in her throat. "It did for me."

"I will. Now I think we had better get back. Maybe we can eat these sandwiches later."

They started back to the Performing Arts Center, each with her own thoughts.

The psychic told Tristana she saw danger around her, Emma thought. *I wonder what she meant by that. Guardian Angel, tell me how to help this woman. I can feel so much of her pain.*

TWENTY-FIVE

THE FOLLOWING DAY Emma decided to stay home. She had neglected the housework a little too long; the film of dust on the furniture was too obvious to ignore. She also had transplanting to do. Some of her plants needed to make the transition out onto the roof garden, and this was a job she thoroughly enjoyed.

She walked outside and breathed deeply. The sensations that accompanied spring never failed to invigorate her: the freshness of the air, the birds darting about building nests and calling to one another. Even Lake Michigan had a different feeling. The waves seemed to dance toward shore in a flowing ballet-like motion.

Trowel in hand, Emma dragged a bag of potting soil outside and began on the large planters, removing debris and roots from the previous season, making a neat pile to dispose of later. After transplanting the hardy herbs, she looked around the area. *It's too early yet for tomatoes,* she thought. *I'll leave them in the atrium a little longer.*

"Emma," Nate called, "phone."

She frowned, slipped off her gardening gloves and walked into the atrium. "Hello," she said, taking the phone from Nate.

"Hi. I hope I'm not bothering you," Tristana's voice came through the instrument.

"Not at all. I'm ready for a break. I've been working since the crack of dawn. How is everything?"

"Fine. Bruce Hamilton was just in here. The forensic examiner said it would take about two weeks to study the documents thoroughly. They appear to be genuine, but first she has to determine the provenance, then find out what type of trees grew in the area at that time. The paper would be made from their pulp."

"I never thought of anything like that," Emma said.

"Something about the ink, too," Tristana continued, "as well as the style of handwriting. It all sounds very complex, and expensive."

"Does he still want to search for descendents?" Emma asked.

"Oh, yes, now he's more intent than ever. He asked the examiner if the documents had any intrinsic worth. The woman said only from an historical perspective. A few collectors might be interested, but she doubted that a professional thief would try to steal them."

"Hmm." Emma thought for a moment. "There's another reason, I feel it."

"What *could* it be?" Tristana asked.

"This is just between you and me, but I believe the attempted robbery is somehow connected to the stranger and that storeroom."

"You do? But how? No one has seen him for quite a while. And—he didn't seem to be…" She left the sentence unfinished.

"I know we haven't seen him, but he's there, just waiting for the right time."

"Emma, you're scaring me."

"I didn't mean to. It's just that sometimes I get these strange premonitions. Let's see what happens. In the meantime, be careful and keep your eyes open for anyone who seems suspicious. If you notice anything out of the ordinary, no matter how small, tell me or James. Promise?"

"Yes, I will."

EMMA WANTED TO PUT the entire situation out of her life, but she knew, all too well, that she couldn't.

Nate found her at the computer staring at the screen and mumbling. "What, pray tell, are you reading so intently?"

She jumped, then frowned at him. "You startled me."

"Sorry." He kissed her on the neck and glanced at the screen. "Earthbound spirits," he read. "Have you suddenly taken an interest in the occult?"

"Just something I was reading in a book. I thought I'd find out more about it." She closed the site, turned off the computer, and scooped up a number of pages from the printer tray.

"Hmm." He sighed, shook his head, and walked out of the room.

Emma picked up an orange highlighter and began to read. *"Why do some spirits remain earthbound? Because of unfinished business; may need assistance from the living."* She highlighted that statement—it was a possibility.

"Some stay near the site of their death, especially if it was violent and sudden." She felt a shiver. What if the stranger had been murdered somewhere in the Performing Arts Center and was trying to ask someone for help? Nonsense. Those things only happened in horror stories.

She thought of the man in the old Water Tower, how he died saving others, how his spirit sometimes appeared in an upper window. Anyone with a vivid imagination could come up with something like that.

Don't discount anything, her inner voice said.

"All right." She screwed up her face and read on. *"There is a superstition in London's Theatre Royal on Drury Lane. During rehearsals the actors look for the 'man in gray' sitting in the last seat in row D. He was believed to be an eighteenth-century patron. A sighting of his ghost meant a successful run for the play. The actors believed he guided them to better positions on the stage."*

Emma took a pad of paper and a pen out of the drawer and began to jot down other possibilities.

1. What if the stranger is an earthbound spirit?
2. What if he either died accidentally or was murdered in the Center?

3. What if he can't rest until his body is found and properly buried?

4. What if he wants to identify his killer?

She knew how fantastic it all sounded. Still… She clipped all the papers together, put them in a folder, and tucked it in the lower drawer, underneath some magazines.

THE RINGING OF THE PHONE pulled Emma's thoughts away from the macabre. She picked it up just as Nate walked in the front door, his arms loaded with packages.

"Hello," she said into the phone, and gave Nate a quizzical look.

"Hi, my long distance friend, long time no talk," came Gladys's booming voice.

"You're absolutely right. I've been neglecting my friends. How are you?"

They carried on their conversation as Emma watched Nate unwrap a number of boxes.

"Just a minute," she said to Gladys. "Nate is opening a rather large box."

She turned to him. "What is it?"

"Never mind, nosy." He picked it up and walked into the kitchen.

"Did you find out what's in the box?" Gladys asked.

"He won't tell me."

"I love surprises," Gladys said. "Knowing Nate, it's probably something fabulous."

This piqued Emma's curiosity even more, but she decided to let him surprise her in his own time. She walked into the atrium and settled in her favorite chair, ready for a nice *chin wag* with her friend.

"How is the new librarian working out?" Gladys asked.

"Just fine. She's a lovely woman. But something in her past is troubling her. She hasn't told me what it is yet, but I'm sure she will when she's ready."

Gladys laughed. "You draw people with problems like a magnet. Do you put a sign on your back—Mrs. Fix-It—bring me your cares and woes?"

"Don't make fun of my 'gift,' or 'curse,' as I often think of it." She lowered her voice. "I think I've passed it on to my new granddaughter, little Robin."

Gladys scoffed. "The baby is only a few weeks old. Don't tell me she's making predictions already."

Emma got off the chair and paced. She looked out over the lake; a strange gray tone reflected off the usually blue surface.

"She has a birthmark shaped like a fish, the same as mine and my grandmother, Lizzie, in exactly the same place. She was born on the thirteenth of the month, just like me and Gram. I tell you, when I look into that baby's eyes, I see a look—I'm not sure what to call it—as if we're kindred souls. I know this sounds crazy, and I wouldn't say it to anyone but you. Now, laugh if you like."

"I'm not laughing. I still think you should write a book. It would be a bestseller, I guarantee it."

"Humph," Emma replied. "On a different note, we had some excitement at the Center."

"I'm all ears."

Emma told her friend about the break-in, the document authentication, and Bruce Hamilton's obsession with searching for descendents of the original owners.

"You know, my youngest daughter, Nora, is so into genealogy. She spends all her spare time researching people's ancestors. Absolutely loves it. I'll ask her if she thinks she can find out anything about these people," Gladys said.

"Thanks, that's a good idea," Emma said. "Now, I want to see just what Nate's doing in the kitchen. I hear an electric drill."

"Oh, oh. You'd better investigate. Bye now."

Emma put down the phone and walked into the kitchen. "What in the world...?"

Nate had just finished hanging an elaborate shelf with hangers dangling from the bottom. He motioned her to stay where she was. "How does that look?"

"Fine, but what is it?"

He grinned. "The Kitchen Store was having a sale." He opened another box to reveal a set of gleaming stainless steel pots and pans. With a flourish, he hung them from the rack.

"What do you think, nice, huh?"

"They're wonderful." She went over and gave him a hug. "Are they very heavy?" she asked, looking at the thick metal.

"Not bad," he said, handing her a pot.

She took it with both hands and smiled, tightening her grip. *I'll have to do some weight lifting before I can use these.*

"What shall we make for dinner?" he asked, standing back and examining his new acquisition with pride.

"We really should invite someone over, to christen the new pots," Emma said.

"Okay, how about Sylvia and James and the boys?" Nate suggested.

"Good call, and maybe Tristana. I'm sure she would enjoy the children," Emma said, warming to the idea. "We'll make chicken *francaise* and I'll bake an angel food cake." She thought for a moment. "We'd better make that tomorrow so I'll have time to prepare."

"You're on. Go make the calls while I make a few minor adjustments here."

Emma walked into the living room half expecting to hear the entire assemblage crash to the floor, but all she heard were a few expletives. She smiled as she picked up the phone.

A MAGNIFICENT angel food cake sat on the counter, pink icing draping the top and sides. Emma looked at it with a discerning eye then decided chocolate sprinkles would enhance the confection.

"Umm," Nate said, coming up behind her, "that's pretty enough to grace the cover of a cookbook." He swiped his finger across a trail of icing that had dripped onto the serving plate.

"Hands off," Emma said. "You're as bad as a child. Now, if you will please reach that large frying pan, I'll get this dinner going." She didn't trust herself to take the oversized pan off the rack. She was afraid the entire thing might come tumbling down on her head.

"These are a little heavy," he admitted, placing the pan on the stove. "But I'll always be here to help you, Sparrow." He kissed her on the back of the neck and circled his arms around her waist.

"All right, lover boy, save that for later." She gave him a mischievous wink. "Now, vacate the kitchen. Our guests will be here in an hour and I have a dinner to prepare."

Tristana arrived a little early, two bottles of wine in hand. "I didn't know what you were serving, so I brought one white and one red."

"You are a dear," Emma said, putting the bottle of Pinot Grigio in the refrigerator.

"What can I do to help?"

"You can make the salad, if you like. I have all the ingredients over there." She pointed to a large bowl surrounded by two kinds of lettuce, a cucumber, tomatoes, green onions and mushrooms.

Nate stood in the doorway watching them. "I see I'm not needed here."

"You can entertain the boys when they get here," Emma said. "Why don't you take those toys out of the closet in the study?"

"Will do."

"He's a very sweet man," Tristana said, a wistful expression on her face.

"I'm a lucky woman to have had two good men in my life. My husband, Frank, was a gem. After he died, I never expected to meet anyone of his equal."

As Emma dipped the thin slices of chicken breasts in egg, then in flour, she watched Tristana out of the corner of her eye. The woman's face was a mask of pain.

"I was alone for a long time," she continued. "Was comfortable living in the house where we had raised our three children."

"When did you meet Nate?"

"About three years ago. I auditioned at the Midwest to be a supernumerary, and there he was. We hit it off right away—like magic." She thought back to the things that had happened in the past few years, hardly believing them herself.

"Last year I sold the old house and moved here with Nate. It was too much for me, the yard, all the repairs that were needed; the stairs seemed to get steeper every year. There's a time to move on with your life." She caught Tristana's eye and held her gaze. "Realize that. We all have to let go of the past and move ahead."

"That's just what the psychic said," Tristana whispered.

Just then the doorbell rang. "Here they are," Emma said, putting the last piece of chicken into the frying pan.

WHEN EMMA INTRODUCED Tristana to Sylvia, she noticed a slight hesitancy. Tristana already knew James from the Center. She gazed at the boys with a wistful expression as they grabbed Emma and gave her hugs and kisses. Emma stroked Frankie's curly hair as he stared up at her with the same huge gray eyes of his mother and grandmother.

"Want to see my new truck?" James Jr. asked Tristana, walking hesitantly toward her.

"I would love to," she said.

"It's red. It's a dump truck. See how it works?" He concentrated on pulling the lever that tipped the bed of the truck.

"That's wonderful," Tristana said. "In the summer you can fill it with sand and make a big pile."

The child nodded, intent on his new toy.

"Come on, Sylvia," Emma said. "Help me in the kitchen."

EVERYONE ENJOYED THE DINNER and agreed that the new cookware enhanced the flavors. Tristana relaxed once she had a glass of wine and seemed to enjoy playing with the children.

"James, don't wrestle with your brother. He's smaller than you are," Sylvia scolded.

"No, no," one-year-old Frankie cried, trying to pull the truck out of his brother's hand.

"Come here," Tristana said softly, holding a jack-in-the-box. "See what I have?" As she turned the handle, Frankie toddled over to her and clapped his hands when the clown jumped out.

"Now you have his attention," Sylvia said.

James Jr. busied himself with a line of trucks and cars, stringing them across the living-room floor.

Emma turned her attention to her son-in-law. "Is Bruce still interested in researching the original family of the building?"

"More than ever. The man is obsessed with the history of that site." James shook his head.

"I was talking to my friend, Gladys, the other day and mentioned it to her. She said her youngest daughter is very passionate about genealogical research. Perhaps she can take on the job."

"That would be great. It might get Bruce back to running the Center. I've had to pick up the slack while he's concentrating on the historical research."

"What about the assistant?" Nate asked. "What does he do?"

"That's a good question. Bruce told him to find the maintenance man we spoke of."

"And has he?"

"He claims he couldn't identify the man. Personally, I don't believe him. I think he's into something else." James blew out a breath and stretched.

"Like what?" Emma asked.

"I think the man is a gambler. I saw him looking at a racing form the other day, and I think he was talking to a bookie when I walked into his office. I overheard just enough to be suspicious." James sighed and looked at his watch. "Okay, tribe, time to go home."

"Have you talked to Bruce about him?" Emma asked as Sylvia put the boys' jackets on and Nate picked up the toys.

"I plan to do that first thing Monday morning."

Emma kissed the boys good-bye, and the family left.

She breathed a sigh of relief as the elevator doors closed on her waving family. "They are exhausting, aren't they?" she said to Tristana.

"Yes, but very sweet and so much fun."

Emma heard the regret in her voice.

"If you're ready, I'll drive you home," Nate said.

"I can take the bus."

"Absolutely not. I wouldn't hear of it," he said, taking her jacket from the closet.

"What about the cleanup?" Tristana asked.

"I'll just load the dishwasher; it'll only take a few minutes. No problem," Emma said.

"Thank you for the lovely dinner and the opportunity to meet your family."

Again, Emma noticed the expression of pain, and something else she couldn't identify.

Later, as she cleaned up the kitchen, Emma thought back over the evening. Tristana seemed to regret the fact that she had no children, but Emma felt certain it went deeper than that.

And Norman Quiller, the weasel, was hiding something, too. *None of it is any of my business.*

But perhaps it is, her inner voice said.

She let out an exasperated breath as she picked up the heavy frying pan with both hands and ran it under the tap. *Why is it that* everything *seems to be my business?*

TWENTY-SIX

TRISTANA THREW HER jacket on a chair and walked to the window. The ever-present traffic drove down Belmont Avenue like a train, heavy tonight because it was the start of the weekend: people going to a late dinner, the theater, any number of places of entertainment in the big, bustling city. A group of young folks walked by, laughing. How she envied them.

I've just had a lovely evening with Emma and Nate and Emma's family. The little boys are precious, so full of life. I should feel satisfied.

Her face contorted in pain. But where did her future lie? Would it be an empty wasteland—no children—no grandchildren? She paced, wringing her hands. I've tried to let go, as Rose told me. And even Emma's story was so poignant. If she could do it, why can't I?

But the situations were different. Emma had been tied emotionally to a helpless old woman, one she had to care for. No one belittled her day after day; no one beat her; no one threatened her...

Perhaps she should go and see Rose again. She did seem to care, and Tristana had felt better after the session. She would go tomorrow.

THE FOLLOWING DAY Tristana found herself again climbing the seven stairs to the heavy oak door. She had called Rose and the woman told her to come in that afternoon.

Before Tristana could knock, Rose opened the door, her cheery face wearing a welcoming smile. "Come in, my dear; you do look better than the last time I saw you."

They walked into the same living room, the same sooth-
ing music playing, the same fragrant tea already on the table.
Tristana sat in the same chair as Rose handed her a cup of tea.
She sat back, inhaled the floral fragrance and took a sip.

"Now, tell me what you have been doing since the last time
I saw you."

She told her about Emma, the previous night's dinner, their
talk about release, and her overwhelming loneliness. This time
the words came tumbling out, as if of their own volition.

"This friend of yours sounds like a wise woman. Stay close
to her," Rose said.

She took Tristana's hand, closed her eyes, and held it still for
a moment. "You're struggling within yourself, and that's a good
thing. I believe you're preparing to release the past and face the
future."

"But what kind of future do I have?" Tristana asked, envel-
oped by the familiar feeling of hopelessness.

Rose let go of Tristana's hand, sat back and smiled. "People
always want to hear that a mysterious *stranger* will emerge and
take them away—to a happy, carefree life. That is the stuff of
fairy tales. We *make* our own future, and that's what you must
do."

Again she picked up Tristana's hand, stroked it and looked
at the palm. "I feel a possible relationship looming, but first, I
see danger. I didn't want to frighten you the last time you were
here, but I feel it stronger now."

Tristana pulled back. Sometimes she felt it, too. She told Rose
about the documents, the break-in, and her attack.

The woman sat, unmoving. Again she closed her eyes. "I see
a dark, tight space. Stay away from there. Someone died in that
place."

Tristana jumped. Someone died? Could it be the stranger?
"There's been someone, or something, roaming around the
Center," she said softly. "Not everyone can see him."

"Tell me about this—apparition," Rose said, leaning forward,
a deep furrow forming between her eyes.

Tristana told her about the sightings, the description, the smells, the upcoming opera, *The Ghosts of Versailles,* the supernumeraries; it all spilled out. "But no one has seen him for quite a while."

"He's there, you can be sure of that, just waiting for the proper time and the right person. From what you tell me, I believe this may be an earthbound spirit unable to cross over because of some unresolved issue." Rose suddenly grasped her head in her hands and moaned.

"What's wrong?" Tristana asked, wide eyed and frightened.

"A sudden pain in my head. That's all I can do for you today, too many vibrations coming all at once." She rubbed her forehead then pulled her hands down her cheeks.

After a few minutes she looked up, smiling at Tristana. "It's all right now. You must come back, next week. And, please, be very careful."

With those words she led Tristana to the door. Again she hadn't asked her name, or for any payment.

EMMA PICKED UP the ringing phone as she walked out onto the roof garden. She glanced at the caller ID; the library number at the Center. "Hello."

"Emma…it's Tristana."

"Good morning," Emma said, noting the hesitancy in the woman's voice.

"First I want to thank you for the lovely dinner Friday night. I did so enjoy meeting your family."

"And we loved having you. I spoke with my daughter yesterday, and she said James Jr. asked about the pretty lady at grandma's house. You seem to have a way with children."

"Yes, they are sweet little boys. I had fun with them."

Emma heard a wistful tone in her voice.

"I saw Bruce Hamilton this morning. He asked if I knew anything about genealogy. I told him I didn't, but I did mention your friend and he liked the idea. I hope I wasn't out of line."

"Not at all. I'll call Gladys today. She told me that when her daughter starts digging into people's pasts, she sometimes un-covers descendents they would rather not know about." Emma smiled as she heard a laugh from the other end of the line.

"Ah—there's something else I want to talk to you about, but not over the phone," Tristana said.

"Shall we meet for lunch?" Emma suggested. "That café across from the Center is convenient."

"Not there," the woman said. "Too many people from here go there. I'd rather not run into anyone."

"All right. It's going to be a lovely spring day. I'm on the roof garden as we speak, and it's already warm enough for just a sweater. I'll pack a lunch and we can picnic where we sat be-fore, on the bench along the lake. I can meet you there at noon."

"You are a dear," Tristana said, a relieved note in her voice. "I have to discuss something with you—in private."

"I'll be there. Now, I have to call Gladys and ask her what information her daughter needs to begin the search."

After Emma pressed the disconnect button, she stood for a long time looking out over the lake. *I wonder if she's ready to open up and tell me what's troubling her?* She shook her head and turned back into the condo.

Nate stood there, watching her.

"What's up? You're making faces."

"Tristana called. She wants to meet me for lunch—in private. She's a deeply troubled woman."

"And you're the one to 'untrouble' her?" He cocked his head to the side, raising his eyebrows in a question.

She answered him with a frown and then a kiss on the chin. "I'm going to meet her for a picnic lunch by the lake and some girl talk. You don't mind, do you?"

"And if I did?"

"Oh, Nate, don't give me a hard time. You'll have a few hours to yourself to do whatever you like." She smiled.

"Go ahead. She's a nice person. Even I can feel that she's suppressing something. The way she interacted with the boys Friday was touching."

"Don't tell me some of my 'gift' is rubbing off on you."

He stepped back. "I certainly hope not. Two of us in one family would be too much. Besides," he said taking her in his arms, "it's my job to keep you grounded."

EMMA PACKED A SMALL BASKET with two bottles of water, two cheese and turkey sandwiches, and two banana-nut muffins. *This should be enough,* she thought as she added a few napkins.

"I'm off," she called to Nate as she opened the front door.

"That statement can be interpreted in a number of ways," he said, smirking.

"Just behave yourself, Mr. Sandler. I shouldn't be long."

"Do you have your cell phone?" he asked.

"Of course. I always carry it, as instructed."

He kissed her, and she saw him watch as she got into the elevator.

I swear, Emma thought, *he is a bit overprotective. He has to be able to reach me all the time, but after those experiences last summer, I'm glad. It gives me a secure feeling.*

The elevator doors opened on the first floor to reveal her neighbor, Claude, standing there, loaded with packages.

"Hello, Claude, have you bought out all of the stores on Michigan Avenue?"

"Just about. I'm glad we ran into each other." He motioned with his head for her to follow him into an alcove.

"What's all the secrecy?" she asked, looking around. There was no one about but the two of them.

"Saturday is Thomas's birthday," he whispered. "I'm having a little surprise party—just a few friends. Would you and Nate like to come?"

Emma's eyes widened. "I'll certainly ask him." She hesitated for just a moment. "I'm not sure what's on the calendar for this weekend." They probably wouldn't know most of the guests, but that didn't matter.

"Let me know," he said, as excited as a child. "Now, I have to hide these."

"I will." She smiled as she watched him. *He's good for Thomas, and perhaps for the boy, too,* she thought.

Emma breathed in the warm spring air as she walked out the door. *We really should put in an appearance at that party. They are good neighbors.*

For the time being she put that thought out of her head and concentrated on Tristana. What did she want to talk about? Was she ill? Did she feel threatened after the attack?

You won't know 'til she tells you, so stop conjecturing.

"Humph," she said, climbing onto the bus.

When she arrived at the appointed spot Tristana was already there, waiting. They exchanged greetings as Emma opened the basket.

"You didn't have to go through so much trouble," Tristana said.

"Nonsense. I hardly call making a couple of sandwiches trouble."

"This is delicious," Tristana said, taking a bite. "What kind of cheese is it?"

"I'm not sure. Nate bought it at the deli. I must remember to tell him to get some more."

When they finished the muffins, Tristana sat back. "I don't usually eat that much for lunch, but those muffins were great."

Emma smiled, remembering the significance of her muffins in the past, how they had almost gotten her in trouble with the neighbor next door. "Now, what's on your mind?" She turned to the other woman and looked directly into her eyes.

Tristana took a deep breath and let it out slowly. "I went to see that psychic again." She hesitated, but Emma said nothing.

"There are things about my past that I haven't told anyone," she whispered.

"My dear," Emma said, taking her hand, "there's no need to relive the past if you've let it go, but, if you're holding on to it, sometimes talking about it helps."

She nodded. "I need to verbalize it—stare it in the face—let it know it has no more hold on me."

"That's the right attitude. I'm a good listener," Emma said, "and anything you tell me goes no further, understand?"

For a moment Tristana seemed mesmerized by the lake. "You assume that I've been grieving for my husband, but that's not so. My marriage wasn't a happy one. He was an abusive alcoholic. Why *did* I stay with him?" She looked at Emma as if searching for an answer. "Why do so many women stay? Because he threatened me, and I believed he would follow through with the threats." She stopped for a moment and took a deep breath, then turned toward Emma.

"When I told you I had no children I didn't mention my baby boy born, stillborn, ten weeks early. My husband told the doctor I fell down a flight of stairs. He omitted the fact that he had pushed me." Her voice faltered.

Emma winced at the picture those words evoked: Tristana tumbling down the stairs, crying out, trying desperately to protect her unborn child.

"When I saw your little grandsons, I wondered if my little boy would have been like them." The tears threatened to spill from her eyes.

Emma took a tissue from her purse and handed it to the woman.

She looked up at Emma, her eyes wide and wild. "When I told you I was a widow, you felt sorry for me. I didn't say it was the best thing that ever happened." She covered her face with her hands and sobbed.

Emma gently rubbed her back. No consoling words could ease the pain.

"He died in an automobile accident. We were coming home from a party. He was so drunk, I insisted on driving. He kept yelling at me, said I wasn't going fast enough, that I was a lousy driver. It was raining so hard that I could hardly see the road. Finally I had enough of his ranting so I stopped the car, got out and told him to drive himself. It was a foolish, irresponsible thing to do. He could have killed an innocent person."

She turned to Emma with so much pain in her eyes that Emma fought to keep back her own tears.

After a moment's hesitation, she continued, "I don't know how many miles I walked that night. By the time I got home, I had made my decision. I would leave immediately.

"The phone was ringing as I opened the front door. It was the police. My husband had lost control in the storm. He hit a semi-truck, head-on, and was killed instantly. They said they were very sorry for my loss. They couldn't know that it wasn't a loss but a liberation. I asked if the driver of the truck had been injured. They said he had sustained only minor injuries and would be fine. At that moment all I could do was thank God for that."

The women sat for a long time, neither saying a word.

"You know," Tristana finally said, "I feel better, as though a burden has been lifted from my shoulders."

"It has," Emma said. "Now, do you want to tell me what the psychic said?"

"She said there might be another relationship, but I had to release the past first."

Emma nodded. *They all say that,* she thought.

Tristana frowned. "Then she said something odd. She said she saw a dark, tight place and I should stay away from there. Someone had died there. She felt danger again." Tristana rubbed her arms and let out a soft moan.

Emma's eyes widened. "Did you tell her about the stranger?"

"Yes. She thought he's probably an earthbound spirit, unable to free himself. Maybe he's the one who died?"

"A dark, tight place," Emma mused. "I wonder what she meant by that."

"I don't know. Then she grabbed her head—said it was too much at once and I should come back next week."

"Hmmm." Emma scrunched up her face. "How much is she charging you for these readings?"

"That's another strange thing. She hasn't asked for any money."

"That is unusual."

"Do you think I should go back?"

"I think you must."

"I'm planning on it," Tristana answered.

TWENTY-SEVEN

"HOW WAS YOUR TALK with Tristana?" Nate asked as Emma settled herself into a chair.

"Listening is exhausting."

"Anything you can share?"

"The personal stuff was just between us girls. But I believe it did her good to let it out. I think she'll be a happier person."

"How about some coffee," he said, rubbing her shoulders. "I made a fresh pot."

"Umm, that feels good and the coffee sounds heavenly." She was about to get up from the chair, but Nate motioned her to stay put.

"I'll bring it in here. Just relax."

When Emma had the hot coffee in her hands, she inhaled the rich aroma and let out a long "Ahhh… Why are you looking at me that way?" she asked.

"I like to watch the expressions on your face. You grimace in the most unusual way."

"Am I supposed to take that as a compliment?"

He merely smiled.

Emma put the cup down on the coffee table and looked at him seriously. "Tristana went to see a psychic."

"She did?" Nate leaned forward. "I didn't think she went in for that kind of thing."

Emma ignored the insinuation. "The woman told her to stay away from a dark, tight place. She said someone died there."

Nate said nothing, just shook his head.

"I thought it sounded strange, too," Emma said. "Then Tristana told her about the stranger. She said he was probably an earthbound spirit who can't cross over for some reason. He may be the one who died in the dark place."

"Do you know how ridiculous that sounds?" Nate asked, a note of exasperation in his voice. "All this talk of spirits is ludicrous. This stranger is some homeless guy who found his way into the building for refuge. Now that the weather has warmed, he's probably gone. Has anyone seen him recently? No. So there's your answer. And, I think you should caution Tristana to stay away from charlatans."

"Are you finished with the lecture?"

"Yes."

She took a deep breath. "I ran into Claude. He's having a birthday party for Thomas on Saturday and asked us to come. What do you think?"

Nate looked at her and without hesitation said, "I think we should go. They're our neighbors, and we shouldn't snub them because they're—different."

"All right then, let's go shopping. We'll need to buy a gift."

SATURDAY NIGHT, Emma and Nate dressed casually, she in navy slacks with a long tunic-length sweater in a lighter shade of blue. Nate wore chinos and a beige fisherman-knit sweater. "I think we look presentable, don't you?" he asked.

"Certainly." Emma checked the time as someone tapped on the door. "That's probably Claude," she said opening it.

"Can you come over right now?" he whispered. "Everyone is here and Thomas is on his way."

"We're ready," Nate said, reaching for a box wrapped in birthday paper.

They locked the door and followed Claude into the condo next door. Emma examined the décor. She hadn't been there since the two moved in. The change was remarkable. Three drawings of ballet dancers caught her eyes. The design was simple, but they all depicted movement, tense muscles ready to leap off the paper. A familiar Degas print of ballet dancers hung behind a magnificent Steinway parlor grand piano. A red silk shawl trailed across the top.

"Look at this furniture," Emma whispered to Nate. "Nothing but the best for these two, right out of *Better Homes and Gardens*."

Emma was surprised to see a mixed group of both men and women. She hadn't known what to expect.

Claude added their gift to a pile in the corner and made quick introductions: a man and wife who worked with Thomas; other couples were obviously gay.

A petite blond woman wearing a long flowered skirt and a matching tank top came out of the kitchen carrying a tray of hors d'oeuvres. She put the tray down and walked up to Emma and Nate. "I'm Sharon, Thomas's sister. I believe you and I have met before," she said, extending her hand to Emma.

"Yes, we have. This is my partner, Nate Sandler."

"I've heard so much about you. Thank you for welcoming my brother and Claude."

"They're good neighbors, and that's all that matters to us."

They looked over at Claude who stood with his ear to the door. He raised his hand. "Quiet everybody. I hear the elevator."

They heard the doors open and close, a hesitation, then a key in the lock.

Total silence until the door opened. "Surprise!" everyone shouted at once.

Thomas stood glued to the spot. He stared at the assemblage; his cheeks had turned crimson. He put his hands up to his face and smiled at his partner who stood there grinning from ear to ear. He gave Claude a warm hug, then went around greeting the guests.

"Nate," Claude called from across the room, "I want to introduce you to Joshua. He's a writer."

Nate looked at Emma and she motioned for him to go.

"Why don't I help you in the kitchen?" Emma suggested, looking at Sharon.

"That would be great. Claude is so engrossed in making everyone comfortable, that he's totally forgotten the food."

Sharon led her into a kitchen that was a cook's dream. It was much more elaborate than theirs. An island counter took up the center of the room, much larger than the one in Emma and Nate's condo. Gleaming copper pots hung from a huge rack fastened to the ceiling.

"My God," Emma said. "This kitchen takes my breath away." She studied the appliances, all black with stainless steel trim.

Sharon smiled. "They spare no expense when it comes to their home."

"What would you like me to do?" Emma asked.

"You can start by arranging these pastries on this platter."

"Of course. They look delicious."

"I understand you're quite a baker," Sharon said. "The boys are always raving about your cookies and muffins."

"I do enjoy my kitchen. Nothing makes me happier than getting my hands in a bowl of bread dough, unless it's my plants." She smiled. "The atrium is a wonderful room to garden in all year round.

"What else would you like me to do?" Emma asked, putting the last mini-cream puff on the tray.

"Sit down for a moment. I want to talk to you about something."

Emma wondered if she was going to talk about the boy. A small table with two wrought-iron chairs fit into one corner of the room. Emma sat in one and Sharon took the other.

"Claude told me about that stranger at the Performing Arts Center. I was in the audience for the ballet performance. I, too, saw him lurking in the shadows." She looked at Emma for a long time, her eyes wide and questioning.

"No one has seen him in quite a while," Emma said. "Nate thinks he's a homeless man who found refuge in the Center and is now gone."

"Do you believe that?"

"No, I don't."

"I feel a kindred spirit in you," Sharon said. She stopped for a moment, stared at the wall, then continued, "I have a friend who sometimes exorcises haunted places. Remember that. If you feel her services are needed, call me." She took a card from her pocket and handed it to Emma. It advertised a catering service, *Sharon Aherne, Proprietor.*

"Now, we had better get back to the party," Sharon said.

Emma hesitated for a moment before picking up the pastry tray.

Oh, Guardian Angel, I have a feeling this whole stranger thing is about to resurface. She felt a prickling up her arm as an answer.

TWENTY-EIGHT

THE FOLLOWING EVENING Emma and Nate sat watching the news. "Someone's at the door," Emma said, hearing a soft knock.

"I'll get it," Nate said. "It's probably Claude." He walked to the door with a smile on his face.

Emma rose from her chair when she heard his surprised greeting. "Thomas, Claude, please come in."

As they walked inside, Thomas looked down at the boy clutching his hand. "Nate, Emma, I want you to meet my son, Oliver."

"I believe Oliver and I have already met," Emma said warmly. "Do you remember me, the lady in the elevator?" She gazed down at the boy and smiled.

He knit his brow and rubbed his free hand over his crew cut. Then he smiled triumphantly. "I remember. I pushed six and you got off, too."

"That's right," she said. "Please sit down, all of you. I'll make us some tea, with milk and cookies for Oliver."

"Please don't go to any trouble," Thomas said. "I just thought I should talk with both of you."

"It's no trouble." Emma bustled into the kitchen as the men sat on the couch with the boy between them.

Nate, who was a natural negotiator, began talking about a new exhibit at the Art Institute and soon the other two relaxed and joined in the conversation.

Emma returned shortly with the refreshments. Oliver's eyes widened as he saw the round cookies with chocolate chips poking out at every angle. He looked at his father.

"Go ahead, son, take a cookie," Thomas said, his face wreathed in a smile.

The boy reached for the largest cookie on the plate while Claude fussed, spreading a napkin on his lap.

"Now, be careful of the crumbs," he cautioned.

Emma watched the two, obviously comfortable in their role. When they finished, Oliver walked over to the piano and touched the keys. "Be careful," Thomas cautioned.

Claude followed the boy and asked, "Can you find middle C?"

Thomas shook his head. "He's trying to teach Oliver the rudiments of the piano, but I'm afraid it's beyond him."

Thomas turned to Nate and Emma. "I'd like to tell you both about my relationship with my son. I feel I owe you both an explanation. You've been so kind in making us welcome here."

Nate raised his hand. "Thomas, you owe no one any explanations. We certainly don't want to intrude in your private life. You don't have to tell us anything."

"But I want to." He sat back, sighed, and looked off into the distance for a moment. "To put it mildly, I had a difficult time growing up, trying to find out where I belonged in this complex world. My sister understood my confusion, but not the rest of my family."

He rubbed his face with his hands, then reached for the remnants of his cold tea and took a sip.

"Shall I make more?" Emma asked.

"No, no. Now that I've started, I want to finish.

"After I graduated from college with a degree in design, I married Patricia. She was a sweet, sensitive girl and I really liked her, but not as a lover. My family was relieved that I had straightened out my life. But my sister cautioned me not to marry. I should have taken her advice."

At that point Emma wanted to go to him, take him in her arms and take the hurt away, but she knew that *telling* was a form of catharsis.

"We were reasonably happy for a couple of years. I had become a master of pretense, but Patricia knew something was missing in our marriage. We were both delighted when she became pregnant, but Oliver was born prematurely. It was a difficult birth and resulted in Oliver having some brain damage. When he was three, Patricia found my hidden stash of magazines. She was hurt that I hadn't told her, but I think she had suspected for a long time. She said she could no longer live with me. I accepted that, but after the divorce when she moved to Arizona to start a new life, I was devastated. She took my son away. That was nine years ago." Again he stopped for a breather and gazed at the empty tea cup, his face a mask of pain.

Emma went into the kitchen and returned with a large glass of water. He nodded his thanks and took a generous swallow.

"Meeting Claude was the best thing that ever happened to me. I told him everything right from the beginning. You see, his family accepted his sexual orientation right away. He helped me to realize who I really am and focus on the positive aspects of our life together. We've been happy. Can you understand that?" He looked at Nate as if asking for reassurance.

"Of course we do," Nate said. "Don't ever doubt that."

Emma nodded.

"Thank you," Thomas said. He sighed deeply. "The problem is that now Patricia has moved back to the area. She tried other relationships, but her partners couldn't accept Oliver's disability. She wants me to be involved with him." He let out an ironic laugh. "She said since he'll always be a child, he never has to know what his father is." A look of pain crossed his face for only a moment.

"Anyway, Patricia needs extensive surgery to correct a defect in her spine. So Oliver will be staying here with us for a while and part of the time with Sharon. I just wanted you two to understand the situation."

Nate gripped the man's hand. "I want you to know that Emma and I have accepted you two from the beginning."

Tears welled up in Thomas's eyes. "That means a lot to me, coming from a man like you."

Emma swallowed the lump in her throat. "And, if we can help in any way, just let us know."

"Thanks." Thomas turned to his son who labored with the notes on the piano. "That's enough for tonight. Time for your bath."

"Oh yes," Claude said. "We have to try out that new boat."

"Thank the lady for the cookies and milk," Thomas said to the boy.

Oliver rubbed the top of his head with his hand, lowered his eyes, and murmured, "Thank you" as they walked out the door.

TWENTY-NINE

For the next few days Sharon's words about dispelling spirits kept repeating in Emma's mind. She didn't dare tell Nate. He would completely disregard such nonsense, as he called it. But was it? Were some people really able to exorcise spirits from their earthly surroundings?

Don't disregard something just because it's not proven scientific fact, her inner voice said.

"That's true. I've had premonitions all my life. Why not go one step further?"

"What are you muttering about?" Nate asked, coming up behind her.

"Don't sneak up on me like that. You startled me. I'm just talking to myself, as usual." She grabbed a potted plant and tried to lift it.

"Wait a minute, let me do that. Where do you want this?" Nate asked, picking up the large pot.

"Out here on the roof garden." Emma opened the sliding glass door and indicated the area where she wanted the planter. She looked at the row of dwarf junipers in huge pots that grew along the wall that separated their portion of the roof from their neighbors'. She noticed the new growth already sprouting from the branches.

Emma breathed in the warm spring air, stretched her arms, and danced around. "Isn't it heavenly? It won't be long before we have tomatoes and herbs and flowers blooming all over."

"Humph," Nate said, rubbing the small of his back. "I hope you put the other pots out here before you fill them with soil."

He walked up to her, slid his arm around her small waist,

and pulled her close. They looked out over Lake Michigan and watched the gulls swoop down looking for a meal, listening to their squabbling calls. Only small wavelets rippled toward shore over the unusually placid water.

"It is nice," he said. "And you know what's the best part?"

"What?" She turned her large eyes to him.

"Sharing it with you." He held her close, nuzzling her neck. "Damn, there goes that infernal phone."

"You don't have to answer it," she said.

He peered at her from the corner of his eyes. "Your curiosity wouldn't allow it."

He walked into the condo and picked up the ringing instrument. "Hello?" he answered in a gruff tone.

Emma heard only Nate's side of the conversation and her curiosity was piqued.

"What was that all about?" Emma asked.

"The super captain from Midwest. They need more supernumeraries for the opera and she wants me to help with the auditions." He stood up tall, preening like a peacock.

"You've been a super for so long that I can well understand that," she said, giving him a kiss on the chin.

"They're also going to need women, so that will include you and Tristana."

"Great. James said that would probably be the case. It will be a good experience for her."

"I'm going to call a few friends and see if they're interested," Nate said, looking for his address book.

Emma went back out onto the roof to transplant a few more seedlings. Something about this production bothered her. Was it the fact that it was about ghosts? Would the stranger reappear?

A few clouds obscured the sun casting a shadow over the roof. Emma sighed.

Guardian Angel, please keep me out of trouble, just this once.

"Oh, Emma, I don't know if I can do it," Tristana said, rolling her eyes and clasping her hands.

"Of course you can. You did fine at the audition, remember? You don't have to act or say anything. In this production we're simply part of a crowd of revolutionaries. I suppose we might have to wave our arms about, but that's all."

"What's the opera about anyway?" Tristana asked, her eyes wide with what appeared to be genuine fear. "With ghosts in the title it sounds eerie." She shook her head and wrung her hands.

"I'm not really sure," Emma said, trying to sound matter of fact. The word "ghosts" bothered her, too. "From what I understand the ghost of Marie Antoinette is unhappy in the hereafter. The playwright, Beaumarchais, is in love with her. I assume he's a ghost, too." She shrugged her shoulders. "He contrives a plot to rewrite history and bring Marie Antoinette back to life."

"Oh, my God," Tristana said, a shocked look on her face. "How could he possibly do that?"

Emma shook her head. "I don't know, but in opera, as Anna Russell said, they can do anything as long as they sing it. In the end Marie Antoinette realizes history is as it should be and contents herself with her state of being. Does that make any sense?"

"It sounds bizarre," Tristana said.

"Yes, some operas really are, especially the modern ones. But we have to be willing to accept new concepts. At least, that's what I'm told."

"I'm still not sure. I might pass out." Tristana gripped her hands so tightly they turned white.

"Relax," Emma said. "Take a few deep breaths. There, that's better." She took the other woman's hands and pried them apart. They felt cold as death.

"Just give it a try. I assure you that after the first couple of rehearsals you'll be completely relaxed." Emma smiled as she remembered the many mishaps during her first few experiences as a supernumerary. *I'd better not share them right now,* she thought. *That would really freak her out.*

WHEN EMMA RETURNED to the condo, she heard Nate's muffled voice muttering and cursing. She hurried into the kitchen to see him lying on his side, his head and shoulders disappearing into the cabinet under the sink. Tools and pieces of pipe lay hit and miss on the floor.

"What are you doing?" she asked, standing with her hands on her hips.

"What does it look like I'm doing? Certainly not enjoying myself."

"Perhaps you should call a plumber?"

No answer, only more mumbling.

I'd better stay out of this, she thought. She tiptoed out of the kitchen to answer the ringing phone.

"Hello."

"I've left three messages. Why didn't you call me?" Gladys asked, a slight note of exasperation in her voice.

Emma looked at the light blinking on the answering machine. "I wasn't home and Nate is up to his ears in a plumbing job that, by the looks of the kitchen floor, isn't going well." She plopped into a chair and heard more muttering from the kitchen.

Gladys laughed. "I remember when Cornell tried to fix the plumbing. When he finally conceded defeat, the bill was twice what it would have been if he had called a plumber in the first place."

"I have a feeling that's what's going to happen here."

"The reason I called," Gladys continued, "is that Nora found something about the descendents of that house."

"Really?"

"Uh huh. I don't think your director is going to want to advertise this line of folks."

"Why is that?"

"A few were shady characters. Some actually did prison time."

"Oh my word, Bruce won't like that."

"I didn't think so. She's still hunting. I swear that girl must have been a bloodhound in a former lifetime. She's e-mailing you what she's found so far. I'll keep you posted. And, take my advice and call a plumber."

"Thanks, my friend. Bye."

She looked up to see Nate coming out of the kitchen, a silly grin on his face. He was streaked with black grease, and the few remaining hairs on his head stood at odd angles.

"I got it all back together," he said, puffing out his chest. "I had to replace one of the pipes. Come and see how well it works now."

With a feeling of trepidation, Emma followed him.

"See?" He locked the drain and filled the sink. "Now, voila." He opened the drain and they watched the water flow smoothly down.

Emma saw a trickle of water trailing out of the cabinet and onto the floor. "Nate, why is water coming out?"

"What?" He looked under the cabinet at the water seeping out of all the pipe joints. "Oh God." He shut off the water then sank into a chair, blew out a deep breath, and held his head.

Emma went to him, put her arms around his neck and kissed the top of his head. "It's all right, dear. You tried. I'll call the plumber."

He nodded and let his head sink down to his chest. "And while you're at it, make an appointment with the chiropractor."

THIRTY

Dressed in black, he made his way to the familiar rock. He cursed at the full moon as he crept among the thorny bushes that obscured the access.

Damn, it's a good thing business is booming, he thought. *A few more trips and I'll have enough dough to blow this place—go where it's warm—make a new start.*

At that moment, a dark cloud crossed over in front of the moon plunging the area into blackness. Good, now no one can see me.

He pushed the rock aside and slid down into the opening. More dirt and rocks had fallen since his last trip.

"Pretty soon this whole goddamned place'll collapse," he muttered, as he shone the flashlight along the rocky walls. He came upon the familiar niche, cut out long ago. He felt inside with his gloved hand.

"What the…?"

He shone the light into the crevice but saw nothing.

"That son-of-a-bitch! What kinda game is he playing? No dough, no merchandise." But he was counting on that money. He needed it.

He pulled a cell phone out of his pocket, flipped it open and punched in a number. "What? No signal?"

Expletives flew out of his mouth as he crawled back the way he had come. As soon as he was out in the open, he tried again. It rang once, twice…five times before a voice answered.

"Yes?"

"Where's the dough?"

"I—I had a problem. Money's tied up. You'll get it as soon as I sell the merchandise."

"Uh uh. That's not the way I do business. No dough, no merchandise. Don't jerk me around, pal. I can always sell somewhere else."

"No. No, I promise. Give me two weeks. I swear I'll have the money then."

He hesitated. "Okay. Two weeks, but it better be here." His finger pressed the disconnect button and he flipped the phone closed. "You got two weeks, or it's all over."

THIRTY-ONE

EMMA PUT DOWN the phone, and with a deep sigh, walked out into the atrium. She looked at the lake, tall waves pounding the shore.

"What's wrong?" Nate asked from behind her.

"My sister's coming."

"Your sister?"

She turned to see the startled look on his face. Again she sighed and nodded. "She and Nolan are going to Missouri to visit one of his relatives, and Clara thought a short visit here might be in order."

"Short is a good choice when it comes to your sister," he said, raising his hands in the air.

"I'm sorry." She shook her head, as if the impending visit were her fault.

"Take that look off your face. I promise to be my usual charming self," he said, suppressing a grin.

KNOWING HER fastidious sister, Emma fussed and cleaned.

"We're not expecting royalty you know," Nate said, watching her.

"Oh, you know how Clara is. When I lived in Brookfield and she visited she criticized everything from the flowers, to the vegetable garden, to the way I looked. She's always been like that."

"Well, this is *our* home," he said, putting an emphasis on the *our*. "If she says anything I'll give her the evil eye. How do you say that in Italian?"

Emma laughed. "The *malocchio*." She remembered her neighbor, Maria, attributing every mishap to the *malocchio*.

She missed Maria. They had been good neighbors for twenty years. But this was a new life. She was here with Nate in this lovely condo, and Maria was living happily with her daughter now. Emma made a mental note to call her soon and maybe go out to lunch.

"When did Clara say they'll be here?" Nate asked. "I hope it doesn't coincide with rehearsals for the opera."

"No, it won't. I told Clara we would be busy starting next week. They'll be here late Wednesday and leave on the weekend."

"Early on the weekend, I hope."

EMMA SET ABOUT baking a nut cake Wednesday morning as soon as she finished her yoga exercises. It was their mother's recipe, and one of Clara's favorites.

"That looks nice," Nate said. "I can't recall you ever making that before."

"I haven't made it in years, because it's loaded with butter."

"Umm," he said, looking longingly at the cake.

"Hands off. I have to decide whether to make roast chicken or beef." She puttered around picking up one item and putting it down again. Then she sat in a chair and began perusing a cookbook.

"Why don't we just go out to dinner and simplify everything?" Nate suggested.

"We can do that tomorrow night. I figure they'll be tired after the long drive and will enjoy a home-cooked meal. After all, Minneapolis isn't around the corner, you know."

He shrugged and raised his hands in surrender.

"THEY JUST CALLED from their cell phone," Nate said. "They'll be here in about an hour. I'd better go down to the garage and tell the attendant we have guests so they can give Nolan a parking permit."

"Oh, dear," Emma said. "I'd better hurry." She checked the

chicken roasting in the oven and estimated it would be done on time. "Now, for the potatoes and vegetables."

When the doorbell rang a little over an hour later, Emma jumped. Nate motioned for her to stay on the couch where she had just sat down. He pressed the intercom and was greeted by Clara's booming voice. "We're here," she sang out.

"Come up to six," Nate said as he buzzed them in. Then he turned to Emma. "Relax. Remember, she is your sister."

Emma went into the kitchen and took the chicken out of the oven. The skin crackled a rich, golden brown. It smelled delicious. She nodded her approval, then put a tent of aluminum foil over the top to keep it warm.

Emma heard Nate open the door, then cringed as she heard her sister's voice. "Nathaniel, how good to see you." She walked reluctantly into the living room.

"Emma." Clara lumbered toward her, her arms held wide. She clasped Emma in a bear hug that took her breath away. When Emma finally extricated herself, Clara examined her critically, a frown on her face. "Oh, dear, you're still so thin." She made a *tsk* sound as she examined Emma's body.

"Nonsense," Emma said. "I've gained ten pounds in the last two years." She forced a smile. *I look thin because you've gained at least twenty since I last saw you.*

"I think you look great," Clara's slight husband, Nolan, said, coming out from behind his wife to hug Emma.

"Thanks, Nolan. It's good to see you both. Now, I'm sure you're starving after your long ride. Dinner is ready."

"Oh, no," Clara said. "We stopped on the way and had a late lunch."

Emma turned away, clenched her fists and counted to ten.

"I'm sure you can eat a few bites," Nate said. "Let's get you settled in the guest room, then I'll show you around while Emma puts the finishing touches to dinner."

By the time they sat down at the table it was eight o'clock. The chicken was a bit dried out, but Clara ate everything on her plate.

"That was a wonderful dinner," Nolan said.

"Thank you. Now, if anyone has room for dessert, I made Mom's nut cake." Emma looked at Clara.

"Oh, dear, you know I have a cholesterol problem," she moaned, "but maybe just a sliver."

Emma brought the cake in, setting it on the table. When she poised the knife over it to cut a small wedge, Clara grabbed her hand and moved it to a very generous slice.

NATE GRACIOUSLY VOLUNTEERED to load the dishwasher while Emma visited with her sister. Nolan joined him. Emma knew they were pouring a brandy and she, too, longed for one.

"I'm working on a new play," Clara said.

"Really." Emma had seen two of her sister's plays put on by a local community group and hadn't understood either one. "What's this one about?" She was almost afraid to ask.

"A haunting," Clara said, her eyes opening wide in her round face.

Emma felt goose bumps climb up her arms. Another ghost?

"There's an old country house where a man was murdered in a most gruesome way." Clara sat forward in her chair.

"Oh?" was all Emma could say.

"His body was dismembered and buried in the basement."

"Oh, my God!" Emma was horrified at the premise. A body buried in the basement. Could the stranger's body be buried somewhere under the Performing Arts Center?

"This ghost roams around for years," Clara continued. "You see, he can't rest until his murderer is caught and punished." She sat back, her bulk filling the wing chair.

"How do you resolve it?" Emma asked. Maybe Clara had some solution that would help her.

Clara sighed. "I haven't figured that out yet, but I'm thinking about talking to a psychic."

Psychics and ghosts again. When would this all end?

FOR THE NEXT FEW DAYS Emma and Nate acted as good hosts and took their guests to a number of new sites Chicago had to offer. They spent a day visiting Emma's children and fussing over the new baby.

Friday night Emma and Nate took them to the opening of a new play at the Performing Arts Center. It was advertised as a tragedy, and Emma thought Clara might enjoy it.

During the final scene, when the heroine lay on her death bed, Emma saw a figure standing at the foot of the bed. She recognized him immediately.

He's associating himself with death. Why? What does he want?

When they left the theater Clara took Emma aside. "Who was that ragged black man in the last act? He didn't look like he belonged there." Her look demanded an explanation.

"So you saw him, too," Emma said.

"Yes, who is he?"

"Not everyone sees him. I'm convinced he's a spirit lost between two worlds."

"Oh," Clara exclaimed, clasping her hands to her bosom. "You have a real ghost. How exciting."

"Shush," Emma cautioned. "I don't think anyone else saw him. Nate believes he's a vagrant who took refuge in the Center."

"But we know better, don't we," Clara said, her eyes wide with excitement.

"Don't mention it, please," Emma said.

"Mum's the word, but you must let me know how it all turns out. It might help me with my play."

By Saturday afternoon the sky began to fill with ominous clouds. The weather channel predicted stormy weather.

"We had better get going," Nolan said. "You know I don't like to drive in the rain."

Reluctantly they took their leave with hugs and promises to visit again soon. The women gave each other conspiratorial looks as the elevator doors closed.

Emma went back into the condo, sat in a chair and blew out an exhausted breath. "Thank you, Nate, for being such a good host. You're a dear."

He gave her a mock frown. "You owe me, big-time."

THIRTY-TWO

A VIOLENT SPRING STORM lashed the area on the afternoon of the first rehearsal of *The Ghosts of Versailles*. Winds whipped the rain into such a frenzy that it looked as though it was falling sideways. *Is this some sort of omen?* Emma wondered.

Some of the supers didn't make it to the rehearsal. One of the singers, drenched in the downpour, wasn't able to sing. She claimed her throat had closed up and feared she might contract an infection.

Emma and Tristana watched from the wings as the stage director talked to the principals; they had been rehearsing for a week, but now it was time to get the entire production synchronized.

"This is a strange set," Tristana said.

"It's a strange opera," Emma said. "It starts out in the world of ghosts where they put on a play, a stage within a stage. Then it proceeds to the world of mortals. We're in the ghostly realm now." She shivered as she voiced the words aloud. They looked at the filmy pieces of light gray fabric hanging from unseen cables and dancing in areas of the stage. *The lighting will do wonders with those,* Emma thought.

"Where's Nate?" Tristana asked.

"He's talking with the stage manager. He comes on as a footman in the prologue and in act one. We're not on until the second act. We might as well go to the community room and have something to drink."

As they made their way toward the community room, Emma watched the lighting crew positioning the lights in strategic places. She heard the designer call to one of the men.

"Move that one over here. No, a little further. Good. Need to make it look otherworldly."

That's a task I wouldn't want, she thought.

They entered the community room, poured themselves a cup of tea and sat in comfortable chairs, but Tristana didn't seem able to relax. She kept fidgeting. Emma watched her out of the corner of her eye and wondered if she would go through with this venture or balk at the last minute.

"Hello, ladies," she heard Nate's familiar voice say. Emma greeted him with a smile. Then her eyebrows raised in surprise as she saw a good-looking man accompanying him, the one they had seen at the auditions.

Tristana turned and almost dropped her tea cup.

"Here, let me take that. You look a little flustered," the man said.

"I am," Tristana stammered. "In fact, I'm terrified."

Emma noticed that the man touched her hand as he took the cup. She exchanged glances with Nate.

"Let me make a proper introduction," Nate said. "This is Marshall Baxter."

The man gave a theatrical bow before the women, his wavy black hair bobbing slightly with the movement. When he looked up, he smiled.

That looks like an honest face, Emma thought, *a genuine smile and beautiful dimples as well as a cleft in his chin. I like him, and it appears that Tristana does, too.* She noticed the blush on the other woman's cheeks.

"This is Tristana Morgan," Nate continued, "and Emma Winberry." He snaked his arm around Emma and pulled her close.

"I'm looking forward to performing with you three. This should be fun," he said in a deep baritone voice.

"Have you done this before?" Tristana asked, her eyes locked on Marshall Baxter's.

"I was here last year as a backup, but didn't get to go onstage. But I have been an extra in a number of movies."

Emma's eyes rolled toward the ceiling.

Nate cleared his throat. "We tried that last summer. It was a disaster, swore never to do it again."

"Amen to that," Emma said.

"Sometimes it gets rather tedious," Marshall said, "but you can meet some interesting people."

Emma remembered the not so interesting people she had met the previous summer and was in no hurry to repeat the experience.

A call from the stage manager alerted the men.

"Show time," Marshall said as he and Nate made their way to the stage.

"He seems nice," Emma said but felt a familiar nudge. *Don't make snap decisions,* her inner voice said. Emma frowned and decided to ignore it.

"Uh huh," was the only answer from Tristana, but Emma saw her eyes watching his departing figure.

"Come on," Emma said, "let's watch. We don't go on for quite a while."

They walked into the auditorium and sat down. The stage director was instructing the supers as to their positions and when they were to enter and exit the stage.

Tristana's eyes darted from stage right to stage left. "They look so relaxed," she whispered.

But Emma wasn't listening. She was staring at a darkened corner of the stage. A shadowy figure stood, watching. No one seemed to notice him. A chill ran up Emma's spine. As soon as the stark notes of the opening music began, he disappeared.

AFTER THE PROLOGUE and the first act finished, the director called a break. The ladies met with Nate and Marshall in the community room. Tristana kept her hands clutched; Emma said nothing.

Nate pulled her away from the other two for a moment. "What's wrong, Sparrow? Have you contracted Tristana's nervousness?" He hugged her to him.

"No, I'm all right."

"Come on, I know you too well. Out with it."

She raised her eyes to his, deep creases forming between them. "I saw the stranger."

"Where?"

"He was standing in a dark corner, stage left. He seemed to be watching the action onstage. When the music began he—left."

"Damn. I thought he was gone now that the weather has improved." Nate blew out a deep breath. "He probably came in again because of the storm. I'd better tell James."

She put her hand on his arm. "No, there's no sense in anyone searching. You won't find him."

Nate shook his head and let out a frustrated breath. "I'm almost beginning to believe you."

DURING THE SECOND ACT, scene three, Emma led a trembling Tristana onto the stage. They took their assigned places among the many others portraying revolutionaries. Nate and Marshall took the parts of footmen.

"Hang in there," Emma whispered. She studied the pallor of the other woman's face and wondered if she might pass out. *I'll stay as close as I can,* she thought.

The scene proceeded amid a great deal of confusion. The director kept changing his mind: he wasn't satisfied with the positioning of the supers; one of the singers was off key; a dancer slipped during the prison scene.

Finally he called a halt. "Stop! That's it for today. We have to rework some of these scenes. I'll notify everyone of the next rehearsal." He waved his hands as the performers left the stage amid grumbling and cursing.

"This is a farce," the outspoken Dominic Orso said. "That director doesn't know what he's doing. I could do a better job."

Emma nudged Nate.

"I don't think that one will be around much longer," he said. "I'll speak to Cecily Cunningham about him."

She nodded. "He's just an overblown know-it-all."

The four of them decided to go to the café on the corner for coffee and scones. The rain had abated for the time being, but heavy, low-hanging clouds heralded more. Again Emma nudged Nate as they watched Tristana and Marshall talking animatedly, their heads together, each apparently comfortable in the other's personal space.

When they were seated in the café and had given the server their orders, Marshall asked, "Is there always this much confusion?"

"No, definitely not," Nate said. "This is a particularly difficult opera to stage, and I'm beginning to wonder if Midwest is up to it." He sat forward, elbows on the table, his chin resting on his hands.

Emma said nothing. Her thoughts were in a jumble. *Maybe the opera is cursed; maybe the stranger has something to do with it; maybe…*

"What's going through your head, Sparrow?" Nate asked.

"Nothing in particular, just random thoughts."

"Why do you call her Sparrow?" Tristana asked.

Nate smiled. He hesitated for a moment. "When we first met, Emma was much thinner than she is now. She reminded me of a tiny bird."

Emma grinned. "Actually I was shaped like a stick. I even bought enhanced—" she hesitated for a moment, felt her face flushing "—you know, what we once referred to as unmentionables."

The others laughed.

"But, since I met Nate, I've filled out a bit. All that wining and dining has been good for me." She looked at him, her eyes sending a message only he understood.

Tristana sighed. "That's so romantic."

Marshall looked at her. "Yes, it is." His eyes also seemed to be sending a message. Then he looked down and frowned.

I wonder what's in his *past?* Emma thought. *Everyone seems to have secrets.*

THE NEXT REHEARSAL was worse: missing props, missed cues, missing supers. To compound the problem, the whole Midwest area was locked in a weather system that sent torrents of rain pounding the city. Basements flooded; underpasses became impassable; cars stalled, embedded in water up to their doors.

Emma called James to ask about the Performing Arts Center.

"It's bad," he said. "There's a foot of water in the basement. Bruce hired a crew to pump it out, but if it doesn't stop raining, it'll just fill up again.

"We've already lost quite a few props. The stagehands have moved as many things as possible into the rooms on the upper floors. It's a mess."

She heard his frustrated sigh.

"According to the weather forecast, this front is supposed to pass in a few days," she said.

"Yes, that's what we heard. The director plans to resume rehearsals by Wednesday. Now, I have to go. There seems to be another crisis. Talk to you later."

Emma's face reflected her mood; a frown creased her forehead; the sides of her mouth drooped.

"It's that bad, huh?" Nate asked, circling her with his arms.

"Poor James, everything is going wrong. I wonder if they'll have to cancel the production."

"That would be a terrible financial loss for the Midwest Opera." He shook his head and frowned, lifting his arms from around her.

Emma walked away from Nate and into the atrium. She watched as sheets of rain obscured Navy Pier and even the lake. She felt a heaviness weighing her down.

Guardian Angel, this doesn't bode well. Something bad is going to happen. I know it.

THIRTY-THREE

THAT NIGHT THE unrelenting rain continued. Power failed throughout the entire northeast area of Chicago.

A figure dressed in a black slicker and boots waded through the water and debris at the rear of the Performing Arts Center. He expertly dismantled the security system, forced the lock on the back door and quietly entered the building. Leaving his slicker and boots in a corner, he made his way to the box office.

That particular night the cash box had not been emptied; no bank deposit made; no money transferred to the safe. He picked the lock on the door, let himself in, and collected the money that was banded and ready for the next day's deposit.

Someone was coming, probably the guard making his rounds. He ducked down behind the counter as far as he could. Would the guard check the back door? Would he notice the wet floor? Would he find the slicker and boots?

He couldn't take the chance. Too much depended on this money. He grabbed the sap he carried for just such a possibility.

Carefully he followed the guard. He saw him check the door, look at the wet floor, take his cell phone out of his pocket and flip it open. Before he could punch in the numbers, the sap came down on his head with a skull-crushing blow. The guard crumpled to the floor.

The figure retrieved the slicker and boots and disappeared into the deluge.

"MY GOD!" EMMA SHOUTED into the phone. "How bad is it?"

"The guard is in Intensive Care in critical condition—a subdural hematoma—taking him to surgery," James said in halting tones. His voice mirrored his exhaustion.

"How much money did the intruder get?" she asked.

"About two thousand dollars. Bruce is livid. Quiller was supposed to see that the money was deposited in the bank. I have no idea why he didn't do it."

"Is he there?" Emma paced from one end of the room to the other.

"He hasn't come in yet. He called this morning and said he'd be late, blamed the weather."

"What did Bruce say to that?"

"I can't repeat it, not to a lady."

"James, I can't explain why, but I get a bad feeling around that man. He's up to no good."

At that point Nate took the phone. "James, I'm just getting Emma's side of the conversation. Do you want me to come down? Is there anything I can do?"

"Not right now. If the weather lets up, maybe you can pick up Tristana and bring her in. The library's been closed for three days. We've been getting calls for research material and there's no one here to answer them." He let out an audible sigh.

"Will do. Is the power back on?"

"Yes, thank God."

"See you later." He turned to Emma who was still pacing and wringing her hands. "If it stops raining, we're to pick up Tristana and go to the Center. Give her a call, will you? I'm convinced this is the work of your stranger. It has to be."

TRISTANA WAS EAGER to get out of her claustrophobic apartment and back to work. Emma accompanied her to the library, and Nate went directly to James's office to see what he could do to help.

As the women walked through the halls, they glanced into rooms filled with props hastily carried up from the basement. Emma wrinkled her nose at the smell of wet, molding fabric.

Huge fans oscillated back and forth circulating the air, but most of the items appeared irreparably damaged.

"What a shame," Tristana said. "Look at that ornate wooden table, all warped and discolored." She shook her head.

They heard raised voices before they reached the library. Emma pulled Tristana into the vending machine area and listened.

"Goddamn it, Quiller, I told you to find that maintenance man. What have you done about it?" Bruce Hamilton's voice rose an octave higher than normal.

"He was only a temp. I, I couldn't find out where he was working after he left here," Norman Quiller whined.

"It was your responsibility to see that the money was deposited in the bank," Bruce continued in the same accusing tone.

"I told you I couldn't take it because of the flooding." More whining.

"That's no excuse. Now, the money is missing and a man has been seriously injured. He might even die." Bruce's voice rose a few decibels. "I'm holding you personally responsible. Get to the bottom of this. Find that maintenance man. Find that stranger. I'm certain they're one and the same. Your job is at stake, Quiller. Now, get out of my sight until you bring me that man."

Emma and Tristana turned to each other and shrugged. They each got a cup of coffee from the machine and went into the library.

"Well," Tristana said when they closed the door. "I wouldn't want to be in his shoes."

Emma screwed up her face. "They're on the wrong track. That maintenance man has nothing to do with any of this."

"How do you know?"

"I just know. It goes much deeper. Just how deep remains to be seen."

THIRTY-FOUR

EMMA FROWNED AS she carefully heated milk in a saucepan, then measured the cocoa and just enough sugar to suit her. She stirred the mixture to prevent clumping—no premixed packets of hot chocolate for her. They were too sweet and artificial tasting. She preferred to make it the old-fashioned way. Of course, Nate would add more sugar; he always did.

She glanced at the clock when she heard a knock at the door. *Who can that be at nine o'clock at night?* She heard Nate's voice.

"Claude, come in. You're just in time for a cup of hot chocolate."

Emma smiled. She always enjoyed Claude's visits. *Thomas must be out,* she thought. *Claude does get lonesome.*

When she walked into the living room carrying a tray with three cups of steaming cocoa and a dish of cookies, Claude jumped up from the sofa.

"Emma, Nate, you're too kind." He took the tray from her hands and placed it on the coffee table.

"It's always a pleasure to see you," Emma said. "You haven't been here in a while."

He heaved a deep sigh and crossed both hands over his chest. "I'm working on a new ballet, a daunting task. I've hit a snag and can't seem to go any further." He looked across the room. "Thomas is away until tomorrow." His voice dropped to almost a whisper.

"And where is Oliver?" she asked.

"He's staying with Sharon for a few days. Thomas and I have both been so busy lately." He shook his head. "I never realized just how much time a child requires."

Emma nodded. She knew only too well.

"You're always welcome here, you know that," Nate said, handing him a cup.

"Thank you." He sipped the rich mixture. "Umm, delicious."

Emma watched Nate spoon more sugar into his cup. She shook her head and picked up her own.

"I heard about what happened at the Performing Arts Center," Claude said.

"Yes," Nate said through gritted teeth. "Something must be done, but I don't know what, and neither does anyone else."

Claude's eyes darted from one side to the other. He leaned forward and said in a soft tone, "I think the place is cursed."

Emma looked at him and tried to suppress a smile. "I don't think so. I think there's a rational explanation for all the things that are happening. We just haven't figured it out yet."

"And who, pray tell, is going to come up with the answer, Mrs. Sleuth?" Nate asked, raising his eyebrows.

"Get that note of sarcasm out of your voice, Nate Sandler. Perhaps I shall." She pursed her lips and raised her chin.

"That opera you're rehearsing is filled with ghosts," Claude said with a visible shiver.

"They're only singers portraying the ghost world," Nate said. "There's nothing supernatural about it."

"I still worry about you two," he said, reaching for a peanut butter cookie. "I wouldn't want anything to happen to either of you."

"Don't worry, Claude," Emma said. "We're perfectly safe. Any time we're at the Center, we're surrounded by other supers and cast members. Remember, there's safety in numbers. Now, tell us about your new ballet."

CLAUDE'S WORDS PLAYED over and over in Emma's mind as she tossed and turned, unable to sleep later that night. Were they in danger? Who was responsible for the trouble and why?

Look to the stranger, her inner voice said. *He will lead you to the answers.*

Guardian Angel, are you telling me that the stranger is involved in all this?

Look to the stranger...

REHEARSALS RESUMED the following day. Tristana seemed more relaxed, but her hand was icy cold when she grabbed Emma's just before they went onstage.

Everything went reasonably well this time. All the mechanical devices worked, the singers sang the difficult music on key, and the dancers outdid themselves. The director still wasn't satisfied with a few minor details, but they could be worked out.

During the final scene, a number of ghost dancers dressed in tattered, gauzy costumes appeared. Amid the swirling mist that surrounded the supernatural world, Emma saw a figure standing at the back of the stage. Tristana grabbed her hand. The women exchanged glances. When they looked back, the figure was gone.

"That's all for today," the stage director said. "This is finally coming together. I think we'll be ready for the opening night in three weeks."

Emma, Nate, Tristana, and Marshall went over to the café. It had become a routine after each rehearsal. Emma noticed a relationship growing between Tristana and Marshall. She tried to see it as a positive thing, but something bothered her. She felt Marshall was harboring a secret. Sometimes he seemed about to say something, then drew back. Did he have a wife somewhere?

As they sat at the table waiting for their order, Marshall asked Tristana, "So how did your parents choose such a Wagnerian name for you?"

She laughed. "They were obsessed with his music. 'The Ride of the Valkyries' resonated through our house for as long as I can remember." She looked out the window, a half smile on her face.

"They called the dog Brunhilda. We just called her Hilda for short. If I had been a boy, they would have named me Tristan.

When my younger brother was born, seven years later, they called the poor child Sigfriend."

Strange, Emma thought. *She never mentioned a brother, or any other family.*

Marshall threw his head back in a merry laugh. "I'll bet he had a hard time when he went to school."

Tristana looked down, fingering her napkin. "He never went to school. He died of meningitis when he was four."

"Sorry." Marshall took her hand and held it for just a moment.

Tristana smiled; her eyes brimmed with tears. "It was a long time ago. I've learned to let go of the past." She glanced at Emma, their eyes exchanging a message.

Nate cleared his throat. "I think the director finally has this production on the right track. The lighting was perfect. It lent just the right amount of mysticism to the set."

"Yes," Emma agreed. "It did go well today."

THE FOLLOWING DAY Emma had just left the library and decided to watch the ballet practice for a few minutes. As she walked toward the auditorium she heard Claude shouting.

"Oliver!" He ran off the stage and down into the auditorium.

"What happened, Claude?" Emma grabbed his hand.

"Oliver was with me—had to go onstage for only a minute. When I looked back—gone!"

"He can't be too far," Emma said, trying to calm the near hysterical man.

A few stagehands came to his aid. "What's wrong?" one of them asked.

"Oliver, the young boy who was with me. Did you see where he went?" Claude's voice rose with each word.

The men shook their heads then began searching the entire first floor of the auditorium including underneath the seats. But he was nowhere.

Claude ran out into the foyer shouting, "Oliver. Oh, my God, I'm responsible for that boy. If anything happens to him…"

James and Bruce Hamilton came out of their offices when they heard the commotion. They began looking in the rooms on the second floor. Tristana ran down the back hall. Claude and another dancer ran toward the dressing rooms, the community room, then headed for the wardrobe room.

"I'll check the basement," one of the stagehands said.

"I'll go out in front," another called.

Emma joined the search. When she heard Claude's cry of joy, she retraced her steps. She joined him as he ran toward Tristana who was holding Oliver's hand. He dropped to his knees and grabbed the boy.

"Oliver, where did you go?"

"I found him walking toward the back door," Tristana said. "He was mumbling something."

"Where were you going?" Claude asked again. His entire body shook.

"I was going with the man," the child answered.

"What man?" Claude's voice rose an octave. "What did he look like?"

Oliver shrugged and looked as if he were about to cry.

"Claude, you're upsetting him," Emma said. "Why don't Tristana and I take him to the library and settle him down. You go back to your dancers and come and get him later. We'll take good care of him."

Claude nodded and tried to compose his face into a smile, but his entire body trembled. "All right." He took a deep breath. "Go with the nice ladies, Oliver, and I'll come by in a little while for you."

The boy took Tristana and Emma's hands and walked with them toward the library. Emma stopped at the vending machines and purchased three cups of hot chocolate. Then she followed Tristana and Oliver into the library and sat next to them at one of the tables.

They were quiet while they sipped the chocolate. Emma thought it was a bit watery, but Oliver didn't seem to mind. When he took the last swallow, he sat back and looked at the women.

"Do you want to tell me about the man?" Emma asked. Again he shrugged.

Tristana thought for a moment. "Oliver, do you like to draw?"

He nodded, his eyes widening.

She took the box of crayons she had tucked in the drawer and a sheet of paper and set them in front of him. "Why don't you draw a picture of the man for us?"

He thought for a moment, then examining the crayons, chose a brown one, and drew a round circle. He colored the entire inside brown then chose black for the hair. He proceeded to draw a stick figure for the body. When he had finished he frowned, as if unsatisfied with the result. Again he picked up the brown crayon and drew some vertical lines roughly indicating clothing.

"That's very good," Tristana said. "Can you tell me why you followed the man?"

"He told me to." His eyes looked at her with the innocence of youth.

"Did he talk to you? I mean in words?" Emma asked.

"Uh huh."

"What did he say?" This was the first time anyone claimed to hear the stranger actually speak.

"He's sad," the boy whispered, looking down at his drawing.

"Why is he sad?" she persisted.

"He wants to go home."

"Where does he live? Did he tell you?"

Slowly the boy turned his head from side to side.

"What happened next?"

He shrugged. "He wasn't there anymore. I couldn't find him."

Oh, Lord, Emma thought. *This is getting too spooky. I'd better tell Claude to keep this child out of the Center until this mystery is solved.*

THIRTY-FIVE

AFTER THE EPISODE with Oliver and the stranger, Emma was more confused than ever.

Dreams and portents of danger plagued her sleep: she floated through clouds of mist unable to find Nate; she felt herself crammed into a tight, dark space, alone and terrified…

"Emma, wake up. What in God's name are you dreaming?" Nate shook her awake.

She grabbed him. "Oh, such nightmares."

"You're trembling," he said, turning on a bedside lamp and circling her slight body in his arms. "It's all right. I won't let anything bad happen to you ever again." He cradled her head in his hands, smoothing down her unruly hair. "Do you want to tell me about it?"

She heaved a deep sigh. "You're going to think I'm mad."

"Is that something new?" he asked, grinning.

"All right, I'll tell you what I think, but don't interrupt me until I've finished."

He nodded.

She sat up in bed, pulled up her knees, and rested her arms across them. "I think that stranger who's been roaming around the Center is a troubled spirit who can't rest until he tells us whatever it is he wants us to know." She held up her hand at Nate's gaping mouth. "I'm not finished yet. The stranger had nothing to do with the break-in at the library or the theft of the money. Spirits aren't able to pick locks and knock people on the head. That's the work of someone mortal." She gave her head a sharp nod, pursed her lips, and turned to Nate.

"You're right, you are mad. So Oliver claimed that he spoke

to him? Doesn't that prove that he's a mortal man? I didn't think spirits could talk. I'm sorry, my dear, but I don't believe in ghosts. I think the stranger is a flesh-and-blood man and is responsible for all the problems at the Center. Find him and everything will be solved." He returned her determined look.

"We shall see," Emma said, swinging her legs over the side of the bed and looking at the clock. The hands pointed to five. "I'll put on a pot of coffee. Go back to sleep if you wish."

"No, I'm getting up, too." He got out of bed and made his way to the bathroom.

Emma thought for a moment. *Where did I put that card?* She searched her top dresser drawer where she stored odds and ends—not there. *Ah, the jewelry box.* She retrieved the card that Thomas's sister had given her at the party. *I think I'll call her and get the number of the psychic.*

Later that day Nate went out to the hardware store. It was one of his favorite places to browse. Emma knew he would be gone for quite a while.

She paced, fingered the business card, then walked into the atrium and looked out over the lake. A few lazy clouds sat unmoving in a clear blue sky. The storms had passed for the time being. *I should be out walking on this lovely day, not stewing about spirits.*

Oh, Guardian Angel, what should I do? Is Nate right? Is my imagination running wild?

Call the woman, her inner voice said. *She can help.*

With renewed resolve Emma walked back into the living room, picked up the phone and called Sharon who gave her the number. Emma punched it in.

"How can I help you?" a soft voice asked.

"Hello, is this Rose? I'm afraid I don't know your last name," Emma said, hesitating just a bit.

"No need for last names. Do you wish to schedule a reading?"

"Uh, no, I'm not sure what I need. Sharon Aherne gave me your number."

"Oh, yes, I know her well."

Neither woman spoke for a long moment.

"What is your problem?" Rose asked.

There's no way but to blurt this out, Emma thought. "I'm a supernumerary for the Midwest Opera at the Performing Arts Center, and I think there's a spirit roaming around, trying to tell us something." *There, now this woman probably thinks I'm mad, too.*

"Tell me about the spirit," Rose said, her voice remaining soft and calm.

Emma recounted all the times the stranger had appeared, beginning with the incident in Gina Rienzi's dressing room.

"How many people have seen him?"

"Only about five or six claim to see the man. Perhaps there are more who haven't admitted it. And a young boy claims that the spirit spoke to him, but this child has developmental problems." Emma didn't know how else to explain it.

"What did the entity tell the child?" Rose asked.

"He said he wanted to go home."

Rose was quiet for a long time. Then she asked, "Would the management allow me to walk through the Center and see if I can pick up anything paranormal? It would have to be at a time when there is a minimum of activity."

Emma thought for a moment. *Tristana has a key. Maybe I can enlist her help.* "Let me get back to you. I need to talk with someone about that."

"That's fine. Get back to me when the time is right."

That's strange, Emma thought, as she replaced the phone on its base. What did she mean by that? And she didn't even ask my name.

"TRISTANA, THIS IS EMMA. I want to run something by you."

Emma held the phone a little too tightly and paced as she spoke.

"I'm all ears," the other woman said.

"I've been thinking more and more about the sightings at

the Center. Last month when Claude gave a party for Thomas's birthday, I met Thomas's sister there. She's a very sensitive woman. Apparently her brother told her about the stranger, because she brought up the subject. She said she knew a psychic who is sometimes able to exorcise spirits trapped in this world." Emma hesitated for a moment.

"What are you suggesting?" Tristana asked.

"I'm not sure. I called the woman and explained the situation to her. She said she would be willing to walk through the Center."

Emma heard a sigh from the other end of the line.

"I guess it wouldn't hurt, but we'd have to get permission from Bruce, wouldn't we?"

"I doubt that he would consent," Emma said. "No, it's better to beg forgiveness than ask permission, especially when you know it won't be granted."

"You're right."

"You have keys to the building," Emma continued. "Come up with a time when there isn't likely to be anyone around, and we'll ask this Rose if she can make it."

"Did you say Rose?" Tristana's voice mirrored her question.

"Yes, no last name."

"I believe that's the same woman I went to see. I also mentioned the stranger to her."

"Really? Oh, I hear Nate's key in the door. He won't agree with any of this. I'll talk to you later."

Emma quickly put down the phone, grabbed her watering can and hurried into the atrium.

"What mischief have you gotten into while I was gone?" Nate asked, planting a kiss on her cheek.

Emma put her hands on her hips and tried to look indignant. "I've been tending to my plants." That wasn't really a lie. She did have time to pour a few drops of water on the growing tomato plants. "Look at these. I think by next week we can safely transplant them out on the roof."

"The weather does seem to be settling down nicely," he said. "How about a walk along the lakeshore?"

"Perfect. I'll be right with you."

"HI, GLADYS, I've been thinking about you," Emma said, picking up the phone.

"We do seem to have some type of extrasensory communication between us," Gladys said. "I always call when you claim to be thinking about me and vice versa."

"Yes," Emma agreed. "I suppose you might say we're soul sisters."

"Nora has finished searching that family line. The only living person she could locate is a George Perkins. He's been in and out of jail and is living somewhere in the Chicago area."

"How did she find all that out?" Emma asked.

"Don't ask me. From what I gather you can glean just about anything from the Internet, if you know where to search. I'll e-mail you these pages and you can do whatever you want with them."

"Send me her bill and I'll give it to Bruce Hamilton. She must be paid for her time."

Gladys laughed. "There's no charge. She loves doing this kind of stuff. She says it's good experience in case she ever decides to open her own business."

They spent the next half hour catching up on each other's families. When Emma put the phone down, she went into the study to print out the information.

Nate, who had heard her end of the conversation, peered over her shoulder. He picked up the pages as they spit out of the printer. He frowned and made a grunting sound. "Bruce is not going to like this. I doubt very much if he will attempt to contact this George Perkins."

"That's for sure."

"Let's just e-mail all this information to him and let him make the decision," Nate said.

"Good idea. We certainly don't need to be contacting criminals with everything else that's going on," Emma said. "I'll make a cup of tea while you send the messages."

TRISTANA LOOKED UP from her desk as Bruce Hamilton stormed into the library.

"Mrs. Morgan, did…did you see this information on the genealogy search?"

Tristana shook her head. "No, I didn't."

"This is scandalous. Why…why the only living relative has a criminal record. We can't have someone like that involved in our exhibit." He blew out a breath and paced, his limp more pronounced with each step.

"Why not forget the genealogy and leave the exhibit simply an historical one. I'm sure the people on the tour would accept that," she said. "And, no one with a criminal background is likely to come here to the Center. So you wouldn't have to worry about this man 'accidentally' showing up."

Bruce dropped his head and moved it slowly back and forth. "I suppose we'll have to do just that." He made a *tsk* sound through clenched teeth. "I was hoping to be able to trace the family to someone respectable."

"Think of it this way," Tristana said, cocking her head to one side. "As we discussed earlier, if you perhaps did find a businessman, he might claim the artifacts as their rightful owner." She raised her eyebrows and gave him a half smile.

"Hmm. That's a possibility. I suppose I shall have to be satisfied with what we have. It is a significant find." He turned and limped out of the library, muttering to himself.

Tristana smiled. *He does seem a bit obsessed with this whole thing,* she thought. *But, he's rather a sweet man.*

Her thoughts returned to the conversation with Emma about the psychic. How ironic that it should be Rose. She didn't like the idea of trying to exorcise the ghost, but she knew nothing about the occult. Was it possible to do something like that? She shrugged. There seemed to be only one way to find out.

She examined the schedule of events at the Center for the

next week: an opera rehearsal at four that afternoon; a play by a visiting acting group that evening. *That takes care of today,* she thought. The next three days were crowded with rehearsals and events. Saturday morning seemed to be clear. There wasn't anything on the agenda until late afternoon.

She picked up the phone and called Emma. Nate answered.

"Hello, Nate, this is Tristana. Is Emma around?"

"Hang on a minute, she's out on the roof. I'll bring her the phone."

Tristana tapped her fingers nervously on the desk as she waited. In a few moments Emma answered. "Hi, what's up?"

"I've checked the calendar for the week, and next Saturday morning is the only time that might work. This is kind of scary. What do you think?"

"I agree, but what else can we do?" Emma asked. "Saturday is best. Let's bite the bullet and do it. Probably early. I'll call Rose and see if she can make it. Shall we say eight?"

"What are you going to tell Nate?"

"I'll think of something."

THAT WEEK THE OPERA rehearsals began in earnest, with one mishap after another. The filmy curtains of the ghost world swayed back and forth. The ghosts moved through these as if gliding through the air.

"Stop, stop!" the director shouted. "Too much distraction. The audience won't be able to see the performers."

Emma and Nate, along with Tristana and Marshall, stood at the back of the auditorium with James watching as the stagehands removed some of the curtains; the lighting director adjusted the intensity of the lighting while general chaos reigned onstage.

James shook his head. "I'm afraid we've bitten off a little too much with this opera. It's difficult to stage."

"Nonsense," Emma said. "They'll get it right. It looks pretty eerie from back here." She felt a sudden chill, as if someone had opened a door. A corner of the stage caught her attention. The figure of a familiar man stood watching. Was it the stranger, or her imagination? There were too many props to be certain. She squeezed her eyes shut and looked again, but he was gone. She noticed a startled look on Tristana's face. The women exchanged messages with their eyes, but said nothing.

"Come on," Nate said. "Let's get some coffee. They won't be ready for us for a long time."

"I'm going back to my office," James said. "See you folks later."

Emma watched him walk away, his gait shuffling, his shoulders hunched. *Poor James, this job is so stressful, it's taking years off his life. I'm going to suggest that he and Sylvia take a restful vacation when this season is over.*

When the rehearsal resumed, the wind machine refused to work properly.

"Somebody fix that damn thing!" the director yelled. "How can we put on a production with such archaic equipment?" He ran his hand through his thinning hair and paced back and forth. A technician ran up to him and whispered something. He shook his head in resignation. "We'll have to do without the wind until tomorrow I'm told. Let's go on."

The supers did not appear until the second act. Then they marched across the stage against a backdrop of dark gray. The atmosphere was charged with excitement as the ghost of Marie Antoinette stood to the side, reliving her execution, her pale face reflecting the horror. She clutched a handkerchief in her hand, wringing it. Her costume was of grayish-white reminiscent of the splendor of the court, but the bouffant skirt hung in tatters. Her wig was in disarray, the curls escaping from their comb. No jewelry adorned her neck, nor her ears.

The stage filled with revolutionaries shouting and waving their hands. Some carried clubs, others spikes topped with skulls. On the back of the stage the words, *Liberté Egalité Fraternité* were scrawled in red on a wooden board, supposedly in blood. Nate and Marshall joined a band of revolutionaries beating drums and marching across the stage. They wore red caps flopping to the side, baggy trousers, and stained worn shirts.

Emma and Tristana, dressed as peasant women with mob-caps on their heads, waved banners and followed the men. They wore shawls and some carried knives and staves. Confusion reigned as both chorus members and supers shouted.

Emma glanced to the side and saw the stranger behind the ghost of Marie Antoinette. She kept her eyes on him as she marched off the stage.

Finally the director called a halt to the rehearsal. "All right, everyone, that looks better. We'll reconvene on Thursday at four."

He turned to a technician, his fists clenched, and said, "Please have the wind machine repaired by then." It sounded more like a command than a request. The man reassured him he would have it in working order.

Emma's eyes scanned the stage looking for the stranger, but he was nowhere in sight.

"LET'S GO TO THE CAFÉ for a bite," Nate said to Tristana and Marshall.

Marshall looked at Tristana with a question on his face.

"Sounds good to me," she agreed.

The four of them hurried across the street between the raindrops that had begun falling. They found a comfortable booth and settled in. After ordering sandwiches and coffee, they began to discuss the production.

"Hi, there," a loud voice called out. "Mind if I join you?"

Emma looked up to see Dominic Orso, their fellow super, looming over them.

Nate frowned. "As you can see, we're in a booth for four." His look was far from welcoming.

"Sure." The man leaned his beefy hands on the table. "Just thought I'd say hello." He looked at Nate, then stared at Marshall, a little too long Emma thought.

They sat without saying anything for an awkward moment, then the man stepped back, said good-bye, and left.

"He's not very likable, is he?" Tristana said.

Marshall sat quietly rotating his coffee cup in his hand.

Emma turned to Nate. "I thought you were going to suggest dismissing him when the stage manager asked for your help."

"I did," Nate said, a furrow creasing his brow, "but the director insisted he stay." He shrugged. "I don't know why. At least he hasn't made anymore boorish remarks."

Emma watched Marshall as he continued to stare at his coffee cup.

THIRTY-SIX

SATURDAY DAWNED TO an overcast sky, the clouds filled with rain. "I'm sorry," Nate said, "but I have to rewrite this article for the investment journal. The editor wants it from a different slant. It'll probably take me most of the morning." He looked at Emma as if asking for her approval.

Emma had just finished her daily yoga exercises. She took a deep breath and stretched. "Don't worry about me. I want to go to Water Tower Place and look for a few things. In fact, I think I'll leave early and take a walk, get some exercise. It's been raining so much lately that I haven't been able to walk along the lake as much as I'd like." She gave him an innocent smile, but was that a suspicious look he returned?

When she reached the Center, Emma saw two women standing at the stage entrance: Tristana and a unique-looking woman who had to be Rose. Emma was momentarily taken aback by the stark white hair surrounding the middle-aged face. Only when she got closer and saw the pink irises did she realize the woman was an albino.

Tristana introduced Rose, then nervously inserted her key in the lock.

"Remember," Emma said, "if anyone sees us, tell them you have an out-of-town guest who wanted to see the Center."

They nodded in agreement and made their way to the library. When they were inside with the door closed, Rose turned to them.

"You two sit in that corner and let me walk around. I need to feel for changes in temperature and for vibrations."

Emma and Tristana did as requested and watched Rose. After

circling the room twice she shook her head. "I don't feel any presence in this room. There is nothing out of the ordinary that I can discern."

"Let's go out on the stage," Emma suggested. "That's where most of the sightings have occurred."

As they walked quietly down the empty corridors, Emma felt a heaviness in the air. Their soft footfalls were the only sound. Every so often Rose stopped, closed her eyes, appeared to be listening for something, then shook her head.

When they reached the darkened stage, Emma hesitated. It was so different from rehearsal time when the lights blazed and people milled about. Here their footsteps echoed loudly on the bare wooden floor. Emma shuddered, then clicked on the flashlight she held in her hand.

"No lights," Rose whispered. "Let me walk around, alone."

Emma stood at the edge of the stage fearful that the woman might fall into the orchestra pit. But Rose seemed to know exactly where she was going. She held out her arms and circled the stage twice. Every so often she stopped, sniffed the air and mumbled something.

When she rejoined the other two, she shook her head. "There's nothing here that I can sense. Where else has he appeared?"

They walked through the halls along the dressing rooms where Gina Rienzi had screamed that first night, but still, Rose said she sensed nothing.

She frowned, scratched her head, and looked around. "Is there a basement?"

"There is," Emma said, "but it's pretty damp down there. It flooded twice and the water had to be pumped out. I think they have some large fans still going in an attempt to dry it out."

"I must go down there," Rose said. "I have a feeling the entity is there."

Emma and Tristana stared at one another, then led the way to the basement door. So far, they hadn't run into anyone, but Emma was getting nervous. They were bound to meet the guard eventually.

They found the basement door unlocked. As Emma opened it, a loud squeak issued from the rusted hinges. She cringed and looked about expecting to see someone coming around the corner at any moment.

Quietly, they slipped through the door and closed it after them. Smells of must and mold permeated the air. Tristana coughed and covered her mouth and nose with her hand. The whirring of the fans emitted a chilling sound. Emma turned on the flashlight; the beam penetrated the darkness in a small circle, the only light in the windowless area.

"I feel something here," Rose finally said as she slowly made her way directly to the storeroom door. She stopped, put her hands on the door, and closed her eyes.

Emma held her breath.

Tristana stood motionless, a look of fear on her face.

"Oh, my God," Rose moaned. "So much pain and suffering behind this door." She rocked back and forth, moaning softly.

This was the room where the slaves were hidden, Emma thought. She felt it, too, but it appeared, not as acutely as Rose.

The psychic turned around. "We can't go any farther. This is where your spirit is earthbound—somewhere behind this door. I can't reach him. I seem to be blocked by some force I can't identify." She stood still and listened, her face tilted to the side. "I sense danger there. Do not try to follow the specter. I can't emphasize that strongly enough. Stay away. I'm afraid there is nothing I can do for this spirit. Now, we must leave." She turned and walked away from the door holding the sides of her head with her hands.

Emma felt something, she wasn't sure what it was, but it was frightening. All she wanted to do was get out of there.

They left the basement quickly, making their way back toward the library. Suddenly a figure turned the corner, saw them, and stopped. Emma recognized the pungent smell of his aftershave even before he came into view. It was Norman Quiller.

"What are you doing here?" he demanded, his usually twitchy face locked in a scowl, his fisted hands at his sides. He looked them each directly in the eye. This was something Emma had rarely seen him do.

"I—I have an out-of-town visitor," Tristana said, not very convincingly. "She wanted to see the Center. I thought it would be all right."

"Well, it isn't. Did you get permission from Bruce?" He stood his ground, looking very different from the cringing weasel Emma knew.

"We're just leaving," Emma said. She wanted to say "don't get your drawers in an uproar," but thought better of it.

They quickly exited the Center, feeling Quiller's hostile stare all the way. When they were outside, Rose looked at the two of them. "Don't trust that man. I felt bad vibrations coming from him."

"I felt it, too," Emma whispered.

For a moment she and Rose looked at each other. *The woman appeared exhausted,* Emma thought. *This experience must have taken all of her energy.*

"Is there nothing we can do to free this spirit?" Emma asked.

"Perhaps," Rose said, "but as I said inside, I'm not the one." She looked directly at Emma sending her a message that Emma did not quite comprehend.

"Let me repeat my warning." She stared from one to the other. "Be careful. There is something evil going on in there." She motioned with her chin toward the building. "I see danger around you both."

Emma felt a chill run down her spine. She thanked Rose for her efforts and headed for home.

Oh, Guardian Angel, what did Rose mean when she looked at me like that? I cannot possibly be the one to release that spirit.

For the first time there was no answer from her inner voice. That was more frightening than anything else.

WHEN SHE WALKED in the door, Nate stood there, looking at her.

"You're pale as a ghost," he said, then looked at his watch.

"Since the stores opened about a half hour ago, do you want to tell me where you really went?"

Emma bit her lower lip and lowered her eyes. She plopped in a chair and realized her hands were trembling.

Nate walked up behind her and began massaging her shoulders.

"Oh, that feels good," she murmured, closing her eyes and taking deep breaths. She felt the tension in her muscles drain away.

When he finished, he patted her forehead and her cheeks. "You relax while I brew a cup of tea, then, if you're ready to talk, I'm ready to listen."

Emma heard the comforting sounds as Nate puttered around the kitchen.

Oh, Guardian Angel, what shall I tell him?

The truth, of course.

He'll be angry.

If you begin lying to him now, when will it stop?

"You're right, as usual," she said aloud.

"Who's right?" Nate asked, walking into the living room. He carried a tray with two tea cups, sugar bowl, creamer, and a plate of coconut macaroons.

Emma's eyes widened. "Where did those come from?"

He looked down at her, a deep crease forming between his eyes. "My dear Sparrow, you are a terrible liar. I knew you had no intention of going shopping at eight o'clock on a Saturday morning. Unless you had a liaison with another man, I presumed that you and Tristana had some scheme in mind. I went out to the bakery. Had a feeling you'd need a treat when you got back. Now, drink your tea and 'fess up."

"Oh, you are a dear, and you know me too well." She took the cup in her hand, put in a half teaspoon of sugar and a little milk, and began to sip. "Umm, good."

For the next half hour, between swallows of tea and bites of macaroon, Emma told him the unvarnished story.

When she finished, he simply shook his head and raised his eyes to the ceiling. "When are you going to stop all this ghost nonsense?"

"He's a troubled soul. All we wanted to do was send him on his way."

"Emma," he took her shoulders in his hands and gave her a gentle shake. "Let it go."

She heaved a deep sigh. "I suppose we're going to have to now. All right, no more talk of the stranger." She gave him one of her deceptive smiles.

No more talk, she thought. *That's all I promised.*

THIRTY-SEVEN

WHEN REHEARSALS RESUMED the following week, the wind machine worked properly. The strategically placed props along with the lighting gave the stage an unearthly look. Emma and Tristana stood back and watched the beginning of the opera.

The curtain opened to reveal a gauzy scrim of loosely woven fabric hanging in front of the performers. They could see the ghost world through the scrim, figures moving and floating back and forth through the air. Eerie music contributed to the ethereal atmosphere. Emma felt the familiar goose bumps crawl up her arms.

The scrim slowly rose up into the fly space and the figures appeared more clearly. The stranger mingled with the ghost figures. They moved like marionettes, their heads bobbing, their hands and arms flailing. They don't look like real people at all. Emma marveled at their ability to move in such a fashion.

The director nodded his approval. With Claude's modifications, the ballet blended perfectly with the scenes. The director seemed pleased with that as well.

"It looks great," Emma said, coming up behind Claude. He stood at the back of the auditorium moving his head in time to the music.

He turned to her, a relieved smile on his face. "It does, doesn't it. All that hard work paid off in the end."

"It usually does," Emma agreed.

Claude's smile turned to a worried frown. "Emma, have you seen him?" he whispered.

"The stranger?"

"Yes."

"I have, a number of times," she said.

"He disturbs me," Claude said. "What does he want?"

"He wants release," she said, emphasizing the word release. She proceeded to remind him of the encounter with Oliver, and then told him about the psychic and what she had said.

He shivered. "Oh, God, we'll never be free of him. He'll haunt this place forever."

Emma sighed. "We have to free him."

"But how?"

"I have no idea."

OPENING NIGHT LOOMED. Storms returned in an unending deluge. Properties too close to the water lost as much as a foot of land as the greedy fingers of the lake claimed the shoreline. Basements flooded again. Despite all their efforts, many families lost whatever was stored in them.

As Emma looked out the atrium window, she felt as though Thor's hammer was wreaking havoc on the Midwest. She thought of her old house in Brookfield. Was the basement flooded there? Probably. She hoped that young family who bought it wasn't suffering too much.

She picked up the phone and punched in her daughter's number. "Sylvia, how is your house holding up?"

"Pretty well, so far. We have standpipes in the basement and two sump pumps. They've been running constantly."

"How are the boys coping?" Emma was almost afraid to ask.

"They're driving me crazy. They keep looking out the window and James Jr. recites 'rain, rain go away...' over and over and then wonders why it doesn't work."

"I don't ever remember so much rain in this area. I saw on the news that some homes in the flood plains are a total loss," Emma said, commiserating with those folks.

"Stop watching the news," Sylvia said. "It's not going to get any better in the foreseeable future. You're lucky you're on the sixth floor."

"Yes, we certainly are. I spoke with your brothers, no problems there, thank goodness."

"That's good," Sylvia said. "Stephen and Pat live on a hill and Martin and Bertie are in a third-floor condo." She hesitated for a moment. "James is worried about opening night. If it's still raining this hard, people might not show up." Sylvia's voice trailed off as she reprimanded one of her sons. "I have to go, Mom. The boys are fighting. Talk to you later. Bye."

Emma stood mesmerized by the rain, the phone still clutched in her hand. What about opening night? Is the production cursed as people think? More problems had occurred with each rehearsal. The other day, in the dramatic final scene where Marie Antoinette's ghost relives her execution with the guillotine in the background, the blade got stuck and didn't fall. The director was beside himself. Emma shook her head wishing Midwest had chosen a simpler opera.

"What are you thinking about?" Nate asked, snaking his arms around her.

She turned to him and planted a kiss on the cleft in his chin. "I'm remembering the director's reaction yesterday when the guillotine failed to function. His face was so red I was afraid he was going to have a stroke."

Nate shook his head. "The poor man will probably never work at Midwest again. He did come especially to direct this opera. I think he must have stock in the antacid companies the way he's been popping them in his mouth."

"Why have so many things been going wrong?" Emma asked, screwing up her face and cradling the phone to her chest.

"I haven't a clue. Now, unless you have permanently laid claim to this telephone, I would like to make a call," he said, taking the instrument out of her hand.

"Oh, I didn't realize I was still holding it."

He smiled at her as he walked into the living room.

Emma stood there a while longer trying to come to some conclusion as to why all the mishaps.

Perhaps the ghost is trying to get someone's attention, her inner voice said.

That's ridiculous. Spirits can't control the physical world, Emma thought.

Don't be too sure.

THIRTY-EIGHT

THE DRESS REHEARSAL performance exceeded all expectations: all the props worked, including the wind machine and the guillotine; the ballet fit perfectly into the production; and the singers received many "bravos."

During the second act, when the supers went onstage, Emma gripped Tristana's hand. "Take deep breaths. We've done this a hundred times. I'm right here."

The woman nodded, but Emma felt her tremble. Nate and Marshall beat their drums with the enthusiasm of men with a purpose and marched with a band of revolutionaries. The women waved banners and followed them across the stage with other supers and chorus members.

It seems so real, Emma thought, *as if we've actually been transported back to the French Revolution.* She could almost smell the dirty bodies and the blood from the guillotine.

In the melee that accompanied the scene, Emma saw the stranger lurking at the rear of the stage like a spectral visitor. Would he always be there?

"That wasn't so bad, was it?" Marshall asked Tristana as they walked to the community room.

"I made it," she said, beaming. "I actually appeared on the stage in a real production."

They helped themselves to tea and sat around relaxing and discussing the performance.

"Emma, you're so quiet," Nate said.

"I'm just a little tired, that's all." She turned around to see Claude coming toward them.

"Did you think the ballet went well?" he asked, clutching a program in his hands.

"It was perfect," Nate said. The others agreed.

"What do you say we change and all go out to dinner?" Marshall suggested.

"Great idea," Nate said, looking at the women who nodded and smiled. "What about you, Claude?"

"No thank you, Thomas and I have plans. Now that Oliver has gone back to his mother, we can resume our normal lives."

Emma raised her eyebrows in question.

"Thomas and his ex-wife came to an agreement," Claude said. "We'll have Oliver one weekend a month and more often, if she needs a break."

"That sounds like a workable arrangement," Nate said.

As they began walking out of the room, Claude took Emma's arm and held her back. "Did you see him?" he whispered.

"Yes, I did. I think we're just going to have to get used to him. He's not going to leave."

Claude hung his head. "He's so sad. I feel him calling to me for help." He gave Emma a pleading look.

"We'll try, some way," she said, attempting to placate him.

He nodded and left as she hurried to catch up with the others.

During dinner they discussed their roles and how authentic everything felt. "I noticed that Dominic Orso isn't causing any more trouble," Emma said, frowning. "I wonder why the stage director wanted him so badly." She looked at Nate with a question in her eyes.

He shrugged. "As I said before, the director gave no explanation." Nate smirked. "He does look like a rabble-rouser."

Emma smiled, then noticed a worried look cross Marshall's face. In a moment it faded. Was it her imagination?

After dinner Marshall asked Nate to take Tristana home. He claimed to have some business to take care of.

They drove off in sheets of falling rain, Emma and Tristana ensconced in the backseat.

"Tristana," Emma said with a frown on her face, "do you know what Marshall does for a living? I know you're becoming fond of each other, but do you know anything about the man?"

Tristana sat still, her hands clasped in her lap. "You're right. I don't know anything about him. When I asked, he answered rather vaguely that he ran some type of consulting business."

She looked at the falling rain and then back at Emma. "And I am becoming fond of him."

"I don't want to see you get hurt," Emma said. "I know you're vulnerable right now."

Tristana nodded. The women said no more, each occupied with her own thoughts.

WHEN NATE PULLED INTO the underground parking garage of their own building, he breathed a sigh of relief. "Driving in this weather is hard on the nerves."

Emma nodded but said nothing. Something was troubling her.

When they were back in their living room, each cradling a cup of tea, Nate said, "I heard your conversation with Tristana."

"What do you think?" Emma asked.

"I don't know." Nate wrinkled his brow and rubbed his hand over the emerging stubble on his chin. "The man is rather secretive. I've asked him a couple of times about his business. He claims he and a partner are just starting this venture, and he'd rather not discuss it." Nate shrugged. "I didn't push it. After all, it's none of my business." He gave Emma a serious look.

"It does sound plausible," she said, getting up and taking their cups into the kitchen.

Oh, Guardian Angel, what is it? What's bothering me about the man?

Watch everyone, her inner voice said.

Emma breathed a sigh of frustration as she put the cups in the sink.

"I'm going to bed," she said, walking into the living room. "Are you coming?"

"In a little while. I want to catch the late-night news first," he said.

Emma undressed and was about to don her cotton pajamas. *No,* she thought. *I need to wear something else.* She took out a pair of red silk pajamas from the drawer and slid into them. Then she crawled into bed enjoying the feel of the silk against her body.

In the background she heard the droning of the television. She was almost asleep when she heard something familiar. She jumped out of bed and went to the door.

"suspected drug smugglers…linked to…crime family…"

What was the name he mentioned? She knew she had heard it before. She hurried into the living room. "Nate, what was that on the news about drug smuggling?"

"Huh?" he asked.

"The commentator mentioned some crime family, but I didn't make out the name. Something about it sounded familiar."

Nate scratched his head. "I was in the kitchen getting a glass of water. I guess I missed it." He shrugged. "Someone is always involved with drugs somewhere."

"I'm sure I'll remember it sooner or later." She stood with her hands on her slim hips alternately frowning and biting on her lip.

Nate raised his eyebrows. "You look fetching in those red pajamas, Sparrow. I think I'll come to bed right now."

He turned off the television and the lights and followed her into the bedroom.

THIRTY-NINE

THE PUMPS WORKED nonstop churning water out of the basement of the Performing Arts Center as fast as it seeped in. The huge fans whirred day and night in a vain attempt to dry out the structure. But a musty, damp smell crept up through the walls and invaded the hallways on the lower level of the building.

"No matter what we do, that musty smell is all over the place," James said. "I hope it doesn't seep into the auditorium."

Emma sat in her favorite chair in the atrium, the phone cradled in her neck. "What does Bruce say?" she asked.

"He says some of the singers are right. This production is cursed. And, he also said he's sacking Quiller as soon as the season is over."

"Really." Emma's eyes widened.

"Yep. He's giving him his notice on Monday with two weeks' pay. I don't think he'll even give him a reference."

"I wonder how he'll take that," Emma said.

"I don't think Bruce cares. The man's not dependable. Right now, he went out to get more deodorant and has been gone for two hours. I'd better go now. Have to check on a few things. I must say, Emma, I've never dreaded an opening night as much as I do this one."

EMMA TOSSED and turned. Every time she dozed fantastic dreams invaded her sleep: she was lost in a dark, constricted space, couldn't move; she was engulfed in floodwaters; the stranger stood before her, ragged and despondent. He seemed to be trying to get to the other side, but something held him back.

She sat up with a start. Why? What's holding him back? She

swung her legs over the side of the bed careful not to disturb Nate. He continued snoring as she crept out of the bedroom, warmed a cup of milk, and snuggled in her favorite chair in the atrium.

Guardian Angel, you and I need to have a serious talk. That spirit cannot keep roaming around the center forever.

You must help him cross over, the voice said.

Me? How am I supposed to do that?

Think. He didn't surface until you and Nate disturbed the artifacts in the basement storeroom.

That's true, but what does he have to do with that?

He's a black man, isn't he? Dressed in rags.

A light bulb suddenly switched on in Emma's head. *A slave. Of course, he was a runaway slave. That has to be the answer. But...but...*

Not so fast. Remember there was a tunnel from the storeroom out to the lake.

Oh, my God. He must have died in the tunnel trying to escape. Perhaps he can't rest until we recover his remains and give him a decent burial. That's it, that's got to be the answer. But how do we do that? Dig up the entire area?

You'll find a way. Watch and listen.

Emma clutched the cup in her hands as she watched the sheets of never-ending rain whipping down outside the window.

FORTY

"Hello." His voice was subdued as he looked around to make certain he was alone.

"When is the next drop?" a coarse voice asked.

"I told you never to call me here. It's too dangerous."

"I gotta move this stuff. If you don't want it, I'll find somebody who does."

"Not so fast. I've got the money. Been waiting for the right time. I'll try tomorrow, before opening night, but it's been raining so hard I don't know if it's safe."

"Don't give me no more excuses. Tomorrow, or maybe I'll send a letter to the police. I'm sure they'd like to know who stole that money from the Performing Arts Center."

"Wait a minute." But he heard only the dial tone from the other end.

He began to tremble as he flipped his phone shut. Would the man really dare to call the police?

FORTY-ONE

On the morning of the opening of the opera, the clouds rolled away and the sun shone down on a soaked earth. Emma breathed a sigh of relief as she stood looking out at the lake from her atrium. Tiny wavelets danced in the sunlight replacing the roiling waves of the past few weeks.

"Isn't it beautiful?" she said to Nate as he walked into the room carrying two mugs of coffee.

"Enjoy it while you can. There's another storm brewing just west of here predicted to hit late tonight."

"Spoil sport," she muttered as she took the proffered mug in her hand. "Maybe it'll wait until the performance is over."

"Perhaps it will. Anyway, according to the weather map on TV, that will be the last of it." With a grunt, he sat in one of the lounge chairs and looked out at the horizon.

"This is the first time we've been able to see the Ferris wheel at the Pier in over a week," Emma said.

"Uh huh." He took a swallow of coffee and grunted again.

"I'm worried about Tristana and Marshall. I've been watching them. They seem to care for each other," Emma said, "but we know nothing about that man."

"It's none of our business," Nate said for the umpteenth time. "But, if it will relieve your mind, I'll try to talk with him again."

"Oh, Nate, you are a dear."

He sighed. "I don't want to see Tristana hurt. She's a nice woman and seems so sad all the time."

"Am I rubbing off on you?" Emma asked, a smirk on her face.

"Perhaps you are, Sparrow." He smiled, reached over and took her hands in his, kissed the palms.

They sat for a long time, enjoying the sunshine and each other's love.

When the phone rang, Emma motioned to Nate to stay put and went to retrieve it. She saw her daughter's number on the caller ID.

"Hello."

"Emma, it's James."

"I'm glad to see the sun shining," Emma said. She knew how concerned he and Bruce were about tonight.

"Yes," he said, a tone of relief in his voice. "I hope it persists. I wanted to let you and Nate know that the guard who was injured in the robbery is well on the road to recovery."

"That is good news," Emma said. "I'll tell Nate. See you tonight, and am I supposed to tell you to break a leg?"

He laughed. "I think that's only the performers, but thanks for the thought."

She went back into the atrium and told Nate about the guard.

"That's good. With everything that's been going on, we need some good news."

"Maybe it's an omen," Emma said. "Tonight will be a huge success, the season will close on an upbeat note, and we can enjoy the summer." She checked her plants in the atrium. They almost begged to be put outside in the spring sunshine.

THAT EVENING as Emma and Nate walked the four blocks to the Performing Arts Center, a feeling of impending doom surrounded her. It was so intense that she stopped and grabbed Nate's arm.

"What's wrong?" He looked at her in concern.

"I don't know. It's passing now, just a momentary feeling of—I'm not sure." She felt confused. "I'm fine now. Let's go."

I mustn't let Nate know, but something is going to happen tonight. This whole business is coming to a head, like a pustule about to rupture. What will happen when it breaks?

Guardian Angel, are you here? Keep me on track, please.
She felt the warmth engulf her, but the feeling of foreboding
persisted.

AN AURA OF GAIETY surrounded the entrance as crowds of people
disembarked from cars, cabs and limos. The dry weather held
throughout the day, but overhead storm clouds gathered for yet
another onslaught.

Emma heard snippets of conversation as they walked to the
stage entrance. "…heard this is a fabulous production…some-
one said it's cursed…wonder how they will portray the ghost
world?…"

A shiver shook Emma's body. "I'll be so glad when this opera
is over, and we can stop thinking about ghosts," she said to Nate.

"That will be a relief." He opened the performer's door and
they went inside. "No matter how much deodorant they use, this
place still smells musty and damp. It'll take weeks of ninety-
degree weather to dry it out."

Emma wrinkled her nose and sniffed. She smelled something
else—an odor of decay, a sign that the stranger was nearby. "I'll
help you if I can," she whispered.

"What are you mumbling about?" Nate asked.

"Nothing, just muttering."

They met Tristana and Marshall in the community room, each
holding a bottle of water, their heads together deep in conversation.

Emma smiled. "Are you still nervous?"

"Not too bad," Tristana said. "The dress rehearsal seems to
have broken the spell."

Emma shivered again at the word *spell*.

"I saw Claude and Thomas on the way in," Tristana said.

"Yes, I spoke to Claude this afternoon," Emma said. "He's
such a perfectionist, wants to make certain the dancers perform

exactly as he choreographed the scene. He's probably backstage lecturing them right now."

"I wouldn't doubt it," Nate said, laughing.

"Since we don't appear until the second act, maybe we can find a couple of empty seats and watch the first act," Marshall suggested to Tristana.

"You can try," Nate said, "but I don't think there's an empty seat in the house."

"You two go ahead," Emma said. "I want to talk to James. I think he may be in his office. Nate, why don't you go with them?"

Nate looked at her and frowned. "Are you up to something?"

She put her hands on her hips and gave him an innocent look. "Now, what would I be up to?"

"I wouldn't even hazard a guess. I'll stay here, see if I can find that fellow who marches beside me. He's always out of step. I'll wait for you right here." He gazed into her eyes and emphasized the last words.

"Yes, milord," she said with a theatrical curtsy. She kissed his cheek and left the room.

As she walked through the hallways, Emma heard the voices of the performers in their dressing rooms, some vocalizing, others talking quietly.

Where am I going and what am I looking for?

A lost soul, her inner voice said.

Great, here I am wandering the halls looking for a spirit, and if I do find him, what do I do?

Help him.

Emma was becoming annoyed with her Guardian Angel. All these directives and no means to accomplish them. She jumped as she saw a maintenance man mopping the floor, muttering to himself. He looked up at her and smiled.

"Careful, ma'am, floor's wet." He shook his head. "Somebody comin' and goin' with wet boots all the time."

A thought occurred to Emma. "Have you been working here a long time?" she asked.

He stopped and leaned on the mop. "Been here since the place opened."

"Have you ever seen anything—unusual?" Emma persisted.

"Seen all kinds o' things, good and bad."

"Have you seen a black man in ragged clothing roaming around?"

"You mean Ol' Fred?"

Emma's eyes widened, her mouth opened. "Who is Fred?"

"That poor old ghost," the man answered. "Been seein' him on and off ever since I can remember. Ain't seen him in a couple years until lately. Now he's around all the time."

"Why do you call him Fred?" Emma asked, screwing up her face.

"No reason. He just looks like a Fred to me."

"What does he want?" Emma asked.

"Darned if I know. He just comes and goes. Never hurts nobody. Poor Ol' Fred." He shook his head, picked up his mop and bucket and shuffled down the hall.

Emma was more convinced than ever that the stranger's remains lay somewhere nearby. She was about to turn around and retrace her steps when she neared the back door and heard it opening and closing. She flattened herself against the wall and watched someone sneak inside. She saw a man wearing overalls and carrying a pair of boots. They were encrusted with mud, and so were the overalls he wore. *Who was he? And what in the world could he be doing out in back?*

Emma couldn't see his face, but his walk reminded her of someone. Who? He sidled along the wall and disappeared around a corner.

Should she follow him? No. She sniffed and wrinkled her nose and suddenly knew exactly who he was. But what was he doing out there? Checking the grounds. That had to be it. But something told her that wasn't the only reason.

FORTY-TWO

He crept through the muddy terrain, tripping over the rocks and inching toward the familiar bush. The persistent rain made navigating difficult. He swore under his breath. This is the last drop, he thought. *I'll have enough money to go where it's warm—away from this never-ending rain—away from the cold—and away from the cops. Didn't like that business on TV,* he thought. *They used my real name. Got to get away from here, fast.*

He fumbled with the rock. It had imbedded itself in the oozing mud as if in a deliberate attempt to bar his access to the opening. He was forced to find a heavy branch to pry it out.

"Damn! It's starting to rain again."

He pushed and slid back, and pushed and slid back again, his boots sinking deeper into the mud. He lost his footing and grabbed a nearby shrub. Finally the rock began to move. He threw all his weight against it as it budged just enough for him to squeeze through the narrow opening.

As he slipped down inside the tunnel, he realized part of the structure had collapsed. "Great, I hope I can get to the dough. It better be there."

He clicked on the flashlight and looked around. The passage was deep in muddy water. Clods of earth and rotted wood had dislodged from the walls and ceiling making navigating treacherous.

"This place ain't safe no more. This'll have to be my last drop," he promised himself.

The light danced along the walls as he searched for the niche. A wide grin creased his face. There it was—the envelope, in a clear plastic bag. He grabbed it, quickly checked the contents, then nodded in satisfaction. He placed the two packets wrapped in heavy plastic in the niche.

As he turned, he thought he saw someone. He froze. A black man dressed in rags stood before him, pointing an accusing finger.

"Who the hell are you?" He closed his eyes for a moment and when he opened them again, the man was gone.

"What the? Now I'm seeing things. I'm outa' here."

He quickly retraced his steps, fumbling and falling until he was outside. He pushed the rock back in place and fell in the mud, got up, and in his haste, fell again. Finally he gained his footing and disappeared into the misty night.

FORTY-THREE

As Nate had predicted, there were no extra seats to be had, so Tristana and Marshall stood against the rear wall and watched as the curtain rose to reveal the gauzy mesh scrim. The dim lighting shimmering through the fabric produced the effect of ghostly bodies floating across the stage. The costumes of a washed-out gray color added to the illusion, as well as the pale makeup. The haunting note of an oboe added to the realism.

Tristana grabbed Marshall's arm. "God, that's spooky," she whispered.

He slid his arm around her and pulled her close. "I'm here," he whispered. "I wish I could always be here for you," he said, a wistful note to his voice.

She turned to him, her eyes brimming with tears, and nodded.

As her gaze returned to the stage, she stiffened. There he was, in a far corner blending in with the cast. She squeezed her eyes shut, but when she opened them, he was still there. She felt a deep sadness for the poor spirit trapped between two worlds. Would he ever be free?

She nestled closer to Marshall feeling his warmth. Was this the lasting relationship Rose had suggested? She brushed off the warnings of dark, constricted places. Marshall would protect her. She had nothing to worry about. She breathed a sigh of contentment.

Emma hurried back to the community room to encounter Nate's frowning countenance.

"James was just in here looking for you," he said.

"I—I couldn't find him. His office was locked," she stammered. That was plausible. If he was in the community room, his office would be locked.

"He and Sylvia have seats on the main floor," Nate continued, his eyes boring into her.

"That's nice. I remember Sylvia saying they had a sitter for tonight."

"They want to go out after the performance and want us to join them."

"Of course. That sounds like fun. Nate, will you stop looking at me like that. You're making me nervous." She fidgeted from one foot to the other.

"Is there some reason you should be nervous, my dear?" he asked, raising his eyebrows.

She smiled, a disarming grin. "Just opening-night jitters, that's all. Now, I'm going to tuck myself into my favorite spot in the wings and watch the opera." She pranced out of the room feeling his eyes on her until she was around the corner.

AT INTERMISSION Nate and Emma met up with James and Sylvia in the foyer. Sylvia looked radiant in a deep-red, opera-length velvet dress.

"What do you think of the production?" Emma asked her daughter, wondering how she had managed to produce this elegant creature. She noticed James, clad in evening wear, admiring his lovely wife and felt a surge of satisfaction.

"It's fantastic," Sylvia said. "I've never seen anything like it. The director deserves all the praise he will receive."

"I think the poor man developed an ulcer over this one," Nate said. "He was popping antacids every time I glanced at him."

James chuckled. "There did seem to be an inordinate number of problems."

Bruce Hamilton walked up to them escorting a nondescript woman in a plain black evening gown adorned only with pearls. He introduced her as his wife.

"I think it's going well, don't you?" Bruce asked, looking

from one to another. "I'm worried about that musty odor coming from the basement into the auditorium."

"It doesn't seem to be," James said. "I checked the basement earlier. The floor was dry and the fans seemed to be doing their job."

Bruce frowned. "I put Quiller in charge of that. Has anyone seen him?" He looked around as if expecting the man to miraculously materialize.

"I saw him earlier," James said. "He claimed to have an important errand to run."

Bruce let out a deep sigh. "I'll be glad when the season is over, and I can get rid of that man." He turned to his wife. "Come, my dear, we must greet the critics. I've noticed one from each of the major newspapers here tonight."

When they walked away, Emma realized the woman hadn't uttered a single word. But James's words kept repeating in her mind. Where had Mr. Quiller gone? What kind of errand would take him away on opening night? Something didn't add up.

At that moment Tristana and Marshall came up to them. Her flushed face said more than any words.

"Come on," Nate said, "time to get into costume. The second act will be starting soon."

As EMMA SLIPPED into her ragged dress, tied the old shawl around her shoulders, and adjusted the mobcap on her head, she felt a vague connection to the stranger. He, too, had been struggling against cruelty and poverty—running toward freedom.

"What are you thinking about?" Tristana asked. "You look so solemn."

"Nothing in particular," Emma said, catching her reflection in the mirror as she applied makeup to her face. Then she looked at Tristana. "Here, let me help you." Emma took the cosmetic sponge out of the woman's hand and began rubbing.

At that moment they heard the stage manager call for the chorus members and supers to take their places. They took one last look in the mirror and headed for the stage. Emma felt the adrenaline rush that always accompanied her entrance in front of hundreds of patrons. She grabbed Tristana's cold hand and the two joined the other revolutionaries as they marched across the stage. She held her banner high and raised her fist in defiance as the chorus sang their shouts of rebellion. Tristana carried a stake, and Emma noticed her hands tremble just a little.

Nate and Marshall preceded the women, pounding on their drums. For a few moments Emma felt she was actually part of the revolution. She was a commoner, protesting the power of the throne. Beside them four chorus members carried pikes with huge skulls on the end. They lent a frightening reality to the scene.

Then she saw another figure walking beside her—a black man in ragged clothing. She shuddered and looked away, but when she glanced to her side, he was still there. He beckoned to her with such a look of pleading that she almost stopped in mid-stride.

Concentrate, she told herself. *Pay attention to your part. Forget him. You can't help him.*

But, perhaps you can, her inner voice now said. *The time is right.*

Oh, God, Emma thought, *now what am I getting myself into?*

At that point they exited the stage.

In the next scene they again marched with the crowd accusing Marie Antoinette of treason. The men pounded their drums and shouted "death to the traitor." The women yelled and waved their arms along with the others.

In the final scene the four of them stood in the background with the crowd of revolutionaries, their voices muted. The ghost of Marie Antoinette stood at center stage watching the tumbrel carrying her to the guillotine. Everything appeared in silhouette lending mystery to the scene. Suddenly the blade fell. Shouts from the crowd. The ghost of Marie Antoinette smiled, held out her arms, and returned to the ghost world.

The stranger still stood beside her, his arms also outstretched, as if beseeching someone to set him free.

The curtain fell. Most of the patrons rose to their feet shouting "Bravo." The entire cast assembled for the collective curtain call, as the curtain rose and fell numerous times.

"That was certainly a success," Nate said as they walked toward the dressing rooms. "We'll meet you in the lobby," he said to Emma as he and Marshall turned off toward the men's room.

"Emma," a whispered voice spoke.

She turned, but saw no one.

"Emma, Tristana, over here."

They looked again to see Claude beckoning to them.

"What is it?" Emma asked.

"We must go," he answered mysteriously.

"Where? What are you talking about?" Emma was completely bewildered by his strange actions.

"The stranger—we have to follow him—now—tonight." Claude began walking rapidly down the hall.

"Wait a minute." The two women hurried after him. "Why?" Emma asked.

"Because—he spoke to me." Claude stopped and placed his hand dramatically over his heart.

"What do you mean, 'spoke' to you?" Emma asked. "Did you hear his voice?"

"I can't explain it. The voice wasn't mortal, kind of a telepathic message. Does that make any sense?" Claude seemed confused, a kind of wild expression in his eyes.

"There he is," Tristana whispered.

They turned to see the stranger waving them on.

"We must follow him," Claude said.

Emma's inner voice said, *Yes, you must go.*

As if mesmerized, they cautiously followed the fleeting image.

FORTY-FOUR

WHEN NATE AND MARSHALL met Sylvia and James in the lobby, Sylvia asked, "Where's Mother?"

Nate shook his head and smiled. "The women haven't surfaced yet. They're probably busy making themselves beautiful after taking off all that makeup."

Marshall laughed. "It was pretty difficult getting that stuff off."

Nate noticed a nervousness about Marshall. He kept glancing from side to side, clenching and unclenching his fists. Was he simply eager to see Tristana, or was it something else? Thomas stood off to the side. Nate waved him over and introduced him to the others.

"Where's Claude?" he asked.

"He went backstage to talk with the dancers. There was one movement that didn't satisfy him. You know what a perfectionist he is." Thomas tried to smile, but he, too, kept looking anxiously around.

The group stood waiting, conversing about the success of the performance for a long time.

"Shouldn't they be out by now?" Sylvia asked, a worried frown crossing her face.

"They should," Nate said. He spotted one of the female supers and called to her. "Are Emma and Tristana still in the dressing room?"

The woman gave him a vacant look. "I don't remember seeing them after the performance. There's no one left in the dressing room except the wardrobe mistress."

Nate and Marshall exchanged anxious looks.

"Let's check it out," James said. "They have to be some-where." He turned to his wife. "Sylvia, you and Thomas stay here in case they come back. We'll look for them, and Claude, too." He nodded to Thomas who was beginning to pace.

"All right," Sylvia agreed, her hands gripping her evening bag.

The men hurried backstage. In the dressing room, they saw the wardrobe mistress checking the costumes.

When she saw James, she smiled. "Hello, Mr. Greene. What brings you back here?"

"We can't seem to find Emma and Tristana. Do you have their costumes?"

Her eyebrows came together, and she bit the side of her lip. "What are their last names?"

"Morgan and Winberry."

The woman riffled through the rack of costumes, the name of each performer attached to the top of the hanger. "No." She looked confused. "Those two are missing." She turned to the worried men. "Of course, sometimes they don't put them where they belong. I'm always picking up after someone."

"Where are the lockers with their street clothes?" Nate asked, the cold fingers of fear creeping up his spine.

"Over here. A few bring their own locks, but most leave them open."

James began opening one locker after another. Nate and Marshall started on the other end.

Nate stopped. His hands grew cold. All color drained from his face. "These are Emma's clothes," he said in a rasping voice.

"And these must be Tristana's," James said, opening another full locker. "They never came back to the dressing room."

"But where could they be?" Marshall almost shouted.

James grabbed the phone on the wall and called security. "We have a situation," he said as calmly as he could. "Two supers are unaccounted for, and possibly, the choreographer. I want a complete search of the building, immediately."

Nate almost fell into a chair; his breath came in short gasps. All the fears and anxiety of the previous summer resurfaced.

Marshall put his hand on his shoulder. Nate could feel the man trembling. They both turned to James.

"What do we do now?" Marshall asked.

"We wait."

Outside, claps of thunder rent the air as the storm returned with the vengeance of Thor.

THE STRANGER REACHED the door to the basement, waved the three on and seemed to melt into the structure.

"What do we do now?" Claude asked.

"I guess we follow him," Emma answered. She hesitated for a moment, then opened the door; the hinges let out a protesting squeal. It was pitch black inside.

"Where's the light switch?" Tristana asked, clinging to Emma.

"It's over here, somewhere." She slid her hand down the wall until she felt the toggle. She flipped it up and the room filled with an eerie light. The whirring of the huge fans lent an unworldly atmosphere reminding her of the ghost world in the opera.

Emma noted that the floor was dry, just as James had said.

"Now what?" Claude asked.

They looked around the vast storage area. "Over there," Emma said. "He's standing at the door to the storeroom and waving to us."

With no thoughts to their safety, they followed the apparition as he again disappeared through the door.

"Do we really want to go in there?" Tristana said, pulling back.

"We can stop right now, go back to the dressing room and forget all about this," Emma said, looking at the other two.

"No," Claude said, a determined note in his voice. "He's calling to me. I hear him, and I must follow." His eyes stared ahead with an almost vacant look.

This type of behavior is definitely out of character for Claude, Emma thought. *He seems to be hypnotized or in a trance.*

Guardian Angel, do we go on?

You must, or he will never be free, her inner voice said.

It could be dangerous but she, too, felt the pull of the stranger. "All right, then we all go."

Emma grabbed the knob, opened the door, and turned on the light to reveal the empty storeroom. Spiders had reclaimed the area since Emma and Nate emptied it of boxes. The specter stood at the panel that had disguised the passageway for the slaves. Again she felt the heaviness that still lingered after so many years.

"We have to take off this panel. Whatever he wants us to see lies behind it," she said.

Only a few loose nails held the panel in place. They easily pulled it off.

"This is where we found the trunk," Emma said. "There's no light in there. We won't be able to see anything."

"I have a penlight," Claude said. He switched it on and carefully stepped into the small enclosure. It was empty. The smell of dampness and decay filled their nostrils. The dirt floor was a mass of wet mud. Droplets of water seeped through the walls and the roof. The trio began to cough and take deep breaths, but the air they breathed was more dust and dampness.

"Where do we go from here?" Tristana asked.

Claude shone the light around the small enclosure. "Look, there's a pile of stones in that corner." His hand shook as he pointed the penlight.

The apparition stood, pointing to the stones. As if guided by an unseen force, they began moving them, one by one.

"There's some sort of trapdoor here," Claude said, breathing hard as he removed the last stone. He grabbed the rusted metal ring on the door and pulled, but it didn't budge. Tristana put her hand over his, and between grunts and groans, they managed to pull the ancient door up. Small pebbles and clumps of damp earth loosened and fell into the space below. With a shaking hand Claude shone the light down on a number of earthen steps leading into the darkness.

"The tunnel," Emma whispered. "This must be the escape route the slaves used. We assumed it had collapsed years ago."

"Come on," Claude said. "We have to follow him." The stranger was ahead of them leading them onward.

She, too, felt compelled to complete the venture. Without a further thought to the safety of the structure, the three cautiously descended the stairs, Claude in the lead, Emma following, and Tristana in the rear.

Ahead the stranger continued to beckon.

FORTY-FIVE

"WE'VE SEARCHED the building, Mr. Greene," the guard said. "There's no sign of them anywhere."

"Oh, my God," Sylvia whispered, almost collapsing into her husband's arms.

"They must have left the building," Marshall said. "But why? And where would they go in this downpour?" He began to pace, seemed to be about to say something, then stopped himself.

Nate and Thomas stood immobile, neither one of them able to say a word.

Finally Thomas spoke. "It's that stranger. Claude has been obsessed with him—talks about releasing his spirit, or some other nonsense."

"So have Emma and Tristana," Nate said, looking down at the floor.

"I'm calling the police," James said. "If they did follow this man somewhere, there's no telling where they may be."

Nate turned to Thomas. "Is Claude carrying a cell phone?"

"Yes, yes. I'll call the number." He fumbled in his pockets, then frowned. "I guess I didn't bring mine with me."

"Here," Nate said, handing him his cell phone, "use this."

With shaking fingers Thomas punched in the numbers. After a moment he closed the phone and looked at the others in alarm.

"The message says that the user cannot be contacted at this time."

"He must have it turned off," Marshall said. He had been lingering in the background. His face wore a mask of fear. Again he seemed about to say something but held back.

"Claude never turns off his cell phone." Thomas's eyes bulged wide with fear.

"It may be the storm," Nate said. "It might be interfering with the signals." But, deep inside, he didn't believe that for one minute.

"I THINK WE'VE GONE far enough," Claude said, a note of fear creeping into his voice. "And I'm tired. Oh, God, what are we doing?" He suddenly seemed to realize the danger involved in their headlong pursuit down this treacherous route.

Don't stop now, Emma's inner voice said, *you're almost there.*

"Let's go just a little farther," Emma said, nudging Claude.

He whimpered as they crept, stooped over, through muddy soil, their shoes quickly becoming caked with the wet clay. Moisture dripped from the top of the tunnel onto their heads.

The air was thick; heavy dust filled their noses and throats. Emma's eyes smarted from the particles making their way under her contact lenses, but she dared not rub them. That would be disastrous.

Claude coughed and grabbed his throat. "I'm choking," he croaked.

"Bite down on your tongue," Emma instructed. "That causes more saliva to flow." The others followed her example.

Emma watched the form of the stranger leading them onward. She thought of the psychic's words to Tristana about dark, narrow places. Fear surrounded her, but she had to keep her wits about her. She knew the other two would fall apart in a minute.

"Oh, God," Claude moaned. "Why am I doing this? I must be out of my mind. I have to go back. I'm dirty and soaked and— terrified. Thomas will be so worried." The light danced in the trembling grasp of his hand.

"A little farther," Emma urged. "Then we'll go back." Perhaps they should stop now, while they still could. *This is madness,* she thought, feeling the tunnel closing in on her. She took a few deep breaths in an effort to calm herself. Drops of water rhythmically fell on her head. Tristana clung to Emma, too frightened to speak.

"I see something," Claude said, an excited note in his voice. "Right up ahead—a mound of something."

Rats climbed over the mound and ran ahead. Emma shuddered. They quickly reached an area with a small alcove on the side. The spirit stopped and pointed to the ground.

"Look," Emma said.

Poking out of the mud lay a human skull. A rat poked its head out of an eye socket.

"Oh God, oh God," Claude moaned, covering his eyes with a muddy hand.

"Shoo!" Emma shouted. It seemed a desecration.

"These must be the remains of this poor soul," Tristana said sadly, staring at the mud-covered bones.

"What do we do?" Claude asked, his voice rising an octave.

"Be quiet," Emma said with authority. She closed her eyes and went back in time, could almost hear the voices of the slaves as they crawled toward freedom.

"HURRY, MOSE, hurry! The boat's here."

"I'm comin' as fas' as I can."

She could see the old man prodding the younger ones ahead of him. He knew he would never make it across the lake that had no shore. He groaned as he pulled along his injured leg, the festering wound smelling of rotting flesh.

"Go on," he said to the others. "I can't."

"Come on, Mose, come on."

"I wait for the nex' boat. Be along in a day or so. By then I be better. Ain't 'nuff room for all of us no wise."

He stopped, could go no farther. He felt the side wall and lay as close as he could. He gave a deep sigh and closed his eyes. She almost heard his words. "Oh, Lord, I tried to live by the Good Book. Take my fambly to freedom and someday let somebody find my old bones an' bury 'em in a graveyard."

MY GOD, Emma thought. *He was hurt and unable to go with the rest.* She shuddered as she saw him in her mind, curling his body next to the wall, waiting for death.

Guardian Angel, what do I do next?
Send him on his way.

Emma cleared her throat. "Spirit," she said, her voice trembling. "Go—cross over to the other side. Join your family and friends. I promise you we'll give your remains a proper burial and everyone will remember your sacrifice to freedom."

The apparition didn't move, merely shimmered, next to his mortal remains.

Tristana gripped Emma's arm. "Why doesn't he go?"

"Make it go," Claude moaned.

Emma freed herself from Tristana and shushed Claude, then held her hands out in supplication. "Go," she said softly. "They're waiting for you. You're free."

Oh, Guardian Angel, what more can I do?

Slowly the apparition wavered for a moment, then surrounded by a blinding light, melted into the wall.

In the excitement they didn't notice the large chunks of clay that began to fall from the top of the tunnel. Instead of wet soil, they now crouched in two inches of water.

"Oh, God, is it finally over? Can we go back now?" Claude whined.

"Yes." Emma gasped as the energy drained from her body. She felt so exhausted she could barely move. Her breath came in gasps as she reached for the wall to steady herself. Suddenly she realized the possible danger that surrounded them. *We must get out,* she thought, *now!*

"What was that sound?" Tristana whispered.

They listened.

A rumbling sound. Large clods of earth hit their heads. They squeezed themselves as close to the wall as possible and watched in horror as, chunk by chunk, their escape route collapsed behind them. Water began seeping up into their shoes as the tunnel slowly began to fill. *They were trapped.*

FORTY-SIX

MARSHALL PACED BACK and forth muttering something to himself. Nate sat in a chair, his hands folded between his knees, his head down. Sylvia stood behind him with her hands on his shoulders. Thomas shifted his weight from one foot to the other, his eyes darting back and forth.

"Yes, officer, the guards have searched the building. We tried the cell phone but were unable to get through." James stood off to one side explaining the situation to the police.

Suddenly Norman Quiller came rushing in. "What's happened here? Why are the police outside?" He looked around wildly.

James turned, wrinkled his nose, and shot him a look that made the man step back. "Where have you been? Bruce and I have been wondering where you went off to."

"I—I had an important errand to run. I was here for the second act. I missed Bruce, though."

James noticed his tie askew. He looked as though he had thrown his evening clothes on in a hurry. "Mrs. Morgan, Mrs. Winberry, and Claude Doran have gone missing," James said, staring at the cringing man.

Quiller's eyes widened. "Where are they?"

James let out a loud breath. "Don't you understand? 'Missing' means we don't know." He narrowed his eyes and scrutinized Quiller's twitching face. "Do you have any idea where they might be?"

"Me?" He stepped back and almost tripped over a chair. "How would I know? Did you check the basement?"

"Why would they be there?" James walked toward the man and grabbed his lapels. "What made you say that?" He spat out the words.

"I—I don't know. They were always lurking around there, in that old storeroom…" He left the sentence unfinished.

Nate looked up. "Did anyone check down there?"

"Security checked it out," James said.

"Let's check it again," the officer said.

"Sylvia," James said, "you and Thomas stay here. And Quiller," he turned his attention back to the quivering man. "Don't leave."

During the entire time Marshall stared at Quiller but didn't say a word.

EMMA, CLAUDE, and Tristana stood huddled in the small alcove until the clay stopped falling around them. Hoards of rats scurried frantically trying to escape the mud and rising water. "Ugh," Claude whispered. "I'm going to faint. I think I'm dying." He whimpered like a baby. Tristana clutched Emma's hand so tightly that it soon became numb.

"No one is going to die," Emma said in an authoritative voice. But at that point she wasn't so sure about anything. She, too, was numb with fear.

"Claude, do you have your cell phone?" Emma asked.

"Yes, yes I do." He struggled to get the instrument out of his pocket and handed it to Emma. "You call. I'm too nervous."

"Shine the light here." She noticed the glow had dimmed noticeably since they started out. *If that battery dies, we're sunk,* she thought. She turned on the power and examined the readout. No signal available.

"We can't get through," she whispered trying to keep the disappointment out of her voice. *We're too far underground,* she thought.

All right, Guardian Angel, now what? Emma closed her eyes and waited for the answer.

Since you can't go back, you must go forward.

Emma sighed. "I guess we don't have much choice," she said aloud.

"What do you mean?" Tristana asked.

"The way back is blocked, so we have to go forward as quickly as possible before this whole structure falls on top of our heads. The rats seem to know the way out. We'll have to follow them."

"Oh God, oh God," Claude wailed again and again. "I can't breathe, I'm dying."

"Claude," Emma said in as commanding a voice as she could muster. "There is air in this tunnel so there must be a connection to the outside. You're hyperventilating. Stop it! Take slow, deep breaths. That's it—slowly, in and out, in and out. Isn't that better?"

He coughed as he inhaled more damp, dirty air, then blew it out. "I think so," he whispered.

"You're in the lead," Emma said. "Start crawling and we'll follow. And, I think you'd better turn off the flashlight before the batteries die completely."

"But—but we'll be in the dark," he moaned.

"We'll feel our way. Now get going."

They climbed over the pile of mud that had fallen from the top of the tunnel, and when they saw where they had to go, Claude switched off the light and put it in his pocket. They began to crawl through the cold, muddy water. The swimming rats unnerved them, but they continued on.

JAMES OPENED THE DOOR to the basement, turned on the light, and looked around the cavernous room. "Emma, Tristana, Claude, are you down here?" he cried.

The whirring of the fans drowned out the shouts.

The officer quickly scanned the room. "No sign of anyone here."

"The storeroom," Nate said, hurrying over to the open door.

"Wait a minute, stand back," the officer said. He drew his gun and cautiously shone his flashlight around the empty room.

"There are footprints on the floor," he said, shining the light down. "More than one person."

"Look," Nate said. "The panel's been removed. There's another small room back there."

"Stay back," the officer said. "You'll contaminate any evidence that may be here."

He went in alone carefully checking the area. "The footprints lead to a trapdoor back here."

Nate and James craned their necks to see inside.

"There seems to be a passageway of some kind," the officer said as his voice trailed off.

"Shall we follow him?" Marshall asked, pushing up against Nate.

"No," James said. "Do as he says."

The officer returned a moment later. "No way anybody could get through there. The whole thing's collapsed, and it looks recent."

FORTY-SEVEN

AN INVESTIGATIVE TEAM was called in to help. One of them dusted for prints and another measured the footprints and recorded the measurements in a notebook. "It appears that these were made by at least three different people who went through that opening before it collapsed. These prints lead through the basement into the storeroom and through the trapdoor."

"Why?" James asked in utter frustration. "Why would they do such a foolhardy thing?"

Nate shook his head. "I'll bet that stranger had something to do with this. Maybe he coerced them at gunpoint or something. He could have been hiding down here going in and out through that tunnel."

The policeman looked from Nate to James. "What are you two talking about?"

"A strange man has been seen around the Center. Security has tried to apprehend him, but he seems to—disappear," James explained.

The officer turned back to the remains of the tunnel. "One thing is for sure, there's no way anyone's going to get through there now."

"Come on," James said to Nate and Marshall. "I want to talk to Mr. Quiller and so will the police. I think he knows more than he's admitting."

AT A SNAIL'S PACE as water and chunks of mud continued to drop on their heads, Emma, Claude, and Tristana crept forward in the dark. The tunnel narrowed making it more difficult for them to get through. It was getting harder and harder to breathe clearly.

We want to get out, Emma almost cried aloud. *Guardian Angel, please help us through this tunnel to freedom.*

"I can't crawl anymore," Claude sobbed. "It's getting narrower." He stopped and was silent for a moment. "We're going to die in here!" he shouted, his voice rising in hysteria.

Guardian Angel, help me to control this man. If he faints, we're all doomed.

She tried desperately to control her own rising anxiety. She must rely on her celestial guardian. There was no other choice.

"All right, listen to me, both of you," she said. "Our only chance is to keep going. If we have to slither on our bellies like snakes, that's what we'll do. The slaves did it in their desperation for freedom. We're in the same predicament. Now move!" With those words she prodded Claude in the backside as hard as she could.

"Ow!" he yelled. "I can't…I can't…"

"Yes, you can, and you must."

"Maybe we should sing," Tristana suggested.

"Good idea," Emma agreed. "How about 'Row, Row, Row, Your Boat'? Move forward Claude, and sing."

He began to inch his way along and sobbed out the words. Emma picked it up and then Tristana.

They continued their perilous journey knowing the tunnel was slowly collapsing behind them.

EMMA HAD ALL she could do to keep the other two on track. She was beginning to give up hope herself. Only the voice of her Guardian Angel kept her moving forward. *A little farther, only a little farther.* She didn't dare think of her family or Nate.

It seemed like they had been crawling for hours. They stopped singing. Claude moved only when Emma prodded him. He was no longer whining. She was afraid he had completely given up. Light-headedness gripped her. She shook her head and flashes of light danced before her eyes.

I can't faint now. I simply can't.

"Listen. I want both of you to visualize a place of light. Pretend we're exploring a cave and up ahead there's a cavern full of beautiful light. See it in your minds and keep moving toward it."

Oh, Guardian Angel, are they buying this? Do I believe it? How can I keep us all from giving up?

Keep going, the voice said.

They inched farther and farther. "Keep seeing the light," Emma said every few minutes, close to desperation herself.

Suddenly she raised her head. The passageway felt wider. She sniffed.

Was that fresh air?

"Smell you two—do you smell—fresh air."

"Yes, yes," Tristana said, pushing up against Emma.

"Claude, the passage is getting wider. We're almost there. Keep going," Emma said, pushing him as hard as she could.

He groaned. "Yes, I can crawl again." He almost cried, stumbling over his own hands in his hurry to get out.

A burst of adrenaline coursed through the three of them.

"I see light ahead," Claude shouted, weeping with joy. "I see light."

"Turn on the penlight," Emma said. "I think we're in a larger space."

Claude turned on the light, but his hand shook so much that he almost dropped it. He handed it back to Emma who took it from him and shone it around. There was definitely more space.

"Look, there's a niche carved in the wall and there's something in it," she said.

"I don't care," Claude said. "I just want to get out of here." He began crawling ahead as fast as he could.

Emma and Tristana crept closer. Two packets in two plastic bags sat tucked in the niche. Emma reached out and carefully took them. She handed one to Tristana and put the other in the pocket of her muddy costume. They were almost able to stand now.

"Come on, you two," Claude called out. "There's an opening here of some kind."

The rats were climbing on top of each other, squealing and pouring out of the small space. Emma shivered. How she hated rats.

They hurried along only to find the opening partially blocked by a large rock. Ambient light surrounded it from the outside. Behind them more chunks of mud fell.

"Okay," Emma said. "Let's put all our weight against this boulder and push."

They groaned and grunted, but the rock had sunk too far into the mud. It wouldn't budge.

"Claude, give me the cell phone. Maybe, if I hold it up to the opening, the signal can get through."

She tried to wipe as much mud off her fingers as possible. Then, in the faint glow left by the penlight, she punched in the numbers. *Please—please,* she prayed.

"It's ringing."

"Hello," Nate's agitated voice answered.

"Nate, thank God I got through. We need help and fast."

"Emma," his tearful voice said. "Where are you? Are Tristana and Claude with you?"

"Yes, yes, we're in the tunnel, the one the slaves used to get to the lake. It's collapsing behind us. There's a big boulder sunk in the mud at the opening and we can't move it."

"We're coming. Hang on."

NATE TURNED TO the others, and with tears streaming down his face, relayed the message.

"They haven't much time if that thing is collapsing," James said. He turned to Quiller, hardly able to contain his fury. "I know you've been holding back a lot of information. Now, I don't know if you're in league with that stranger or with someone else, but where's the entrance to that tunnel?"

"I—I don't know."

"I think you do." James had his hands around the man's throat when the officer intervened.

"I suggest," the policeman said, "you take us there—now.

If those three people die and we find out you could have saved them, you will be guilty of three counts of reckless homicide. Do you understand?"

Quiller nodded, and without another word, led them outside in the downpour.

"I CAN'T PUSH anymore," Claude said. "I have no strength left."

"They'll find us. They're coming. I know they are," Emma said.

They huddled together, leaning against the rock, their hands scraped and bleeding while the roof of the tunnel kept falling in large chunks of mud and water around them.

"What was that?" Tristana said, cocking her head. "Someone's calling."

"Here, here, we're here!" they shouted together.

"Emma," Nate called. "Are you all there?"

"Here! Behind the rock."

"We'll have you out in a jiffy. Hang on."

They heard shovels hitting against the stone, then saw it budge. Just a little more—moving slowly—someone pushing against the rock. Finally it began to move, just a little at first, then, with one last heave, it rolled over.

One by one they scrambled out and into the arms of their friends.

FORTY-EIGHT

THE GROUP SAT in the community room, the three from the tunnel grimy and muddy, but smiling, as they drank cup after cup of hot tea.

"I'm afraid we've ruined these costumes," Emma said, looking down at the shredded rags covering her body.

"That is of no importance," Bruce Hamilton said. "As long as you three are safe and sound." James had called him back to the Center.

Claude shivered uncontrollably, the cup in his hand spilling its contents on his ruined evening wear. Every few moments he let out a sigh that came across as a whimper.

Emma looked at his dejected face and made a decision. "Claude is the real hero," she said, "a regular 'Tom Sawyer.'"

Tristana looked at her questioningly, but Emma's returning look silenced her.

Claude's eyes widened at her words.

"Why, he was in the lead and guided us through that treacherous muddy tunnel to safety." She decided not to embellish it anymore.

He looked surprised. "I did, didn't I?" He seemed to question his own actions. "I—I hardly remember it."

"You just kept going," Emma continued, "until you led us out."

Claude smiled, pushed his shoulders back, and took a deep breath.

"I'm so proud of you," Thomas said, squeezing his hand.

"We all owe you our thanks, Mr. Doran," Bruce said.

"Emma," James said, his forehead creased in a deep frown,

his arm around Sylvia. "Just what were you three doing in that tunnel?"

"Well," she hesitated for a moment, still shaking from her ordeal. "We followed the stranger."

"I knew it," Bruce said, stamping his foot, "that man again. Did he have a gun?"

Emma held up her hand. "Listen to me, please. There was no coercion. We followed of our own free will."

Guardian Angel, what shall I tell them?

Tell them the truth.

"You may not believe me, but the stranger was an earthbound spirit. He was a slave who tried to escape through the tunnel long ago. We found what we believe were his bones. All he needed was to be free, and I think he is now. I promised we would see that he received a proper burial."

Bruce looked at her in amazement. He wrinkled his brow. "I think there was some legend about a ghost roaming through this area a long time ago. I seem to remember one of the cleaning crew mentioning him. But this is unbelievable."

"Whether you believe it or not, I think that's the last we'll see of the stranger," Emma said. "And we found these just inside the outlet of the tunnel." She took the plastic-wrapped packet from her pocket and handed it to the officer. Tristana did the same.

"Now, I think we should go to the dressing room to shower and change."

"Yes," Tristana agreed. "I feel stiff in these mud-caked clothes."

"I'm going with you," Sylvia said. "Mother, I'm not letting you out of my sight."

Thomas accompanied Claude to the men's dressing room where he could find extra clothes.

At that moment Dominic Orso came forward. Nate recognized him as the loudmouthed super, the one he wanted to dismiss. "What are you doing here?" he demanded.

Orso held up his hands, then pulled out a badge. "Sorry I came over as such a boor, but I'm with narcotics—been working undercover. We've been watching a person of interest for quite some time, but needed proof." His eyes bore into Quiller's.

Bruce turned to his assistant. "Now, to this other matter. Mr. Quiller, are you ready to enlighten us as to how you knew where the entrance was to that tunnel, and what you know about those packets which I'm certain contain drugs?"

"Mr. Hamilton," Orso said, "I think I will take over the questioning."

He looked at Norman Quiller and waited. His size and his stare visibly unnerved the man.

"I—I…" At that point Quiller fell apart, began to tremble and weep. "I made a mistake."

"Would you rather do this at the station?" Orso asked.

He hesitated for a moment. "No, I think Mr. Hamilton deserves an explanation."

Bruce stood frowning, clenching and unclenching his fists.

"I have a gambling addiction," Quiller said. "I can't control myself." He shook his head and rubbed a hand across his face. "Believe me, I've tried. About six months ago a man contacted me; said if I could move some merchandise, we could both make some money."

"Who is this man?" Bruce demanded.

Orso cautioned him to be silent.

"I don't know his name, I only have a cell phone number."

"I'll need that number," Orso said, continuing to stare at Quiller.

He nodded, pulled a slip of paper out of his pocket, and handed it to the detective.

"And how did you dispose of the drugs?"

"A contact in the city. I don't know his name, either. I only have another cell phone number. I would leave the packets in a lock box and call this number." He reluctantly handed a second slip of paper to Orso. "I was only the middle man," he whispered desperately.

"Go on," Orso prodded.

"When I'd get the call, I'd go back and pick up the money,

take my share, and put the rest in the niche in the tunnel." He hung his head and shook it slowly from side to side. "When I'd get another call, I'd go back to the tunnel, pick up the drugs, and put them in the lock box."

Nate noticed a look of pain cross Marshall's face. He felt his gut tighten as an ugly suspicion crossed his mind.

"I don't think we have to go any farther with this right now," Orso said. He turned to Marshall. "Do you have anything to say Mr. Hawkins or whatever you call yourself these days?"

Marshall closed his eyes and clenched his fists. He turned pleading eyes to Nate. "I didn't mean for any of this to happen. My business venture needed extra cash and my partner had some contacts for disposing of the drugs. It—got out of hand."

Nate shook his head, grimaced, and turned away.

Orso returned Marshall's stare. "Don't listen to those lies. You and your partner have a history of preying on weaklings like this guy." He pointed to Quiller. "We've been watching you. I think the narcotics division in New York will be very eager to hear what you have to say."

"Why?" Nate asked Marshall. "Why become a super-numerary?"

"I didn't trust Quiller and thought I ought to keep an eye on him. What better way than to be part of the opera?"

"All right," Orso said, looking at Quiller and Marshall, "you two will have to come down to the station and write out a full confession." He read them their rights as another officer cuffed them and led them away.

"Wait a minute," Bruce said. "Quiller, how did anyone know about the tunnel?"

"The guy who contacted me said something about having a plan of the original house—something about ancestors. I don't know."

Marshall turned to Nate. "Tell Tristana I'm sorry about all this, but that's the way life is."

Nate narrowed his eyes and clenched his fists. He would have liked nothing more than to punch the man in the face. "Don't even mention her name. She deserves better than scum like you."

Marshall shrugged his shoulders as the police led him and Quiller to the waiting patrol cars.

WHEN THE WOMEN came out of the dressing room, Nate took Emma in his arms. His eyes sent her a message she couldn't quite read.

"Where's Marshall?" Tristana asked.

"He had to leave," Nate said. "Come on, I'll take you home."

IN TRISTANA'S LIVING ROOM, Nate poured a glass of brandy for each of them. He had stopped on the way and bought a bottle of the most expensive brand he could find.

"I have a feeling you have something unpleasant to tell us," Emma said.

Nate nodded.

Tristana took a gulp of brandy, coughed and sat upright. "It's about Marshall, isn't it?"

"Yes." He took a drink, let out a slow breath and told them everything.

Tristana sat quietly, tears streaming down her face.

Emma gripped her hand, sharing her pain.

"He's a good actor, fooled all of us. Apparently he's wanted in New York and other states on narcotics charges. Been using a number of aliases." Nate knew how cruel the words sounded, but there was no other way. "You deserve better, Tristana."

She said nothing, just sat with her head down looking at the floor.

"Do you want to come home with us?" Emma asked.

Tristana thought for a moment then shook her head. "No, I have a lot of thinking to do. I need to sort out my life."

"All right." Emma gave her a hug. "If you want to talk, call anytime, day or night."

"Thanks."

LATER, AS EMMA LAY in Nate's arms, she told him about their adventures in the tunnel. She tried to downplay the danger but didn't succeed. "At least he's finally at rest," she said, snuggling closer.

"You've always attracted troubled people," Nate said, squeezing her a little too tightly. "Now you're attracting troubled spirits. I do wish you would stop getting into these life-and-death situations."

"I don't do it on purpose, honest I don't." Emma suddenly sat up.

"What is it?"

"I just remembered the name of that crime family they mentioned on TV that night. Do you recall?"

"You mean the night of the red pajamas?" He snickered.

She gave him a playful tap on the head. "It was Perkins, the name of the original family who owned the house."

"Good, now can we forget about the whole affair and get some sleep? You know, I think it would be a good idea to go away for a couple of weeks, somewhere quiet."

"That sounds nice," she murmured as she drifted off to sleep.

THE FRONT FINALLY passed over the Midwest area bringing sunshine and warm weather. The opera concluded to rave reviews by the critics. Like a trouper Tristana had continued her part in the performances.

James sat in his office making the final arrangements to ship the production back to New York. Bruce limped in and sat heavily in a chair. James put down the phone and looked at his boss.

"I just received a call from the detective. The man who supplied the drugs, who knew about the tunnel—he was the only living descendent of the Perkins family. Now he's in jail—a drug dealer. How could this have happened?"

"Bruce," James said, "why don't you take all those artifacts and donate them to the Chicago History Museum? We can get a reporter to do a nice story for the newspapers, and leave out the drug dealer, of course. Just focus on the safe house angle and the remains of the runaway slave buried in the mud and clay of the collapsed tunnel."

Bruce raised his head, his expression brightening. "Hmm, I like that idea. And we can have a memorial garden planted there with a commemorative plaque. Yes, that's what we'll do." He walked out of the office for the first time in weeks with a spring in his step.

SHORTLY AFTER the last performance Tristana handed in her resignation. "I'm going back to California," she told Emma over coffee and scones. "I've decided to stop running away from my past. I spoke to a friend of mine the other day. There's a position opening in a new school, and I've decided to apply for it."

Emma saw a look in Tristana's eyes she had not seen before from the woman—determination. "I think you're doing the right thing. But I'll miss you."

"I'll miss you, too, and I'll never forget what you've done for me. You've helped me put my life into its proper perspective. We must keep in touch."

"Absolutely," Emma said with a hug for Tristana.

EPILOGUE

"DON'T YOU just love the fall?" Emma said as she and Nate admired the yellow and russet mums lining the front of the Performing Arts Center.

"Yes, I certainly do, and especially this one. We've enjoyed a trip to Lake Tahoe followed by a relaxing summer, free from any adventures."

"Why, Nate, you talk as if I seek out trouble."

"I didn't say that, but it does seem to attract you like a magnet."

Emma smiled. She did have a tendency to find herself in some precarious situations. "I'll try to mind my own business, I promise."

"That'll be the day."

"I got an E-mail from Tristana," Emma said. "She's happy in her new job and has rekindled a relationship with an old boyfriend. They've started dating." She gave Nate a nudge and a smile.

"I'm glad. That woman's had enough trouble in her life. I still can't get over Marshall Baxter, or whatever his name was. I'm usually a pretty good judge of character, but he had me completely fooled. I must be slipping."

"He had us all fooled," Emma said. "I guess that's the definition of a con man."

They made their way to the new memorial garden behind the Center. The area where the tunnel collapsed had been filled in with soil and a fenced garden planted with shrubs and flowers.

"Oh, look," Emma said, "there's the bench we donated." She hurried over to greet James and Bruce. "This is lovely," she said with enthusiasm.

"It did turn out nicely, didn't it," Bruce said.

"Mr. Hamilton," a man with a camera called out, "will you and Mr. Winberry stand over there by the plaque for a picture to accompany the newspaper article?"

Emma looked down at the brass plaque embedded in the ground surrounded by yellow mums.

Here lies a brave man who valued freedom more than his own life.

Bruce made a short speech followed by applause from the group of people present. "Come into the Center for refreshments," he said.

"Are you coming?" Nate asked her as she held back.

"Go ahead. I want to stay out here for a few minutes."

She sat down on the sturdy bench made from recycled plastic and gave a deep sigh. She rubbed her arms as a chill crept up them. "I hope you're free and happy now, dear spirit."

He is, her inner voice said.

Emma smiled, content that her task was finished.

* * * * *

REQUEST YOUR FREE BOOKS!

2 FREE NOVELS
PLUS 2 FREE GIFTS!

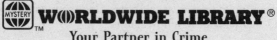

Your Partner in Crime